MW01531921

FIRST EDITION

Life is Better with You

Prologue

What happens when you have your whole life figured out and it is all taken from you in an instant. No one ever prepares for a tragedy, especially one that may or may not ever happen to them. For me, I was just the unlucky idiot standing in the wrong place at the wrong time.

Little did I know my life would change forever. Everything that I though was important to me, suddenly was not. Everything and everyone I thought made me happy, now just made me feel hopeless and unworthy.

My life took a backwards turn, and all I could feel was pain. Pain from my fractured spine, pain in knowing my career may be over, pain of feeling unwanted or unloved, and pain in the uncertainty of ever walking again. This pain was unbearable, and I just wanted it all to end. No one could help me, no one could save me, no one except.... her!

She saved my life in more ways than one. She never gave up on me or let me give up on myself, even when I was a stubborn prick most of the time. She saw the real me, the scared, anxious, hopeless me. She gave me hope when I had none. She showed me how to laugh again and what it means to genuinely love someone unconditionally. Everything that I am now is because of her.

Who knew that the most unusual twist of fate would be the most beautiful blessing in disguise?

Chapter 1

Levi Dawson

"Levi, Emma are you ready", I hear the director shout from the background. "yeah, yeah, we're good" I respond in a more irritated tone than I meant it to be.

"Let's give it another go then" I hear for what feels like the 10th time in the last hour.

I look over at Emma as she rolls her beautiful blue eyes and shakes her head. Normally I would enjoy doing this scene over and over again with my amazingly hot co-star and now fiancé. But its late and I am fairly certain there are tears of sweat forming near my brows. I can also see that Emma's make-up is no longer perfectly set on her face, which tells me she is exhausted.

The room is lit only with the lamp on the dark wood nightstand, and a few camera lights shining on us from above the stage. The camera crew is surrounding us at every angle and the director is sitting about twenty feet away in his tall black canvas chair.

"And go!" is all I hear as I grab Emma's long slender arms and gently slide my hands up to her wrists pulling them over her head and pushing her against the bedroom door, closing it shut. I lean in, taking her full lips into mine. I let go of her wrists and she grabs my white t-shirt, pulling it off over my head. We lock lips again and I reach around to unzip her tiny red dress, letting it fall to the floor. Damn, she is hot in her red lace bra and panties. Looking at her barely

dressed in this way is so tantalizing that I get lost in

my own head, forgetting that there is anyone else in the

room.

I tuck Emma's long blonde hair behind her ear

and rest her face into my palm and kiss her again. This

time it is not as smooth, I can feel her rushing and I

know she wants to get out of here as much as I do after

spending the last 8 hours in this room.

I bring my hand down her back and onto her

hip, then slowly lift her long leg by her thigh and bring

it up to my waist. Her legs are already so long and

slim, these heels she's wearing, makes her almost as

tall as I am.

She breaks free from my grip and places her hands on my bare chest, pushing me back towards the bed. I lay back onto the white duvet cover while she continues to climb up on top of me, kneeling over me and resting both thighs on either side of my legs. We kiss again, this time putting my hands on her shoulders and rolling her over so that I am now on top. I kiss her softly one last time before I whisper, "I love you".

"CUT! that's a wrap for today" the director shouts.

The camera crew scurries around while the set crew collects the props. The director walks over to us and congratulates our splendid performances before he hurries off for the night.

Emma looks up at me and smiles as I help her get up off the bed. "Thank god" she sighs with relief.

"I'm going to shower and change" she says as she storms off.

"Alright? Mate" Mark says to me.

"Yeah, yeah mate" I respond, my voice a little hoarse at this point.

"The Hawley at half eight then, I will send a car for you" Mark instructs.

"Sure, I will let Emma know to be ready" I say.

" I still don't know what you see in her mate, she is sexy as hell but she's demanding and controlling, nothing makes that girl happy" Mark nervously remarks as he brushes his fingers through his hair.

"Well, I have plenty of issues of my own, but she sticks around, and she loves me" I fire back.

Mark may be my manager, but we've become good friends over the past two years, and I know he's just looking out for me. He is not shy with his objections of how Emma is on the outside though, how she acts on the sets and out in public. Mark finds Emma rude and needy, aka "typical actress style" he says. What Mark doesn't see, is her vulnerable and caring side that I get to see when I'm alone with her.

I do not come from a large, well-known family. I have a tight knit group of lads who are like my brothers. Emma does not care much for them she thinks they take my time away from her.

My flat in Camden is small but has more than enough room for Emma and me. I haven't been able to convince her to move in with me yet. Her place is bigger and more luxurious she says, but it is right in the midst of all the noise of all the pubs, restaurants, and shopping. Her building is full of actors, authors, and famous musicians. I would rather reside in a lesser-known place, a home without all the attraction. It is also quieter where I live, but still walking distance to some pretty cool hang outs.

My place is modern yet rustic at the same time. Post and beam accent the vaulted ceilings and the stairway up to the loft. The white walls against the wood floors makes the place feel warm and inviting, just the way I like it.

I do try to make Emma stay here on most nights rather than at her place. Her place has rooms with crimson walls, tile floors, gold crown molding.

Her housemaid is always there picking up after her, I am afraid to touch anything when I am over.

We came up with a compromise; stay at her place the first half of the week and at mine the second half. This will need to change when we get married. Selling both places and settling into a home we will agree on is going to be a challenge, one that I foresee losing.

Chapter 2

In the Blink of an Eye

Levi's POV

I need to hurry and get changed. Emma will be impatiently waiting for us. If she would have only come back to my place like I suggested, she wouldn't need to bombard me with all these text messages.

Half eight and I hear the horn. Outside a black SUV is waiting for me. I open the car door and Mark is sitting in the back seat with a cooler on the floor in front of him. He looks at me all cheerful, wearing a black button-down shirt and black jeans, which go perfectly with his short black hair and green eyes. I climb into the back seat with him. He holds a beer up and looks at me again, "cheers mate!", he laughs, and I already know he has had a fair number of drinks.

I cannot help but chuckle at his intemperance and, also the fact that I am wearing black jeans and a dark button-down shirt, but mine is more of a slate color. Emma likes this shirt she says it highlights my blue-green eyes. She always comments on the way darker shirts or my dark brown hair bring out the blue in my eyes. Yet she can't stand that my hair is a little long on the top and I can never decide if I want to style it up or to the side. Tonight, I'm going for the messy look, that will probably piss her off I'm sure. She will forgive me for my lack of style later, I have no doubt.

Mark gives the driver Emma's address so we can pick her up on the way. As we pull up to her place, she is standing by the door as I expected, with her arms crossed by her chest, I can see the vein in the middle of her forehead throb as she clenches her jaw. Even in distress she is sexy to me. Her long blonde hair is tied back revealing her picture-perfect face and long neck. The strappy black dress falls just above her knees accentuating her tall slender body, and her black heels add the perfect touch. She always wears heels around me, probably so she can feel closer to my 6ft frame. She doesn't like anyone towering over her.

I get out of the car to meet her. "Hey baby" as I give her a kiss on her cheek, "everything ok?".

"You're late" she scowls, stomping her way into the car and sits right next to Mark.

Mark is rolling his eyes of course, so I shoot him over a warning look, and he stops.

"The Hawley Arms" he shouts to the driver.

The driver drops us at our destination. There is a sign at the door that reads "Private Party". Inside the pub a live band is playing, and I look around and see that just about our entire cast and crew from our new movie is here, along with a few other guys I've never seen before. But for the most part, it seems we have the place to ourselves.

" Great! I thought we would have at least one night away from the set" Emma angrily states, then looks at me "please get me a drink".

I leave her at the only empty table we could find then head over to the bar. I order Emma's favorite drink and shot of whiskey for myself.

"I see Emma is beautiful as ever, even if she is ...always angry", I hear a voice say next to me.

I look up to find Liam standing next to me. I don't know why I'm all the sudden so irritated by his comment, usually Liam and I get along pretty well. He's one of my supporting actors. He is generally a nice enough guy. All the girls seem to flock to him wherever we go. He's built like me, muscular but slightly shorter with a chiseled face, blonde hair, and ocean blue eyes.

"Hey mate, lay off of the Emma comments, I don't need her to be mad at me all night because people are talking shit about her" I glare at Liam.

"Sorry, I didn't mean to cause any problems" he says as he gives me an anxious stare.

Then he continues with "I just can't picture you two getting married, I mean, you're so chill and she walks around all high and mighty, expecting everyone to do everything for her".

I can feel my anger creeping up inside me as I try and rationalize what to say to him. I can see he is getting nervous now, rubbing his hand on the back of his neck and looking down at the floor.

" Emma is just a girl who knows what she wants" I begin to explain.

"She came from nothing and has worked awfully hard to get to where she is now and doesn't want anyone or anything getting in the way of that! Not that this is any of your fucking business" I add.

Chill? How does he think I'm chill, I am usually the one telling everyone off. I wave the bar tender over then down another two shots of whisky before heading over to where Emma is sitting.

"Took you long enough" she frowns.

"Sorry Baby, Liam and I got talking, and well you know", I smirk, shrugging my shoulders at the same time.

"Are you drunk already?", she asks me.

"No not yet baby, how about you and I have a dance", I smile at her hoping to change her mood.

"Sure, why not", she beams.

The band is playing "I am Yours" by Andy Grammer, this is perfect, she loves his music and to be honest, we need a perfect moment, just her and I right now.

I grab her hand in mine, while wrapping my other around her waist. She puts her other arm around my shoulder just behind my neck and pulls me closer into her as she leans her head on my chest. This feels comfortable, holding her in my arms, floating across the dance floor.

Our moment doesn't last long enough before I am dragged by Mark into multiple conversations I do not really feel like having with anyone. Someone keeps handing me drinks though, and I find myself too intoxicated to focus on what anyone is trying to say to me now. I stumble my way over to Emma who is giggling at the site of me. I just want to sit here with her and watch her laugh as she runs her hands through my hair.

"Levi, last call and then we are out of here" I hear Mark yell from across the room.

I nod, giving him a thumbs up and then lean my head back on Emma's shoulder. She returns to toying with my messy strands, if she does this for much longer, I might pass out.

Moments later I feel Mark putting my arm around the back of his shoulder as he lifts me from my chair attempting to half carry me out of the pub.

"I can walk, I can walk" I say to him as we get outside.

He lets go of me and I fumble around when I take a few steps forward, trying to gain my composure.

"Where's the car?" I slur.

"It's across the street, wait for Emma, she's right behind us" I hear Mark say.

"Okay, okay" I say.

My uncoordinated feet trip on the curb and I end up taking a few steps backwards into the street. I look up and search for Emma. When I spot her, my body freezes and I will never forget the look of terror on her face as she screams my name.

I am not sure what just happened. I remember my body hitting the ground with a sudden force. All I can feel is pain, all I can hear is Emma screaming and Mark shouting for help. Visions of figures moving all around me. I can't see straight, but I can hear their voices. My head is pounding, people are screaming in every direction.

Emma is standing over me, I think she is holding my hand, but I cannot feel it. Mark is talking to me, asking me questions that I cannot comprehend.

My mind is a haze, everyone is starting to fade away, I am losing consciousness. Why can't I move, why can't I answer them? The pain I am feeling is unbearable. What the fuck is happening right now.

Chapter 3

Charlotte Thomas

"Charlie! what should I do with all these?", I look at the girl working the front desk, waving around a stack of papers that keep coming from the fax machine.

"Try to put them all in a binder for me so that I can look over them, a lot of information will be coming over and I need to go through them all before he gets here" I tell her.

She looks frazzled, but so does everyone here, including myself. I have roughly 3 hours to have everything ready before he gets here. The stem-cell specialist will be here in 20 minutes to discuss options, and I just finished speaking with the London spine surgeon. This is all too stressful and exciting at the same time.

"I can't believe Levi Dawson is coming to our rehab center as a patient!" I hear Sarah, one of my aides say as she runs down the hall carrying sheets and towels.

It's really is hard to fathom, a movie star, no less, is in need of my help I start thinking to myself. Famous or not, the poor guy doesn't deserve everything he's going to have to go through now, no one does. From what I have been told, he was put on a flight here right after his surgery. He probably has no idea what is going on, which makes everything more perplexed.

I'm starting to feel a little nauseous, probably just my nerves. Although, I don't know why I am so nervous, I opened this center for people like him, like my sister, so they can have every possibility of living an active happy life. I have spent all my time in this building, working with patients, perfecting this program. I sleep at home, but otherwise, I am rarely there. I have dismissed most relationships because of my commitment and my goals. My parents admire my work ethic, though still want other things for me. All that I want at the moment is right here. This is the place I feel most needed, most helpful. Helping my patients regain their independence is something I strive for.

This new patient is not an ordinary guy living an ordinary life. He has paparazzi following him, who knows how long he has until they find him here. He was just about to finish a new movie, and he has a gorgeous actress fiancé. He is a particularly important guy to a lot of people, and everything about his life from this point on literally depends on me.

"Hey Charlie! I have got the room all prepared for him, and I have spoken to the staff about keeping it hush. I think they all get it" Nate says.

Nate is my assistant. He has poured as much sweat and heart into this program as I have, and I would not be able to run it without him. He does everything from toileting patients to helping them dress and taking over therapy sessions for me when I do not have enough time.

Everyone loves his honest personality. The women here adore his looks too of course. His dark curly hair and dark brown eyes, his dimples when he smiles, and his perfectly toned body, which is something he acquired from working out every day, and from lifting patients all day I'm sure.

"Thanks Nate", I smile back at him, and he can't help but notice my smile is more an expression of worry.

He grabs my hand, stares at me with his encouraging eyes and says "you are great at this! He may not be a typical patient, and this is not a typical situation, but you are great at what you do. If his family and whoever else in charge of him didn't think you could handle this, they would not have sought you out all the way from London". I allow his words sink in for a minute and my smile turns genuine.

I finish reading all the paperwork sent from the London hospital as the ambulance pulls up. Right behind the ambulance is a black SUV. Nate directs the EMT's to room #5 and tells the SUV full of family, I assume, to follow him to the room.

I did not get a chance to have a good look at him, but I heard him mumbling "Emma, Emma".

"Right here baby" I hear the woman holding his hand say.

She's tall, blonde, and beautiful, and I recognize her from a few movies. She is definitely his fiancé.

An older couple maybe in their 60's are nervously following the stretcher. The woman's eyes are swollen and tearful and she's holding on to the older man's arm for support. This must be his mom.

She has the same expression of worry and fear that all mothers have when something horrible has happened to her child.

Left behind in the front doorway is a well-groomed British guy frantically waving one hand around in the air while he shouts into his cell phone.

"get it done!"

"I don't care what they have to say!"

"It will have to be postponed", is all I hear him shouting in his thick accent to whoever is on the other end.

I feel like this guy calls all the shots and he comes off a bit angry, I am not sure I want to introduce myself.

Just when I am about to head to room five, the angry dark-haired guy walks over to me.

"Do you know where I can find Charlotte Thomas?" he asks, giving me an anxious stare. "

"I am Charlotte Thomas", I tell him.

Immediately his bright green eyes open wide and he jerks his head back slightly while looking me up and down. I already know what he is thinking. I am young, no one expects someone of my age to be responsible for a facility like this.

"I'm sorry, I thought you would be much older" he surprisingly states. "

"Why thank you" I respond back with a smile, I have learned to take reactions like this as a compliment.

"My name is Mark, I'm Levi's manager, I will be here for a while making sure he gets settled in", he says to me as he looks down at the floor and rubs his hand on the back of his neck.

"Don't worry'" I assure him.

"I will go over everything with you and the family once I have a chance to talk with Levi", I tell him.

"Can you tell me who those people are who came with you?' I ask Mark.

It is important that I get to know everyone who will be with Levi, helping him and supporting him. These will be the most important people in his life while he is here. All my patients have thrived when they had someone by their side, encouraging them.

"Yeah, sure, those are his parents Tom and Jenn and his fiancé, Emma", he states.

As I lead Mark towards Levi's room, I see Levi's father standing outside the door with his face resting in his hands.

Yelling is coming from Levi's room.

"Where the fuck am I, why isn't anyone telling me what is going on, and why the fuck can't I get out of this bed".

As I approach his room, I hear his mum softly say, "Levi, sweetheart, you were hit by a car and you are paralyzed, we have brought you to Boston where you will have the best chance of walking again".

Levi starts shouting again. This time louder, more hysterical.

"Walk again! walk again! what the fuck!", he starts screaming again.

Chapter 4

Paralyzed

Levi's POV

Paralyzed! walk again! Those inconceivable words playing over and over in my head. I must be delusional! That has got to be it! The pain killers must be making my mind foggy.

How did this even happen? One minute I am having drinks and dancing with Emma and the next I am here. I have no recollection of the events that took place after Mark dragged me out of the pub. None of this seems real. Like I woke up in the middle of a surreal dream.

All I see above me while I lie here is a white ceiling and when I turn my head slightly, I can see light gray walls. Emma is gently rubbing up and down my arm with her hand and she is whispering, "It's ok baby, everything will be ok", I am not sure I believe her as tears are rapidly flowing down her face.

My mum is sitting by my other side and looks like she has been crying nonstop for hours. I can feel Emma lightly stroking my arm, but I cannot seem to reach for her, my arms feel heavy, so heavy that I cannot move them even though I want to. I look down and see my legs covered by a blanket. I try to wiggle my toes from underneath the covers, but I can't, they do not even feel like they are connected to my body.

This is scary shit! My heart is uncontrollably beating out of my chest now, and my rapid breathing is starting to intensify even more. I can't even focus on anything that is going on around me. Someone please help me! But the words do not leave my mouth.

Emma continues nervously stroking my arm and I cannot take it anymore.

"Stop touching me" I blurt out.

Instantly, the expression on Emma's face turns to shock and she instinctively steps away from me, her eyes filled with even more pity than before.

"Everyone just please stop touching me! and stop crying! you're not the ones lying in this bed", I am practically hyperventilating now.

This is not happening! this is just a terrible hallucination I try to convince myself.

Just then, I am startled by the feeling of my right arm being lifted from the bed. I can feel some pressure up towards my armpit, the pressure then shifts to my elbow down to my fingers. I look over towards my arm and find someone massaging my hand and fingers with hers, then back up towards my shoulder, massaging certain spots and back down my arm again, ending at my fingers. I did not even notice her enter the room just as I was about to flip my shit. But here she is, this strange and beautiful girl, gently yet firmly massaging my arm, and without realizing it, my breathing begins to slow.

"Look at me" her angelic voice says.

With hesitation I try and focus my gaze on her.

"My name is Charlotte Thomas, but everyone around here calls me Charlie", she says to me, and I find myself staring at her with nothing but confusion.

She is looks to be around my age and she is very pretty. Her hazel eyes are studying me, it is not a look of pity for me when she looks into my eyes, it is more of a hopeful and determined look. The way she looks at me is much more calming to me than the way my parents and Emma have been looking at me.

This situation is mysterious and strange, almost resembling an eerie sensation of only her and I alone in this unfamiliar room as everyone else around me has become ghostly silent.

"What are you doing to my arm" I ask her, still trying to determine if she is a figment of my imagination.

"I know you can feel this, now I want to show you that you can move your arm and fingers". She encourages me.

The only thing I can do is shake my head at her. I can feel the image of disbelief forming across my face and I am positive she can see it.

"I want you to only focus on your hand and fingers and nothing else" she calmly says while I nod my head.

"Now squeeze my hand" she instructs.

"I can't" I mumble back.

She gives me the most encouraging smile and says, "yes you can Levi, try one more time, focus...Good!" she says, and at that moment I hear everyone in the room gasp.

"What the hell?", my voice more demanding now.

This feels like an episode straight out of the twilight zone. Who is this girl and what did she just do to me? She popped into my room out of nowhere, distracting me from my fit of rage, and performed some special magic. She is so calm, and she seems to be making me calm as well.

Emma rushes over to my side again and grabs my hand. I give it a little squeeze with mine and she smiles. My mum is crying again but I think they are happy tears now, who knows, this is all so fucked up.

The beautiful calm girl whose name is now forever engraved in my mind, starts speaking again.

"Levi, your family has brought you here to my rehabilitation center because it is the only kind in the world like it, and my program is meant to help you learn how to walk again".

She must see the bewildered look on my face because she continues to explain what happened to me.

"You were hit by a car and the impact broke your back in two places. The lower break caused bruising on your spinal cord which is why you cannot move your legs right now".

My breathing is starting to pick up again as she attempts to make sense of all this. I look around the room and see my dad sitting in a chair with his hands on his lap listening to the girl. My mum of course is still crying, and Mark is pacing back and forth in the opposite corner of the room. Emma is still holding my hand and looking at me with the saddest look in her eyes, like someone just died. I wish I really had died. I can't breathe again; this is too much.

"If you'll allow, I'd like to talk with you alone Levi, so I can explain more, and so I can get a sense of how you feel about my program here", Charlotte asks me.

I nod my head in agreement and she instructs everyone else in the room to follow her assistant to the lounge so they can get some coffee and food.

Charlotte notices the anxiety spilling over my face and the angry scowl on Emma's face after her request.

"I need to access how much feeling and movement Levi has, and I need him to fully understand and agree to this therapy, without any influencing factors", Charlotte directs right at Emma.

Emma crosses her arms like a spoiled little girl. She hates being told what to do.

"It will take about an hour, try to enjoy some fresh coffee and snacks in the lounge, or you are welcome to take a walk along the gardens", she says.

Emma reluctantly nods and whispers to me "I will be back soon babe".

The room is now silent, I don't hear anyone sobbing which is a relief. Charlotte pulls up a chair next to my bed and uses the bed controller to slowly sit me up.

"Let me know if I am hurting you Levi"

She brings the back of the bed up just enough so that I am eye level with her.

" I thought we could just talk face to face, instead of me looking down at you", she says to me with her gentle voice.

Even though my whole body feels like it is shaking inside from anxiety, this girl seems to know how to make everything a little calmer.

Chapter 5

Nothing Works

Levi's POV

"How is your pain level right now? One being the least amount of pain and ten being the worst", Charlotte asks me.

I wasn't even noticing or even thinking about pain or the fact that I have two fractures in my back.

"Umm a four maybe", I lie.

Now that she has asked me, I am in quite a lot of pain. She must notice I lied to her because she gets a few extra pillows from the closet and places them under my arms.

"I am just going to adjust your posture so that you are more comfortable", she says.

Before I can respond, she stands up and leans over me while gently placing her hands behind my shoulders, shifting my upper body slightly to the left. I hold my breath and realize that my body will not lift on its own and she is the one moving my torso.

"Does that help with the pain at all?" she looks worried.

"yes" I reply, not lying this time.

"I am sorry for all the commotion earlier, it must have been scary for you not knowing why you are here", she says to me.

I do not know what to say so I just nod. The events are too unreal to me and I need to be reminded of the details. I gather all the courage I have and ask her, "Can you please tell me what happened again and how I got here?"

She sits back down next to me, "Of course" she says.

She continues to tell me that I was hit by a car while I was walking in the street in London, I was taken to the hospital where they did surgery on my lower spine to stabilize it, then I was immediately flown here to Boston on a med plane. Mark had heard about this experimental therapy program for people with spinal cord injuries and called Charlotte immediately. There was only one spot open, so Mark and my family flew me here right away.

"It was very important that your family get you here quickly, because therapy treatment needs to start immediately so that your nerves stay active and you have the best chance of regaining strength and movement", she says looking straight into my eyes so that she knows I understand.

All I can do is nod and stare at her. Her eyes are so calm, and I am caught trying to figure out what color they are, instead of honestly listening to what she is saying. There is a layer of dark blue, then green and a hint of gold to her eyes, they are mesmerizing! Her face is flawless without a hint of make-up on and her smile is so welcoming. I am curious about her; it is hard for me to look away.

"Is it alright that I try a few things to your left arm like I did to your right one? and to your legs and feet?" she asks me.

I immediately stop staring at her, "yeah, sure" I clear my throat and speak.

She walks over to my left side and gently picks up my left arm and begins to press and massage in the same areas she did with my right arm. She must see the discouragement on my face when she asks me to squeeze her hand and I am barely able to do it.

She looks at me with an encouraging smile and says, "It's ok, you can feel what I am doing right? this is just your baseline, and now I know what we will need to work on".

I should be scared as shit right now, but she seems so hopeful and maybe I should be too.

She moves to my right leg, this time just moving her hand from my thigh down to my toes.

"Can you feel this?" she asks me with a concerned look.

"No" I angrily state, not meaning to sound so angry, but now I feel like I am shaking and hyperventilating all over again.

She firmly presses her thumb into my inner thigh next to my groin and keeps it there a few seconds before massaging my upper leg. She then presses into areas around my knee and into my calf. I can feel that now as she is looking at me and waiting for me to respond.

"Just breathe" she says in a soft yet comforting tone.

I feel my breathing begin to slow again as she massages my leg and foot.

"Try to lift your knee up from the bed", she tells me.

Just then she gives me a huge smile. "That was a good inch up off the bed", she says with excitement.

At that moment I feel myself smiling back at her, and I feel a small sense of relief.

She moves to my left leg, doing the same she did with my right. Only this time my left leg barely moved when she asked me. For some reason, the left side of my body does not want to cooperate, but since she still looks so hopeful, I will too for the moment.

Charlotte then begins to explain that the therapy treatment will be intense. Constant therapy for 16 hours every day. She explained some of different types of therapy they do here and that her and her assistant and one other person would oversee my case.

She informs me that my program will last 12-18 months, and at the end of the 12 months I would probably have gained all the feeling and movement I was going to have. After that, therapy would switch to learning how to live independently. When she informs me that I may or may not need crutches or a wheelchair to help me get around for the rest of my life, my eyes swell up and tears start rolling down my cheeks.

She tucks her long dirty-blonde wavy hair behind her ears and leans over to wipe my tears from my face, since I cannot do it myself. I gape in awe at her, trying to fathom all the things this stranger is doing for me.

We talked for a little longer. she made sure I knew that I would have ups and downs, and that I would need to be on a bladder and bowel regiment to help gain control of those again.

"What do you mean control my bladder and bowels again?" I harshly ask her.

She then takes my hand in hers and looks at me with her beautiful multi color eyes and says," I know you are angry and scared, and 12 months is a long time, but I will do whatever it takes, and I will help you every step of the way, to get you back to an active happy lifestyle".

Charlotte wipes my tears one more time. It is killing me to know that this beautiful girl undoubtedly will need to do everything for me. I cannot even lift my own hand up to my face to wipe off my embarrassment.

"I will send in Nate to get you cleaned up and I will let your family and manager know about the program and the length of therapy we discussed, I will be right outside if you need anything else", she says and walks out the door.

I can feel warmth near my groin area and look down to realize that I have pissed myself. "fuck" I blurt out loudly. Does any part of my body work anymore?

Chapter 6

Disbelief

Charlotte's POV

I walk into the lounge to find Levi's parents sitting together on a small couch in the corner of the room, and Mark on his cell phone again pacing back and forth.

The lounge was designed to be a comfortable place for anyone to relax. The room is well lit, there are two small brown leather couches in each back corner and a large L-shaped brown leather couch in the middle of the room. Two black leather recliner chairs near each end of the large couch. The whole facility, including this lounge room is adorned with Natural wood beams that accent the high ceilings. The contrast of the light walls and wood flooring give the everything a rustic and home-like feeling. An entertainment center with a 75" TV makes the room perfect for gatherings.

Emma sprung up from one of the recliner chairs as soon as she spotted me enter the room and says, "Are you done with Levi? Can I see him now"?

"Just a little longer, my assistant Nate is in the room with him now", I tell her.

Emma's eyes narrow, she huffs loudly, and I can sense that she is getting impatient with me.

"If everyone could grab a seat in front of the TV, I would like to show you a presentation of our place here and help explain what Levi will be doing while he is with us", I instruct.

Everyone cautiously takes a seat on the large couch in the middle of the room. Apprehension clearly expressed on each of their faces. Levi's parents are sitting in the middle of the couch holding each other's hands tightly together. While Mark and Emma take a seat on either side of them.

I began by showing them a video which was more of a virtual tour of the facility and an introduction to the important people who will be working with Levi every day. The second half of the video showed an example about each type of therapy that is offered.

At the end of the video, I take a deep breath and began explaining that because of the extent of Levi's injuries he would need 16 hours of therapy every day and his program would be complete in 12-18 months

I bit my bottom lip while anxiously awaiting their reactions. Immediately Mark stood up and started rubbing the side of his face while pacing again back and forth near the couch. Tears were falling again down Levi's mother's face, while his father just hugged her, then he looked at me and nodded with approval.

"18 months! 18 months!, what am I supposed to do for 18 months, stay here?, go back?, why is it going to take that long for him to walk again", the hysterical words come rushing from Emma's mouth.

I begin speaking as calmly as I can, "I know it seems like a very long time, I'm hoping to have him walking again, whether on his own or with assistance by 12 months, the last 6 months will be for Levi to learn how to function independently with whatever limitations he may have".

"You mean he might never walk on his own again? Why did we bring him here? I thought you were going to make him normal again?", Emma blurts out in frustration.

"Shut up and Sit down, Emma", Mark demands.

That catches Emma completely off guard, and she sits down, but not before giving Mark the most irritating look.

Mark looks at me, "Have you told Levi everything? has he agreed to stay here and go through with this therapy?".

"Yes, I have explained everything to him, and he agrees", I assure everyone.

I continue on, saying, "I want you all to understand, that I can't give you daily personal medical information about Levi, that information has to come from Levi himself if he wants to share it with anyone. You also have to understand that Levi needs your support as he learns how to do everything all over again, not just walking, but moving his arms and legs, learning to sit up on his own, feeding himself...basically everything we do easily on a daily basis, he will need to learn how to do all over again and he will need all the support he can receive from you".

Everyone's eyes stare at me in disbelief, while letting my words sink in, and they start to realize the reality of this whole situation.

This is the hardest part of my job. I have seen this reaction from every family that has been in this room and it breaks my heart every time.

Mark turns to Emma and says", You can stay here with him as long as you need to, we can push back finishing the movie as far as we can push it. It's on the last scenes now and Levi has luckily finished all his scenes already, we just need you for what's left".

Emma nods in agreement, then turns to me, "Can we go see him now?"

Levi's father walks up to me and assures me that he knows that he brought his son to the right place and that this is his best chance. He thanks me before taking his wife's hand and leading her to Levi's room.

Chapter 7

Humiliated

Levi's POV

I am not sure that I can feel anymore humiliated. I just pissed myself and did not even realize it until I felt the warmth run down my leg and see it on my sheets. Now that I am thinking about it, things are going to become quite uncomfortable knowing that this guy Nate must clean me up. I no longer feel like I am me, I am a useless person who can't even use the loo on my own and I am going to need to rely on strangers to clean up my mess. Oh no! am I going to also shit myself without knowing it! That better not happen!

"Hey man, I know this is really upsetting, but it will get better, we will get you on a schedule and this won't happen nearly as often as you think" Nate assures me.

I am sure he sees the horrid look on my face. I'm too embarrassed right now to even speak. I wonder if he is embarrassed for me, although he is probably used to this around here. Normally, I would just curse him out, yell at him, something...but I just lay here silently humiliated and stare out the window.

He starts to put the head of the bed down, so I am lying flat. "Sarah, my assistant is coming in to help me roll you and change the sheets, we need two people for this so we can move you while keeping your back straight, let me know if we are causing you any pain".

A young girl, probably in her early twenties enters the room. Her voice is bubbly, and she is smiling, "Hey Levi", she cheerfully says.

This fragile looking girl with long brown hair and big brown eyes is a bit too happy for my liking right now, but I do not have any choice in the matter. I no longer have any choice when it comes to my body. They can leave me here in my own filth, for all I care, but that will not be an option for me. Everything I was once able to do is now gone, taken from me and I am left with nothing working.

Nate leans over me and puts one hand on the back of my right shoulder and one hand on my right hip and rolls me to my side, as the fragile bubbly girl swiftly removes one side of the sheets and replaces it with a clean one. Nate then switches sides and rolls me the other way while Sarah does the same thing with the sheets on the other side of the bed. And just like that I am lying on clean sheets again. The process of changing my bed sheets was swift and painless, one thing out of this shitty mess that I can appreciate.

"Ok, let me know if you need anything else? nice to meet you Levi", the girl says as she darts out of my room.

"I'm going to clean you up now and get you into some comfortable sweatpants and a shirt instead of this terrible hospital gown", Nate states.

Fuck! I feel my brows pinching together as I glare over at Nate. Just the thought of being fully exposed to this stranger as he cleans my dick and then must dress my limp body is putting me over the edge.

He must see the anguish rush over my face because he quickly starts to wash me with a warm washcloth and says, "This part will be easier if we focus on something else".

Pondering for a second, he then asks me, "What do you think of Charlie so far?"

"Charlie?" I question.

"Oh right, she probably introduced herself as Charlotte", he corrects himself.

"Some of us call her Charlie, she doesn't really prefer one over the other", he tells me.

As soon as Nate mentioned her name, a rush of calm came over me and I suddenly forgot what was currently being done to me. I close my eyes and remember her soft touch, the way she slowed my breathing down, the way she brought me to her eye level so I would not feel so inferior. She has treated me as a competent human being instead of a hopeless freak. Nate is treating me in a similar fashion, not as gentle but he is straight forward, making me feel less inadequate. I can respect him for that.

Nate lifting me forward to put my shirt on, wakes me from my soothing trance. I realize I have not answered his question yet.

"She seems very kind", is all I say.

"Yes, she is probably the nicest, most caring and determined person I know". Nate happily exclaims.

"I'm finished, are you a little more comfortable now?" Nate asks me.

That was not as bad as I thought it was going to be. I nod my head and thank him.

"Good, I will let your family know they can come in now". Nate turns and walks out the door, leaving me alone with my troubled thoughts again.

I do feel a little better now that I am in some comfortable clothes. I do not like this feeling of not being in control of my body. I hate that Emma must see me useless like this. I need to know how she is feeling, what does she think of me now, will she still love me? How can she love a man who cannot even move, cannot even use the toilet, cannot even hold her hand? I need her to love me, without her love, I have nothing at all.

I can't even get my hand to catch the tear I feel falling down my cheek again. I know Emma cares for me, but I don't know what this will do to her now. She is very set in her ways and she has specific goals that she wants to achieve, and I already know she will not let anything get in her way.

The door opens and Emma, Mark and my parents somberly walk in. My mum does not seem to be crying anymore, which is a relief. Emma rushes over to my side and grabs my right hand, I manage to give hers a little squeeze.

"I am going to be ok", I try to assure her while forcing a smile.

"Yes, you are mate!", Mark blurts out from the corner of the room.

"I'm going to make sure you are all settled here, then I am going fix things over in London, get the movie wrapped up, this is a great place here, looks like you will be very busy", Mark rants off.

Mark continues again, " I will call every day and I will be back for a visit next weekend".

"Yeah, yeah, ok thanks mate", I reply.

I look over at Emma, "are you going to stay?" I ask her.

"Yes, I'm going to stay as long as I can", she grasps my hand tighter.

"So are your mother and I", I hear my father chime in.

"Charlotte suggested a hotel close by for us, so we will be going there tonight to shower, eat and get some sleep", my mother finally utters.

They all hung around a little longer, staring at my motionless body, probably waiting for some part of me to miraculously move. No one said much of anything. I think everyone is still too stunned to know what to say, and probably hungry and tired, so I suggested they head to the hotel.

I know they love me and want to stay and help me, but a part of them also wants to forget that the person they love is now crippled. I do not blame them this is overwhelming for everyone.

My mum leans over and kisses my forehead and says, "I love you son", then Emma plants her lips softly to mine and whispers, "I will see you in the morning", then they all turned around and left me desolate.

There is no use trying to hold back my tears. I am not one who cries often, but here I am, wallowing in self-pity.

Chapter 8

Night One

Levi's POV

I am left abandoned now in this huge room. It is the first time I had a moment to inspect everything around me. My bed is much bigger than a regular hospital bed, two of me could fit on here and I don't know if it is my newfound loss of control or sensation of my body, but I can tell this isn't a regular mattress. The material is hard to describe, like an air mattress with hundreds of squishy bubbles, I feel like I'm floating on top of it.

There are two oak night stands on either side of the bed, a leather recliner sits in the corner of the room, and a big screen TV on the wall facing my bed. The walls are light grey, the floors are wood, and two fat wood beams intersect the ceiling, it reminds me of my flat in England.

I have a private bathroom, but cannot make out what it looks like, who knows if I will ever use it. Thankfully, I can lift my head and move it around freely. I can get my right hand to slide left and right over the sheets and my elbow to bend slightly. I do not know if I can handle even attempting to move my legs or other arm right now, just thinking of myself lying here paralyzed is causing my body to tense then release, followed by an internal shakiness. This is what it must feel like to panic. It is an uncontrollable, heart pounding, limbs shaking, can't catch my breath kind of feeling. Isn't it enough that I am paralyzed? Panic attacks are not what I want added to my misery.

Just as I was about to lose my mind, I hear a knock at my door and Charlotte walks in. She is pushing a tray on wheels and what looks like a plate of food on top.

"Hi", her voice soft and sweet. "I thought you might be hungry".

I do feel famished, but how am I supposed to eat, is she going to feed it to me like an infant. I do not know if I can handle that, I have not been able to handle anything else today so far, and for some reason, having Charlotte feed me makes it more futile.

"Is Nate coming in to feed me?" I ask her, hoping she will say yes.

"You are stuck with me", she cheerfully replies.

"Great", I sarcastically grunt without meaning for her to hear that.

I feel my brows squeeze together as I glare at her, even though I know I am being rude, and she does not deserve it.

"And I am not going to feed you, I am going to help you feed yourself, plus you don't look like the kind of guy who wants to be fed", she smirks, trying to lighten my mood.

Somehow it is working, just her being in the room is putting me at ease, I do not want to be alone right now. She pulls up a chair next to me and adjusts my bed, so I am sitting up more.

"I should have asked you what you wanted first, I am sorry, I hope a soup and sandwich is ok? if

not, I will have the kitchen make you something else",
she says.

"No, it's fine", I assure her. I would eat
anything right about now if I could.

She moves her chair so that she is sitting closer
to my bed, but so that we are both facing the same
way. Then she slides her forearm and hand underneath
mine and guides my hand to the plate in front of me. I
silently watch her as she helps me reach for the
sandwich. This is strangely comforting, and I find
myself continuing to stare at what she is doing to me,
this is not what I expected. I feel her place her hand on
top of mine and she wraps my fingers around the
sandwich while using her other hand to bring my hand
up to my mouth. I take a few bites and swallow my
food down.

"Thank you", I say to her.

"The soup might be a little tricky, but we'll try not to make a mess", she chuckles.

I am so thankful for her positive mood; I need things to lighten up a bit after listening to my mum cry all day.

Charlotte picks up my arm and hand again and this time helps me reach an odd-looking spoon. It has a fat handle, and the actual metal spoon part is bent inwards. Once she grasps my hand around the handle, I realize why this spoon is shaped this way, making it easier to grasp and bring it to my mouth without spilling the soup all over me.

This whole eating process was not as terrible as I expected it to be. I felt ashamed at first, having this remarkable girl feed me, but Charlotte occupied my mind by talking about the different things they have here, like the exercise room and therapy pool and spa.

She asked me questions about where I am from and if I had any other family other than who she met today. Our conversation was a nice and a much-needed distraction.

"I'm going to send Nate in now to help you get ready for the night, I will see you in the morning for breakfast, I hope you can get some sleep tonight", she smiles.

I thank her again as she walks out of the room. An uncommon sense of loneliness creeps in as I watch her leave. I have a feeling now that loneliness is going to become a common unwanted friend of mine.

A minute later Nate walks in with the two machines and sets them down on the bed.

"We have got to start the toileting schedule", he reminds me, and brings a urinal to my dick so I can piss in it.

At least it wasn't all over the sheets this time. He then brings the machines over to each of my legs. He places my leg on top of the padding on the machine and straps it in, then does the same to my other leg.

"These machines will give your legs a slow constant movement, bending and flexing your knee, this helps stimulate your muscles, I will leave them on for an hour then come and take them off so you can get some sleep", Nate implies.

"Ok", Is all I muster to say. I am so tired at this point nothing new is going to phase me.

"This whole room is wired into Alexa, so you can just tell her to turn on the TV, and what channel you want to watch. You can tell her to turn off the lights and can also ask her to call one of us if you need anything", Nates tells me.

"Thanks Mate" I say back. He tells me he will return in an hour then leaves the room.

The hour went by quickly as I spent the time trying to figure out the TV, maybe Alexa doesn't understand my British accent because she seemed to ignore the channels I requested. Nate came back and removed the leg machines, made sure I was comfortable and then left me be. I am so tired that even with the annoying ache in my back, I am sure I will be able to sleep.

Chapter 9

Emma Taylor

I didn't sleep at all last night. I cannot wrap my mind around what's happened the last few days. This all just feels like one big nightmare that might never end.

I'm afraid to be alone in the room with Levi, I should not be feeling this way, but I don't know what to do or how to act with him. I am upset, like a mixture of anger and sadness in one. I am sure Levi feels the same, even worse since this is him it has happened to. But this has also happened to me, not the physical part, but every other way about it. We were supposed to finish up our movie and start planning our wedding, even move in together in the next few weeks.

How are we supposed to do that now? Now he must stay here for at least 12 months! What am I going to do, stay here, go home, and come back every few weeks to visit? I must go back to finish the movie, I know that. I will feel awful leaving him here while I am gone, but it must be done.

Today I cannot be selfish, I need to be here for him. I want to help him, I'm just unsure how.

I walk across the hall to Levi's parents' room and tell them I will go see Levi early and have breakfast with him, so they can take their time getting ready.

The 5-minute walk to the rehab center is just what I need to settle my nerves. The weather is beautiful, springtime here in Boston seems nice. The sidewalks are filled with people walking in both directions and the street is busy with traffic, but I don't notice the noise around me because I'm lost in my own head anticipating what this day will be like.

I am greeted at the door by a young blonde girl behind the front desk. She is smiling at me and lets me know Levi is waiting for me. Why is everyone smiling around here? This does not seem like the appropriate place to be smiling, all I want to do is cry, but for some reason I hold it together while that girl continues to smile at me. My mood keeps fluctuating and that assistant guy, Nate passes me in the hall and greets me while also smiling. This has got to be a nightmare, and I want to wake up from it right now.

I find myself pausing right outside Levi's door. I am so nervous, I know I must go in there, but I cannot get myself to move any further. All the sudden I snap out of it as Charlotte walks out of his room and catches me standing there. I expected her to give me some kind of condescending look as I stand like a statue outside his door, but instead she just looks at me plainly like she knows what I am feeling at this moment.

"Good morning Emma", she kindly says.

"Levi is just about to have breakfast, I'm sure he would love to have your company", Charlotte encourages me, then gently places her hand on the back of my shoulder and guides me into his room.

Levi's bed is upright so that he is sitting up to eat. He is dressed in a black t-shirt and grey sweatpants which look comfortable, but I am used to seeing him dressed in jeans. I'm used to him sitting at a table for breakfast too, not in bed with a tray in front of him. His face looks pale and I cannot tell if he looks like he is in pain or if he is tired.

"Hey baby, I'm glad you are here, did you sleep well?" he asks me.

I instantly start smiling back at him when I notice him reaching his right hand up towards me. He can move his arms now, oh thank god! I think to myself, maybe this won't be so bad, and he will be up and moving in no time.

"Come sit here next to me", he pats towards the chair by his bed.

I cannot help staring at what is on his tray. The utensils are bent and have extra thick handles, and the large plastic mug has a large space between the cup part and the handle.

"These are very odd dishes they've given you", I say to Levi.

He gives me a half smile and responds, "I can't grab a normal fork, and this mug is made so I can put my hand between the handle so that you can help me bring the drink up to my mouth without me spilling it everywhere".

"What!", the sound of shock slips out of my mouth.

My reaction must have scared him because he looks down and nearly whispers, "Well that is only if you want to help me eat".

"Um, yes, of course", I recover.

Thankfully, Charlotte saves us from the awkwardness and walks over to show me how to feed Levi.

"Just put your hand over his and help him grasp the fork and use your other hand to help guide his movement towards his mouth, like this", Charlotte instructs.

"Isn't it easier if I just feed him myself?", I question her.

Charlotte smiles while acknowledging my question, "Yes, it is easier, but we want Levi to learn how to do this on his own, it will get easier for him as he gains more strength and movement, plus this gives him a little more independence. I'll leave you two alone for a bit, let me know if you need anything", she says and then leaves the room.

The next 30 minutes I spend trying to help Levi eat. I try to help him one way while he tries to instruct me another. It is all too surreal. Neither of us know what to say or how to act right now, so I decide to ask about his night and how he likes the place so far.

Nate comes in the room just as we finish breakfast. "We are going to start morning therapy now", he tells us.

"You can stay and watch, or you can help with the therapy if you would like Emma", Nate says to me.

I agree to stay and try to help.

Nate instructs me to stand on Levi's right side. "His right side is a little easier, as he will be able to help you a bit", Nate tells me, and I give him a questioning look.

Nate picks up Levi's seemingly lifeless left arm and begins to massage his shoulder down to his elbow, making small circular motions with his thumbs. Levi looks at me and gently touches my hand. He slightly raises his arm for me while nodding at me to take it. I lift it enough for me to get my hands around his upper arm, then I look over to Nate.

"It's ok Emma, just do what I'm doing, press into his muscles, you won't hurt him", he instructs.

I start to copy Nate's movements and I find myself staring at him, not even looking to see if I am doing my part correctly.

"Are you ok?", Levi whispers to me, bringing me back out of my trance.

"Yes sorry, I want to make sure I'm doing it right", I say.

"You are doing fine baby, thank you for helping", he says in his sweetest voice.

Nate disrupts the uncomfortable feeling in the room by asking us about the movie we are making. It felt refreshing to talk about something familiar to us. Levi and I filled him in on all the details about the movie and who all the actors are.

I was too into the conversation we were having to realize I was now bending Levi's elbow, then massaging his forearm, moving his wrist and then his fingers around, as Nate was doing to Levi's left side.

We then moved on to legs. Things got very weird when Nate reached up to Levi's upper thigh near his groin to start massaging, and it got even worse when I was doing the same thing to Levi's right thigh. Levi kept shifting his wide stare from Nate to me then back to Nate. This must be embarrassing for him; I know it is for me. Things got slightly better as we made our way down to Levi's knees and ankles.

Levi was able to lift his right knee slightly for me, but I couldn't help but notice he was not moving his left leg at all. I felt my eyes fill with liquid and looked away quickly hoping Levi would not catch me crying.

"Is this the type of therapy Levi will have every day?", I ask Nate.

"Yes, he will have this type of massage therapy twice a day, but he will also have many other different therapies throughout the day", he continues in his confident voice..."The first two weeks will be similar to this, this passive therapy as we wait for his fractures to heal. After that, we will be able to get him sitting up, swimming, lifting weights and all kinds of other things. It's just slow at first but will get better".

"I'm going to help him with toileting now, then get him up into a wheelchair so he can hang out with you and the family in the lounge", Nate explains.

I look at Levi, and then tell him I will call his parents to come over now. I lean over and kiss his forehead, then head out of the room.

Finally, out of the room, I lean my back against the wall right outside his door and release a long breath I didn't realize I was holding and begin to feel the tears welling up in my eyes again.

Chapter 10

Scared of Me

Levi's POV

My sleep was sporadic and when I woke this morning, I almost started to panic again. I felt trapped in my bed, like my arms and legs were tied down and there was no way out. It took everything I had to try and calm myself down long enough to focus on my right arm. I took a deep breath and willed my brain to make my right arm move. I have never had to conscientiously make any part of my body move before, but here I am, staring at my right arm and telling it to move. Oh, thank God, I exhaled, I can lift my arm up off the bed and bend it slightly. Hesitation stops me from turning to my left arm, and my stomach begins to churn.

Thoughts of my left side not moving start to flood my mind and my breathing picks up again. I feel like my whole body is shaking inside, even though I can see it isn't. Just as I was about to yell for help, Charlotte walks in.

"Good morning Levi", she says with a perfectly calm voice.

Her smile is so genuine, it lights up her beautiful face. I start to release some of the panic that was building inside me from just her presence here. How does she do that?

She must have caught my panic-stricken face when she entered the room because she picks up her pace as she makes her way over to me.

"Are you ok? are you in any pain?', she asks me.

" I... I didn't sleep well", I respond.

"I brought you your breakfast! Emma called to say she's coming in early, so I thought she could help you this morning?", her thoughtful multi-colored eyes are peering into mine, waiting for me to say something.

"Thank you", is all I muster.

Charlotte sets up the food tray in front of me and says, "I will be back a little later, I have a few other people I have to see this morning".

And like a paranoid idiot, I nearly whisper, "when do you think you will be back?"

My chest feels tight and my voice is shaky. I know I must look desperate, but I need her to stay, I need the calm feeling she brings into my room.

She gently places her hand on my right shoulder and her reassuring words lightly flow from her mouth, "I promise I will see you again by lunch time".

I watch Charlotte start to leave my room only to hear her voice again, this time she is speaking to Emma right outside my door.

Why is Emma just standing at my door? how long has she been standing there?

Emma slowly walks in, assessing her surroundings, eying me up and down. Charlotte is guiding her further into my room. She is walking too slow, like she is afraid of something. I am happy she is here, but I do not like seeing her like this, I need to break her solemn mood.

I reach my right hand up towards her and show her a brave smile, "Hey baby, I'm glad you're here, did you sleep well?", I ask her.

"Come sit here next to me", I instruct.

She instantly starts smiling and makes her way over to me. Curiosity sweeps over her face as she looks at my breakfast tray.

"These are very odd utensils", she says to me.

I try to tell her that they are shaped that way so it's easier for her to help me eat, but she instantly jerks back in her chair and yelps, "what?".

My heart instantly breaks, the pain in my chest returns and I put my head down, unable to look at her and sigh, "well that's only if you want to help me eat".

Thankfully, Charlotte hangs around a little longer and shows Emma how to help me with my breakfast. After Emma feels somewhat comfortable helping me, Charlotte leaves the room.

I am pleased Emma is here helping me, but I can't help feeling like she was forced to. I know she must be nervous and doesn't know how to act around me right now. I just want to wrap my arms tightly around her and tell her everything will be alright, or better yet, I want her to wrap her arms around me and let me know she is here for me no matter what. But she barely touches me or looks at me and all I can feel is hurt and anger radiating from me, as we spend the next thirty agonizing minutes eating breakfast.

Nate walks into the room and saves us from emotionally hurting each other any further and lets us know he is doing my first therapy treatment today. Emma hesitantly offers to help Nate do therapy to my right arm.

At least she is trying to be supportive now. She still looks scared as shit, but I give her credit for trying.

I try to help her as much as I can with my right arm as she copies everything Nate is doing with my left arm. All I feel is that irritating pins and needles feeling you get after your arm falls asleep, as Nate massages my left arm. Not only is the feeling aggravating me, but the fact that my left arm is totally ignoring me when I try to lift it, is causing my anger to boil inside me again. So, I focus on Emma instead. Her beautiful face is completely engaged in what she's doing to me right now. Her bright blue eyes looking at Nate then to me waiting for approval.

Nate breaks the silence again and starts asking questions about our new movie. Emma's face lights up as she gladly answers all his questions and then some. I chime in now and then, as long as this keeps Emma's happy mood going.

Nate's next grasp startles me, "What the fuck Nate!"

What the fuck is he doing? He has got his hands up near my groin now, and I am caught off guard with pure embarrassment. Emma is doing the same thing to my right thigh and she looks as mortified as I do, I am sure. I want to plant my fist into Nate's jaw, but I do not want to scare Emma more than she already is. Plus, I cannot get myself to physically punch him anyway and it makes me furious. So, I decide to silently glare at him instead. Nate quickly notices my mood and picks up the pace as he moves towards massaging my lower leg, ankle and foot,

Emma doing the same to my right. Finally, things get a little less disturbing as Nate focuses on bending my knee and moving my ankle, concluding the treatment.

"Are we done?", my voice harsh as I narrow my eyes towards Nate.

"Not yet, we have a few more things to take care of before we get you up into a wheelchair.", Nate adds.

Fuuuuck...I exaggerate in my head as Nate ends therapy and abruptly tells us he is going to toilet me now. Emma's eyes almost pop out of her perfect face. I know she cannot handle this shit, hell, I cannot handle it either. It is not like I have any other choice though.

Emma leaves the room. She either thinks she is giving me privacy, or she is completely mortified by the fact I cannot take a piss in the bathroom on my own. Either way, it is probably better she leaves, I am sure she needs a break from all of this. I want her to stay though, I want her to sit on the bed with me and wrap her arm around me.... kiss me.

Why did this fucking happen!

Chapter 11

Nate Hanson

The first few days after a new patient arrives are always the hardest. They are scared, angry, withdrawn, there is no way around it. I can only stay calm and let them vent in whatever way they need to and be here for them.

Charlie has taught me a lot about compassion and determination, and I have taken what I have learned and applied it to how I interact with patients. Charlie has an incredibly special way of getting through to her patients. She is kind and dedicated and never judges anyone. She pushes everyone to do their best, even her employees and she never gives up on anyone. She is truly remarkable, and I am fortunate to work for her and learn from her.

Levi is a little more challenging than what I am used to. He is an actor, he is used to having things his way, has a beautiful actress girlfriend who has relied on Levi to take care of her, and his manager wants to control everything I'm sure.

"Sorry man", I tell Levi after our first uncomfortable therapy treatment.

He rolls his eyes at me and looks away. "Just get on with the toileting already", he growls at me.

I grab the urinal and do what I need to as he turns his head to ignore me.

"I know this is all unsettling and it will probably get worse before it gets better, but I'm always going to be straightforward with you about everything along the way", I state to him.

Caught off guard, but not totally unexpected, Levi asks me, "What the hell made you want to do this for a job?"

I do get asked that often, being a guy, I can understand why my job is not very appealing. This was not my first choice for a career, but things happen unexpectedly that cause a person to change course. It is better that Levi knows the reason, so I tell him.

"Fifteen years ago, my best friend severed his spinal cord in a skiing accident. There were not any treatment centers like this back then, so I watched him go through whatever treatment options were available.

He couldn't feel or move anything from his chest down, he only had sporadic control of his arms".

Levi seems to be listening to me, so I continue, "I witnessed my best friend go through every emotion possible...anger, denial, hopelessness, depression, and even though I was there for him, it wasn't enough, and he took his own life", I almost choke on the words but go on...." I promised myself I would do whatever I can to make sure someone in his situation does not have his same fate. I did a lot of research, became a physical therapist, and then I found Charlotte, and here I am", I happily explain to him.

I thought of becoming a nurse, but during my first semester in Nursing school, I met Charlotte on the rehab floor of one of the hospitals. I watched the way she interacted with a patient who was paralyzed from the waist down and was intrigued. I started asking her questions and she told me about her rehab center specifically for spinal cord injury patients. She gave me a tour around the facility one day and realized right away that I wanted to be a therapist here.

Levi looks at me with a much more pleasant expression and earnestly says, "oh".

After what feels like a newfound respect for each other, I get the Hoyer lift ready and explain how I am going to use it to lift him into his wheelchair. This process goes smoothly. He stays quiet but no longer angry. I reassure him that we will be able to do more with him as his fractures heal and he acknowledges me with a nod.

"Your parents, Mark and Emma are waiting in the lounge for you, we are all going to take a tour of the place together before lunch, alright? I say to him.

"Yeah, yeah, sure ok" he says as I push his chair into the hall.

Chapter 12

Uneasy

Levi's POV

Once Nate told me he would be putting my
back brace on me, I automatically assumed it would be
some over-sized, extremely uncomfortable contraption.
Instead, it was surprisingly light and thin and wrapped
around my torso like it was specifically pre-made for
me. Not sure when they measured me, but with all the

chaos over the last 2 days, I probably did not notice a lot of things they were doing to me.

Nate then slipped some kind of soft material with handles under me and attached me to a machine. Again, I find myself begin to panic as I watch this machine lift my mostly limp body up off the bed.

"I've got you man", Nate assures me.

Luckily for me, Nate is obviously some kind of expert at this, and quickly gets me adjusted into a wheelchair.

The chair is leaned back, to keep weight off my spine Nate tells me, and my legs and arms placed on top of padded leg and arm rests.

"You ready?", he asks me as he pushes me out of my room.

This is the first time I have seen anything other than my room. Well except for when I was wheeled into this place and did not know what the heck was going on.

I expected to see a plain white hallway with rooms on both sides like a hospital. Surprisingly, this place is not like that at all. It is open with high ceilings and wood beams throughout, as if this place were meant for the country and not the city of Boston.

Nate pushes me a little further down the hall and we pass by a large room with matts on the floor, parallel bars, a large padded table or bed, I don't really know. I scan the room a little more and find Charlotte. She has her hands on some guys hips. He looks like he is in his late 20's maybe, braces are attached to both of his legs and he is using his arms to hold himself up with metal crutches. Charlotte must be guiding him or making sure he does not fall as they both walk slowly in sync across the room.

We get around the corner and enter an oversized room with couches, recliners and a giant TV that takes up an entire wall, complete with surround sound.

"Here is the lounge", Nate exclaims.

Mark and Emma are in the far end of the room and abruptly stop whatever conversation they were having as soon as I enter.

Mum rushes over to me, "Hi son, how are you doing?", she asks me while planting a kiss on my forehead.

"Hey son", my dad nods to me.

"Hey", is all I say and give them a smile.

Mark confidently strides over to me, "Alright? Mate! How was your night? are they treating you well?", he asks me.

"Yeah, yeah of course", I assure him.

"Let's get on with this tour then", Mark adds as he glances towards Nate.

Emma slowly walks over to me and I hold out my right hand to her, hoping she will gladly accept it.

Relief sweeps over me as Emma takes my hand in hers and we all head out of the room together.

Nate continues to lead us around the building, my mum pleased as we admire the pool and spa, a weight room, the expansive kitchen and eating area.

My thoughts were mostly focused on the nagging pain in my back until I realized that Emma was still walking by my side holding my hand.

"I love you", I look up and whisper to her.

She looks at me briefly and slightly smiles, "I love you too".

"How about you and I have lunch together in the courtyard and we can enjoy the views of the bay", I ask her softly.

She quickly releases my hand and starts looking towards my parents. "Um...I..I would love to, but your mum really wants to help you with your lunch today, but maybe dinner?", she responds, keeping her eyes from meeting mine. As soon as we pass a restroom, she darts over and says, "I'll be right back".

Without a moment to process what just happened, Mark is walking next to me.

"Hey mate, this place is fantastic! looks like you'll have everything you need here to get you on your feet again", he cheerfully states. "I'm leaving tomorrow, I have a lot of things to take care of back home with the movie, but I will fly back here Saturday ok?", Mark adds.

"Yeah, yeah, sure, do whatever you need to do, I've messed things up quite a bit I'm sure", I apologetically say to him. "Thanks for taking care of everything", I add.

"You ok I head out?", Mark asks me. "I have about 100 phone calls to make, I will see you in 5 days, but call if you need anything", he places a firm hand on my shoulder before saying his goodbyes to Nate and my parents.

What the fuck! Emma has disappeared into the restroom and Mark took off on me and did not even wait to say bye to Emma. I still have my parents here eagerly following Nate around, so I have not scared them away yet, but I'm sure I will soon.

I would rather be alone to sulk and this chair is really making my back ache now. I am about to ask to be brought back to my room when Charlotte pops out of the gym and into the hall in front of us.

My sour mood immediately taken back by the sight of Charlotte. Her long hair is pulled back into a ponytail. She is wearing a tight-fitting tank top, revealing her slender but toned arms. Her skin is shiny and small beads of sweat have formed above her brows. Was she just working out I ask myself?

She answers my thoughts, "Hey everyone", her multi-color eyes are bright as she turns her attention towards me.

"I told you I'd see you again before lunch", she smiles at me.

Emma finally reappears from the restroom to join us, staring at Charlotte just as perplexed as I was.

Charlotte looks at everyone again and begins to explain herself, "I just fit in a quick work out, so I'm going to have Sarah bring your lunch out to the patio for you all to enjoy while I go take a shower".

"Levi, I will come find you after lunch so we can get going on afternoon therapy", she gladly says to me before Nate whisks us around towards the direction of the patio.

"Are you feeling ok?", I ask Emma as I reach for her hand

"I'm fine, let us go eat", she replies and places her hand in mine.

Everyone is quiet during lunch, except my mum of course who is trying to help me eat, and repeatedly asks for Nate's guidance to assure she is doing it right.

The patio wraps around half the building and overlooks the Boston Harbor. The view gives me a beautiful and peaceful distraction.

After lunch everyone follows me back to my room and silently watches as Nate uses the machine to lift me from my chair and place me in bed. Nate removes my back brace and makes sure my body is positioned correctly in bed. I avoid making eye contact with anyone, I am afraid to find out what their faces will tell me. My parents let me know they will be back for dinner, then head out of the room with Nate.

Emma sits on the chair next to my bed. Now is my chance to talk with her. She has been acting strange towards me all day.

Chapter 13

Alone

Levi's POV

Emma and I are momentarily alone in my room now. It is the perfect time to ask her what the hell is wrong with her today.

"Is everything alright? you are acting strange today", I ask her

She looks at me, her lips pressed together in a firm straight line, eyes piercing through me, "No I'm not alright, none of this is alright", she states, finger pointing around the room. "This is too much for me", she adds

"Too much for you...Too much for you? I angrily repeat back.

My body tenses up and I want to grab hold and shake some sense into her. She is not the one lying useless in this fucking bed while someone must feed me and wipe my ass.

"What about me?", I growl back at her, anxious to hear what she has to say, but she just puts her head down and sits there in silence.

"What were you and Mark talking about in the lounge this morning", I try and change the subject a little.

She looks up at me surprised and rushes out her response.

"We were talking about finishing the movie and how much I have to do back home. He said I can stay here longer, but I have so much to do, I cannot put it all on hold. I'm...I'm ...going back tomorrow", the last part hits me like a freight train as her words slowly roll off her tongue.

She is really going back with Mark tomorrow. It has only been a few days and she is going to leave me here alone. I don't believe this.

"When will you be back?", I quietly ask her

Tears now rolling down her cheeks, "Next weekend", she insists.

I am angry and hurt mostly, but if this is my last day with her for a while, I must do something to make sure she knows I love her and that she loves me.

"Go lock the door" I instruct her

"What?" she looks at me confused.

"Go lock the door, then come back here", and she does what I say

"Now come here on the bed with me", I pat the bed with my right hand.

She hesitates for a moment before sitting on the bed next to me. I tell her to press the button on the bed to sit me up further and she follows my instructions. She looks at me, tears slowly running down her beautiful face. I reach up and cradle her cheek in the palm of my hand, using my thumb to catch her tears and say, "Kiss me".

She leans towards me and I softly press my lips onto hers, capturing her gentle moan with my mouth, I force my tongue to meet hers. I feel my body ignite as her tongue caresses with mine. I take a deep breath and continue pressing my lips harder to hers.

She pulls her mouth away from mine and slowly trails her lips along the crease of my neck, sucking at the sensitive skin at the top of my collar bone. My right hand moves carefully under her shirt and rests on her hip. Quiet gasps release from her mouth.

"You want this, it's what we needed", I groan. My head tilting back into the pillow while she kisses me.

Fuck! I just want to grab both her hips and pull her on top of me, but I know I can't.

She unconsciously starts to slide her hands down to my sweatpants, and just as she begins to slip her fingers under the waistband, I reach my hand down to stop her.

"Emma", I whisper loudly.

Her hand freezes and she pull her mouth away from my neck and looks up at me bewildered. For a moment she stays silent, her eyes instantly turn from passion to pity and she climbs off my bed.

"Shit! Sorry", I immediately blurt out.

I grab her hand knowing all too well what she is probably thinking right now, and gaze into her eyes.

"I just wanted to kiss you", I say softly. My voice pleading, "I'm going to miss seeing you every day".

She takes my hand in hers, our eyes still locked. I want her to still feel a craving for me, but the look in her eyes is confirming my worst fear.... regret!

"I love you Emma", I choke. I can feel the water begin to fill my eyes.

"I love you too", she says and then leans over and kisses my forehead.

"I'm sorry I have to leave, but I will call you every day", she tells me.

"You better", I press. "And we will see each other next weekend, things will be better" I promise her. She turns and walks out the door, leaving me here in this place, Alone.

Chapter 14

Feeling Bad

Charlotte's POV

As I approach Levi's room, I catch Emma hastily walking out, tears streaming down her face.

"What's wrong Emma", I ask her

"Nothing", she lies. "I have to get back to London, I have so much to take care of, I... I... Just can't be here", she sighs, lowering her head.

"Emma, look at me", I calmly demand.

She hesitantly raises her eyes towards me. I understand the look on her face. She is ashamed and confused. He is no longer the same man she fell in love with, not physically anyway, and now she is left to fight this battle inside her. All I can do is remind her that this is just one of the obstacles that they will both overcome with time.

She cannot leave him now, not like this. I know what happened is a shock to everyone, but what kind of person leaves their fiancé alone here after only two days? Yes, I have seen couple break up because of they find they can't handle the situation, but that is only after trying to give it some time, trying to make it work. Emma wanting to leave already is cruel.

I look directly at her and hope my next words sink in, "That is still Levi in there".

She looks down at the floor again then back up at me as I continue. "I know it is terrifying seeing him like this, but each week will get better, he will get stronger. He is still the same person".

Her mood swiftly changes, my words offended her somehow.

"No, he is NOT the same person", she fires back at me.

I'm in shock by her response, her voice is harsh, and she rushes the words out, "He is not the same! he can't do anything on his own, he can't even eat or go to the bathroom! I don't want to do that for him, he's supposed to be the one taking care of me!", she cries. "He's always been the one doing things for me, I don't know how to take care of anyone!"

She takes a deep breath then lets out a long sigh and calmly says, "I'm sorry, I know I look like a bad person, but I just need some time".

I do my best to reassure her, "Emma, you're not a bad person. Take the time you need, but please promise you'll come back and see him and give yourselves one more chance before you make up your mind".

"Okay, I will", she promises and heads out the door.

I contemplated whether I should give Levi some time to himself before bombarding him with therapy but decided it might be better to just keep things going, keep him distracted.

I knock on his door before slowly entering his room. He keeps his attention towards the window when I greet him. He stays quiet as I explain to him that I will be doing his massage therapy now. I decide to start with his left side, since he is content with staring out the window.

I start with his shoulder and upper arm, struggling a little as my small fingers have a hard time grasping around his perfectly defined muscles. His arm flinches a bit as I manipulate his elbow then his wrist, carefully massaging into every pressure point. I do not bother trying to strike up a conversation because I know it is better to leave him in his own thoughts right now. I go about massaging his hand and fingers and suddenly pause when I feel him slightly squeeze my hand, not willing to let it go. I wait for a moment, then he turns his head to look at me.

My thoughts now focused on his perfect face. I haven't really looked at him until now. His eyes are watery and blood shot, but the brilliant blue of his irises penetrate through me and my heart breaks for him.

Emma clearly portrays herself as a stereo-typical entitled, rich movie star who refuses to be burned by anything and expects everything to go her way. What in the world does Levi see in her? Is it because they are both movie stars and those are the people they need to date? I do not understand their world. Levi doesn't seem like he fits that description though. He is understandably angry right now, but he also seems kind and appreciative. So far, he has not been demanding or imperious, he has only been sincere. I feel so bad for him that his girl has left him here like this.

With pure sadness in his voice he asks, "Do you think she'll come back to me?"

I squeeze his hand back with both of my hands and give him an encouraging smile, "I hope so", I tell him.

He turns back towards the window and I finish his left side. He lets me turn on some music. I know we are not going to talk much so it's nice to have a little background noise. I move to his right side and continue moving and massaging his arm. My gaze is drawn to him again and I can see his eyes have dried up now as he shifts his stare from the window to me. His bright blue-green eyes now wary, as he studies my face.

Earth to Charlie, I say to myself, blinking quickly, and forcing myself to look away. I break the silence by going to the corner of the room to grab a small machine.

"This is a nerve stimulator", I explain to him, showing him what all the wires are for.

"I'm going to attach these wires to your arms and legs and the machine will send out impulses" I tell him.

"We've got about an hour until dinner, so I will leave this on and come back before its time to eat".

"What? no wait", he nervously says.

I look back at him with curiosity when he speaks for the first time after not communicating for the last hour.

"Can... can you please stay ...I don't want to be alone", he slowly asks.

Of course, I can stay I let him know. We spend the next hour trying to find a program to watch on the

TV. We still do not talk, but I realize he just needs someone here with him. I know what stage is next for him, and I will do whatever I can to help him get through it.

Thankfully, his parents arrive in time to help him with dinner. I need to catch up with a few of my other patients this evening. I know Nate and Sarah will occupy his time and he needs a shower, so plenty to do, he will not be alone I happily convince myself.

Chapter 15

Here For me

Levi's POV

The next two weeks went by slow. I am still not able to put pressure on my spine, so therapy was consistently the same. Massage, manipulate, leg machine, stimulator, practice eating...

My parents have stayed and ate breakfast and dinner with me every day, and I enjoyed their company. I sent them away during the middle of the day so they can tour around Boston and have some time to themselves. I tried letting them help with therapy treatments, but that did not work out so well for any of us, so we just stuck with helping with meals.

I really focused on getting my left arm moving, I wanted to surprise Emma and show her that I was getting better, moving more before she came to visit.

Mark came during his promised weekend visit. He stayed for two days, asked a million questions, and made sure everyone was doing their jobs here. He said the movie had more setbacks and Emma was needing to stay in London for a while longer before flying out here again.

Emma has called me every night like she said she would, but I wanted her here with me, being the one to cheer me on when I finally lifted my left arm up off the bed, or when I grabbed the big mug and was able to drink from it myself. I felt hurt that she wasn't here to see my small accomplishments, things I worked hard on for her. Our phone conversations became less pleasant, and each day that she was not here with me made me angry. She again promised that next weekend she would visit, so I am going to hold on to that promise and focus on getting my legs to move a little more before she sees me.

It is now Sunday night and my parents are here with me again for dinner. They look tired and worried for me of course. I know this is hard on them, seeing their only son paralyzed. They have been here supporting me, but I know Boston hotels are expensive and they need a break from seeing me like this.

"Mum, Dad", I start talking. "I Love you both and I'm grateful that you've been here this whole time, but it's ok for you to go back home for a while", I say to them.

My mum looks up at me with concern written all over her face.

"I will be alright mum! you can come back and visit in a few weeks", I try and convince her.

"I think that's a good idea son", my Dad adds. "How about we come back every month for a long weekend? will that be ok? will you be ok?", he asks.

I agree with my dad and spend the next half hour settling my mum down, I know she is not keen on this new idea.

"Shower time!", overly joyous Sarah announces as she jets into my room holding a bunch of towels.

"Well, that's our cue to get going son. We will see you in a few weeks then", my Dad states. Both hug me goodbye and head back to the hotel.

"Do I really need a shower every day?", I sourly protest to Sarah. "I don't even do anything to work up a sweat", I add, hoping to deter her from getting me in the shower.

"Levi, everyone showers every day and so should you", she bubbly replies.

"Plus, this is so you don't get any skin breakdowns from lying down so much", she points at me in my bed

"Fine", I growl.

Sarah is so happy and smiling all the time, I like giving her a hard time.

The process of using the Hoyer lift to get me from the bed to the shower chair is such a hassle. Sarah first must undress me and cover me with towels while she transfers me. My useless legs dangle from the shower chair and she has to put a strap around my body, so I do not fall out of the chair when she pushes me into the shower. This whole thing is embarrassing.

The first three times she gave me a shower was so uncomfortable and awkward. She talked annoyingly way too much and having my totally naked body exposed to her while she cleansed my skin with a washcloth, tore away any once of pride I had left for myself.

I must admit though, after going through this a few times now I do not find her nearly annoying anymore. Her constant cheerful chatter distracts me, and I even find myself laughing with her sometimes. The hot water against my tense muscles relaxes me, and I consider my nightly showers a form of calming therapy before I go to bed for the night, that and when Charlotte is with me are the only moments I don't feel like having a panic attack.

I don't know what it is about Charlotte. She willingly stays with me when my anger is out of control and when I make it hard for everyone else to handle, she is always here when I need her. Maybe it's just that I miss Emma, or maybe it's just because Charlotte chooses to be here, and Emma does not.

Chapter 16

Some Independence

Levi's POV

"Morning Levi", a hand tapping on my shoulder wakes me up. Charlotte is here with my breakfast.

" You slept in this morning!", she smiles while sitting my bed up.

"Shit! sorry!... I didn't mean to", I tell her.

Why did I sleep so late, I like to be dressed and my teeth brushed before she comes in. I am sure she does not care about what I look like, but I do. Especially in front of her.

I notice she is not wearing her signature tank top look today. She has got a light pink t-shirt on and tight-fitting grey sweatpants. Her dirty blonde hair is up on top of her head in a messy bun, it's cute!

She notices I am a little upset,

" It's no problem Levi, really! plus this is a big week for you so I'm happy you got some extra sleep".

Charlotte starts setting my tray up in front of me while I am still in bed. Lately I have been up in my chair already for breakfast because it is easier for me to feed myself.

"A big week for me?", I curiously ask her

I can't seem to get my hand to grab any of the food, usually Nate has done the massage therapy before getting me up. Charlotte starts massaging my arm and hand, focusing on my fingers, and helping me grasp my fork.

"Yes, it's a big week", she reminds me. " You're having an x-ray taken to make sure your fractures have healed enough, you'll be custom fitted for your leg braces, and if all works out... we are going to get you practicing sitting up on your own!".

She catches me staring off, "Is that ok?", she looks at me, waiting for me to respond.

"Yeah, Yeah, that sounds great", I say with a little excitement in my voice.

I haven't thought of sitting up on my own, I have only been able to lift my head, arms and mostly my right leg so far. My body has been lifted for me by the machine every time I am transferred out of bed or out of the chair, or to shower.

She squeezes my hand and smiles at me. I hadn't noticed that my random thoughts caused my breathing to speed up.

" I'm going to have Nate come in and help you get dressed, then have the x-rays done", she calmly says while squeezing my hand again, making sure I am ok before she leaves.

I am a little excited for this week, nervous as hell, but excited to start doing different things. The past three weeks have been slow, doing the same things every day, and I was starting to think I would never move forward.

After Nate got me dressed and the x-rays were taken, happy Sarah enters my room with a new wheelchair. She is so excited as she shows me that my new chair is electric. I can sit almost straight up in the chair now she tells me, and I can move my right hand enough now to maneuver myself around using the hand control.

This day just keeps on getting better and better, I think to myself.

I spend the rest of the day doing multiple therapy sessions and getting measured for my leg braces, but during my short down times, I am able to freely wheel around the place on my own. A little piece of independence has found its way back to me, and for the first time in three weeks I feel a hint of hope.

Charlotte helped me with dinner tonight and constantly praised me when I was able to feed myself with barely any help. I still need help grasping things, but Charlotte helped me understand how much of a big step this is for me, encouraging me to do more.

I cannot wait for Emma to see me this weekend. I am making progress now and I hope she will be just as excited for me as I am.

Chapter 17

Always on My Mind

Charlotte's POV

It's already Thursday, this week is flying, I think to myself as I hurry into my facility. Nate catches me at the front door.

"Oh, thank god I caught you right away Nate", dropping papers everywhere, I look like a mess. Nate helps me gather the papers from the floor and looks at me puzzled.

"I'm so sorry to spring this up last minute, I wasn't planning on going earlier, but now I have to get to an all-day conference at Mass General", I apologize to him, but go on, "Are you alright to cover everything here today? I've got Kelly coming in to do some PT with my other patients, if you can just focus on Levi today?"

Nate nods, " Yes of course, what should we work on today?", he asks me.

"Try getting him to lift the 2lb weights with his right arm, you can try his left, but don't push it, we know he will just be discouraged", I instruct.

"And get him moving his legs with his new braces on, I'm heading in there now to make sure they fit before I leave for the day". Nate accepts and continues to where he was heading before he saw me.

I walk into Levi's room with the new leg braces, "Morning!", I greet him.

He is dressed but still in bed, which works out better for me.

"look what I've brought", I show him.

"Great", he says back sarcastically while rolling his eyes.

"Oh, I know what you're thinking", I fire back.

"These things are amazing!, we have all this new experimental technology to make these specifically for you", I cheerfully say to him, and continue on..."they are so light, you will hardly feel them on, the material molds and can be adjusted to perfectly fit your legs and feet, the only hard parts are the thin hinges that lock your knees and ankles in place when we want to lock them", I keep smiling at him, showing my enthusiasm about them.

I know he doesn't believe me when he presses his lips into a firm line and just looks at me. So, I bring the braces over and start placing them on his legs.

He looks down at them and bends his right knee a little sliding his heel up and down the sheets.

"Hmm... I guess you're right ", he chuckles

I am relieved that they fit properly and decide to tell him I am leaving for the day and will not be back until tomorrow.

Panic takes over his face as he quickly looks up at me.

" Why?" he asks.

I tell him the reason and then assure him that Nate will be doing all his therapy treatments today and that I will see him in the morning.

He looks down at his braces again and quietly says, "okay".

The rest of this day is dragging on, this conference is so long, and I catch myself feeling worried about Levi instead of paying attention to the monotone lady speaking on the stage.

I call Nate during my break to check in on everything. He sounds annoyed when he tells me that Emma called Levi to say she was not visiting until Monday now, and that Levi has been in a non-cooperative mood since. I apologize and thank Nate at the same time and promise to be back there in the morning.

This is not going to be good... there goes any chance of me paying attention to anything taught at this conference today.

I call to check in one more time before I can get any sleep. Sarah answers and lets me know Levi was too angry to eat tonight and nearly all but refused his shower, but was in bed sleeping now.

Ok, I can deal with that I try and convince myself. Tomorrow is a big deal, we are going to finally get him sitting up on the side of his bed, no machine to help.

Chapter 18

Panic

Levi's POV

Anger... that is all I feel right now. I am angry with Emma for leaving me here alone, angry with myself for being so drunk that I stupidly walked into the middle of the road, angry I am here in this place and I am completely useless.

I did not sleep at all last night. I was so frustrated after Emma called me yesterday that I took it out on everyone who tried to help me. Charlotte was not here to calm me down, and I want to feel guilty for being mad at her too, but I cannot shake this angry feeling boiling inside me.

I am hungry, but I feel like I might be sick if I eat anything, and my head is throbbing... I think I am going to lose it!

Where the hell is Nate? I should be up in my chair by now, I just want to wheel myself out of this place.

My body feels so tense, I'm agitated, and my limbs stiffen up every time I try to move them.

Nate and Sarah appear in my room without the Hoyer lift I notice. Great... what are they going to do to me now I wonder, I am not in the mood for any of this, and Sarah is not in her normally chipper mood, she looks nervous... I do not like it.

"We are going to get you to sit on the side of your bed for a bit this morning and then transfer you into your chair", Nate assertively states.

" Where is the lift?", I ask him

" No lift", he replies

"What! No... no, I'm not ready for that", I state harshly

"Yes, you are ready, and we are going to help you ", he argues back.

My body once again goes rigid as they both grab a side of me to sit me up. My heart is ready to pounce out of my chest and I lose my breath when I feel Nate grab my legs and swing them over the side of the bed, Sarah guiding my upper body.

"Put me down!", I frantically demand.

"Put me down now! I yell louder.

I do not have any control of my upper body, it feels limp. I hate this sensation. Sarah is pressing one hand to my upper chest and one to my back trying to hold me straight. I will surely fall if she lets go. I am sitting on the side of my bed, but it doesn't feel like it, I am terrified now.

"Please lay me back down", I plead.

My whole body is shaking uncontrollably now. I cannot breathe I try to tell them but can't. I am having a full-blown panic attack.

All the sudden I feel someone get up onto my bed behind me.

"Levi", a concerned voice speaks. ...It's Charlotte.

I am shaking so bad now, I can't stop it, I can't speak. Charlotte will lay me back down; I know she will.

But I am wrong, she is not laying me back down... ugh! No one here is on my side, can't they see I am terrified!

A second later, Charlotte's touch sends an indescribable feeling throughout my body and I stop breathing. She is kneeling behind me pressing her body against my back then reaches over me to grab both of my arms with hers, firmly bringing them up to rest against my chest and gives me a bear hug.

"Just breathe", she softly says, her face close to my ear..."just breathe".

Charlotte keeps a firm hold around me. I can smell the sweet scent of her vanilla shampoo, her face and hair touching my neck. My breathing returns and slows down to almost normal and she waits, her arms still wrapped around me until I stop shaking.

When she starts to release me from her hold, I almost start to panic again, but somehow, I remain calm.

" I'm going to help you sit up now", she says softly.

"No! please", I beg her, feeling completely vulnerable now and I have actual tears pouring down my cheeks.

" Don't panic, please! I've got you, I promise", she quietly adds while wiping my tears with her fingers.

She slowly brings herself to the side of me while lifting my left arm and placing it around the back of her neck and sits beside me. Her right arm is around my mid back holding me up while her left hand is on my chest, and we just sit there.

Nate and Sarah have not said a word during this whole ordeal. They are just staring at Charlotte and I, mouths hanging open like their jaws might hit the floor.

"It's ok guys, I've got this", Charlotte says to them. Then tells them she will call them if we need anything.

She sits with me holding me steady on the edge of the bed for a while, letting me stay silent. I cannot help but look at her, her multi-color eyes, her face, so pure. The way she looks back at me makes me believe that she genuinely cares about me. But she can't really, this is her job, right? I think to myself.

Nate left my chair and what Charlotte calls a sliding board close to my bed. She slowly gets up, bringing my arms to grasp both of her shoulders as she stands in front of me.

"I've got you", she reminds me and places her arms under my arm pits and wraps them around my upper back.

I wrap my arms around the back of her neck, and she lifts me onto the slide board and guides me into my chair then adjusts my legs.

I do not have the words to tell her how I feel right now. I appreciate everything she has done for me and I hope when she looks at me, she can see how thankful I am. Thankful that at this very moment I'm not going to panic.

" Emma isn't coming again this weekend", I manage to speak

"I know, I'm sorry" she says back, acknowledging my hurt.

She grabs my hand and says, " I'll tell you what... how about we spend this weekend working on your core and your arm strength, so that if Emma shows up on Monday you can show her how you can sit up, along with all of your other accomplishments so far?"

" That sounds great!" I tell her. " Thank you, Charlotte".

Chapter 19

Unwanted

Levi's POV

Charlotte kept me busy all weekend with therapy. I can completely control my right arm movements, so Charlotte focused on helping me gain enough strength in my arm so that I am able to support some of my body weight or shift my body when I sit up. Plus, if Emma really shows up today, I want to be able to feed myself without her worrying that she needs to help me.

My left arm is another story. I can move it around but when I try to grab hold of something or use my arm to push anything, it just gives out on me.

I got into the pool for the first time this weekend, which was a nerve wracking and calming experience at the same time. It was not to swim or anything like that. There is a wide swim out in the deep end where the water comes up to my chest when I sit in it. Charlotte was right when she figured that the water would make it easier for me to learn how to balance myself upright.

I am surprised and relieved when Emma finally calls me to tell me she's landed in Boston. Nate finished up my morning therapy and helped me get into jeans and a light blue t-shirt. I actually managed to style my hair too. I know I should not have to, but I feel like I am back to the stage where I need to impress Emma all over again.

Charlotte agreed to let me take the rest of the day off from therapy as long as I promised to work extra hard tomorrow.

I decide to wait in the lobby for Emma to arrive. I can't help but smile when she walks through the door covering her face from the small swarm of photographers hoping to steal a picture of her... or me.

"Levi! ", she squeaks, either surprised or happy, I can't really tell by her expression, but I hope it's happy.

"Hey baby! I say back, holding out my hand for her.

She walks over and accepts my hand. I pull her towards me and plant a kiss on her cheek.

I feel a little nervous and start rambling off questions without giving her time to answer, "How was your flight? are you hungry? do you want some coffee or tea?"

Not sure she was listening to me because she was just standing in front of me examining me up and down and then staring at my chair.

"Emma", I call out her name, so she looks at my face.

" Yes, some coffee would be great", she says

I lead her outside to the patio. It's a beautiful day and we can drink our coffee and enjoy the view of the sailboats on the water instead of her focusing her thoughts on my wheelchair.

She smiles while we sit together silently drinking our coffee, neither having the courage to speak first.

Surprisingly, she grabs my hand from across the small table, " You look great", she says, and courageously keeps going...

" You've told me all you've done here so far, but's it's nice to see it in person".

" Yes, it is nice to see it in person", I politely remind her while biting my tongue so she can't hear my annoyance.

I want to tell her that she should have been here in person this whole time.

Changing the subject, I maneuver my wheelchair around to her, still holding her hand and ask her to come for a walk with me. I am appreciating every moment of her pleasant mood while she follows me to the small garden area. I bring her to a cushioned iron framed love seat among the flowers.

" We should sit here and talk for a while", I point to the love seat.

Her eyes glance at the love seat then back to my wheelchair. She lets go of my hand and says, " I need to go freshen up first, is that ok? I will be right back".

Nodding to her, I ask her to tell Nate to come see me on her way back inside.

Thankfully, Nate quickly comes out to me and I have him help me sit onto the love seat. I know why Emma scurried away; she was looking at me in my wheelchair wondering how to get me onto this bench. So, I wanted Nate to help me before she realized she would have had to pick me up and move my legs for me to sit up properly.

I know she misses me being the one to take care of her, now the roles are reversed, and she doesn't enjoy it, I can see it in her face... the conflict she's feeling inside her. I want it to be love that I see in her eyes when she looks at me... and desire to be here for me helping me get through all of this. I would be here if it were her in this chair.

Emma returned after a few minutes. I smiled when she looked at me, amazement in her wide eyes and happily took a seat next to me.

She disclosed herself to me and started talking about our film and how it was wrapping up, maybe completely finished in a month or two. With slight hesitation, she informed me that Liam has stepped up into a more leading roll with her when the director had to make a few changes in my absence.

That made me frown. So, she quickly decided to tell me about the gala they were having in October in honor of the film's completion, and that she wanted me there for it. I was a bit stunned when she said everyone is looking forward to me attending.

" Yeah! I should be able to make it to that", I impulsively agree.

It is getting a little colder out, I notice her rubbing the goose bumps forming on her arms and suggest we eat lunch on the patio near the fire pit.

She stands up and begins to walk towards the patio until she realizes I am still sitting on the bench. She walks back to me, staring at me waiting to see how I am going to get into my wheelchair.

" Can you help me transfer?" I softly ask her.

"Yes, sure", apprehensively walking to stand in front of me.

I place the slide board on my chair and the edge of the bench next to me.

" I'm going to hold onto the back of your neck so you can grab under my arms and lift me up, then slide me into my chair", I instruct.

She nods, her eyes unsure and places her arms around me. I slide into my chair and get my right leg onto the leg rest. She catches on as I struggle to use my right arm to adjust my left leg and reaches down to move it for me.

Shit ... this was a bad idea; I should have just stayed in my wheelchair and avoided this situation. My left arm doesn't help me any and I still look useless to her I am sure.

We head up to the patio in silence. This time I stay in my chair when we get to the small table by the fire pit. Sarah brings out our meals and quickly leaves us alone again.

I can't stand this awkward silence between us, so I gather all the courage I have left inside me to talk to her about what I fear she might say, but I need to hear it.

"Talk to me Emma... Please! I nearly beg.

" I need to know what you're thinking... what you're feeling"

She grabs both of my hands in hers and looks down and I wait for what feels like hours before she looks up at me.

" I'm so sorry it's taken me so long to come back here Levi, I wanted to, but I didn't know how I was supposed to feel or what I was supposed to do".

Looking at me while she continues, her blue eyes wary, water filling them now.

" I had so much to do back home, finish my scenes, accepting a new role for a new movie".

I look straight at her, fear and hurt take over when I begin to anticipate what comes next. Her next words are more of a whisper and a tear rolls down her check as she looks away from me.

" I only came to Boston today because I'm catching a plane to Los Angeles tonight to start filming"

" Please Emma!", I plead..." I Love you", I tell her.

She stands up and walks over to me. " I Love you too Levi, but we can't be together, I can't be here for you like you need me to be.

I feel the all too familiar feeling of panic building up as she leans over and kisses me goodbye.

I turn my chair to face the bay and just stare out onto the water. My body is shaking and I'm crying.

I stay out watching the sun disappear from the horizon. I am utterly alone.

Not unloved, she reminded me.... just Unwanted.

Chapter 20

Life is Unfair

Charlotte's POV

I frequently glance out the window towards Levi. He has been sitting out there alone for a few hours now, refusing Sarah's and Nates offers to bring him back to his room. My heart aches for him and I let him be alone for a while longer. I figured he would refuse dinner too. Life is so unfair sometimes.

I am worried that it is getting too cold out, so I take a chance and quietly approach him. He does not speak or look at me, but he does not refuse me either when I grab his left hand and hold it in mine. I pull him slightly, persuading him to control his wheelchair to follow me inside.

Once in his room, I head to the bathroom to turn on the shower.

" You don't have to" he quietly tells me.

He needs a hot shower, that will help him. He's already refused any help from Sarah and Nate tonight, so I gently get him undressed, cover him up with a towel and transfer him to the shower chair. I have not done any of this with him before, but he is not putting up a fight, and lets me continue.

After his shower he lets me help him get dressed in a t-shirt and cotton shorts and into bed. He refrains from speaking the entire time until I sit beside him. I want to let him know he is not alone; I am here for him...

" I'm sorry", I tell him. " Do you want to talk", I ask.

He shakes his head no and says in the saddest tone, " Thank you though".

The next two weeks took a downwards spiral. Levi's moods swiftly changed from hurt to anger then resentment, heading him straight into depression.

He fights with Nate every morning, refusing to get dressed or eat on most days.

I hear Levi yelling at him from his room. Nate meets me in the hall and says, " He's getting worse every day, this isn't good, and Sarah is scared to go in there now".

" I know that what he's going through is part of it, and I will keep at him, but I don't know if Sarah will be able to handle much more", Nate informs me.

"I know, I'm sorry Nate and I really appreciate everything you're doing, I will talk to Sarah", I let him know.

" I will take over all of his therapy sessions this week. He does not speak to me, but he does let me do what I need to do with him without yelling at me. Do you mind taking over sessions with my other patients for now?", I ask Nate.

Nate gladly agrees before I head over to talk with Sarah.

The rest of the week is a struggle to say the least. I managed to get Levi into the pool for therapy before lunch every day. I had him sit in the swim out and kept him away from the wall so that he had no choice but to use his muscles to balance himself and sit on his own. I was right next to him of course so he would not fall in.

Every therapy session I changed it up, using the weight room, massage treatments, and different core muscle workouts. He needs to get control of his upper body before I can get him standing, so without him realizing my goal for him, I stayed persistent with every session even when he tried to protest. I wanted him to realize that I am going to be here for him every step of the way.

He did not say a word to me the entire week, so I thought of random things to talk about. I talked more about myself and how my sister who was paralyzed at age fifteen gave me the inspiration to open this place and how she is about to have her 3rd child. I could tell Levi was interested in my story by the way he paused to look at me, even though he never engaged in the conversation.

By the time Friday came I was exhausted. I have only gone home for about six hours of sleep a night. I was here working with Levi every minute of the day, trying to distract him, and praying he would come out of the depression he was in.

He was in his chair staring out the window when I went to check on him this morning. Nate told me he did not sleep all night and refused breakfast this morning.

"Please leave me alone today Charlotte", he quietly pleaded with me when I entered his room.

When I did not move, he tried one more time.

" Please go away, I'm not participating in therapy even if you try to make me", he says.

"Fine, I will give you the morning off, but I at least want you to eat some lunch before I come back this afternoon", I try and compromise with him.

He just nods back and then I let him be. I have so much catching up to do with my other patients, and this gives me a chance to do that.

Lunch time arrives before I have time to catch up on everything and I make my way to Levi's room. He is going to eat lunch even if I must force him.

He is not anywhere in his room or in his bathroom when I get there. Where could he be? I just came from the patio so he's not out there or in the garden, I didn't see him in the lounge when I just passed by and I doubt he's in the gym on his own, but maybe!

I step out into the hall, ready to make my way to the gym and see the pool door closing on its own.

Who is using the pool I wonder; everyone is eating lunch right now?

Suddenly I feel sick, I have this horrible feeling in my gut, and without thinking too much, I run down the hall to the pool and yell for Nate as I get to the door.

I rush inside and find Levi's chair empty and at the edge of the pool.

"Oh my god!", I yell out

Levi is towards the bottom of the deep end, just floating down, he is not even trying to swim, and overwhelming fear takes over me as I realize what he is trying to do.

I dive in after him, grabbing him under his arms and swimming him back up. I drag him up to sit on the swim out and lean him back against the side, waiting with him there until he stops coughing.

Nate rushes in and looks at me, horrified. Flashbacks of when he could not save his best friend probably racing through his mind. He pauses by the pool until I instruct him to leave and get us some towels.

I stay quiet for a moment longer, observing Levi. He's done coughing, his head is down, a mix of real tears and pool water is streaming down his face.

I am so upset with him... but more upset with myself really. How did I not see this coming; the signs were there, and I didn't see them? He was different this morning, he said more words to me than he had in the last two weeks, even if his words consisted of him telling me to leave him alone. I am such an idiot.

I put my hand under his chin to lift his face.

"Look at me Levi", I calmly demand.

He looks at me, his once bright blue eyes now burdened with despair that it shatters my heart in a million pieces.

He tries to look down again but this time I place both my hands on either side of his face and force him to look at me.

I hold my gaze with his and speak in the most meaningful tone I can and slowly say,

" You are not alone in this".

Still looking straight into his eyes, I emphasize even more slowly,

"I... will... Never... give up on you, so you can ... never... give up on yourself"

"Promise me", I say more demanding this time.

Levi closes his eyes for a moment then opens them, "I promise", he softly replies.

Nate hurries back with towels and I get him to take Levi back to his room to help him into some dry clothes.

As soon as they both leave the pool area I break down.

Chapter 21

Feeling Hopeless

Levi's POV

After my absurd pool incident, Charlotte decided she was not going to let me out of her sight.

She stayed with me all night, looking over at me every so often, her eyes sincere, asking me if I am alright.

I really did not know what to say to her. I am still in shock that she jumped in to save me and the fact that she didn't send me away to the psych ward. Maybe she will still, maybe that is where I need to be.

I will never give up on you... Her words burned into my soul, those words that keep playing repeatedly in my head.

I do not know what I was thinking when I pulled that stunt. I wasn't thinking at all actually. The night Emma told me she could not be with me, left me broken on the inside and out.

I was so hurt and angry. Sarah was always so happy, and I made sure to avoid her coming in my room to help me. And Nate reminded me of the man I will never be again.

I gave Charlotte such a hard time the past few weeks, I thought she would just give up on me, but she never did. I just went through the motions. While I was being a jerk, Charlotte was being persistent, pushing me to work harder during every therapy session. I was too absorbed in my own self-pity that I did not realize Charlotte had helped me accomplish sitting up on my own. I was too selfish to notice that she was sacrificing all her time for me.

With Emma leaving me, all that was left was an overwhelming sense of hopelessness.

I was hopeless, ever walking again was hopeless, ever being a real man again or ever finding someone to love me like this was hopeless and I could not take it any longer.

I glance over at Charlotte curled up in the recliner sleeping, and the weight of what I did hits me. Guilt takes over, I feel terrible that I made her cry after Nate hurried me away from the pool area, and I feel guilty that she isn't home in her own bed sleeping, she's stuck here protecting me from myself.

I did not think of what the consequences would be if I had succeeded with my plan, the impact it would have had on my parents.... or Charlotte!... what if she had found me lifeless! Or Nate and remembering what happened to his friend.... Now that I have come to my senses, I realize how selfish I was!

I can't help but stare over at Charlotte. This beautiful selfless girl who is determined to make me better. I do not know why a girl like her is willing to do everything for someone like me... I do not deserve her.

But I promised her I would not give up on myself, so the least I can do for her in return is keep my promise. And with a little bit of time, I may get back a little bit of hope.

Chapter 22

Standing

Levi's POV

I woke the next morning to find Sarah in the recliner, reading a book. Her turn to babysit me I assume. Her eyes are not the cheerful appearance I am used to seeing, they are swollen and blood shot.

"Where's Charlotte?", I ask her. She stands up from the chair barely looking at me and heads for the door.

"Oh hi", she nervously says. " Charlotte went home to take a shower and grab some more clothes.... I will go get Nate for you".

What was that all about? Did I scare her? She is probably upset with me like everyone else is after yesterday.

Nate enters my room right after Sarah leaves.

" Morning", he says to me while he grabs some of my clothes from the bureau.

He seems to be acting like his normal self, so that puts me at ease a little.

" What's wrong with Sarah, she looks like she's been crying", I ask him.

Nate brings my clothes over and starts sitting the bed up but does not look at me.

" She is the one who left the pool door unlocked yesterday, she's been beating herself up about it ever since", he solemnly answers.

Shit! I need to apologize to her, to Nate too... to everyone really!

"I'm sorry Nate, I didn't know what I was doing, what I was thinking... I'm really sorry", I blurt out.

" Listen, I get it man! but you have people who care about what happens to you, people who are here for you every day, and you need to start opening up, not keep it all inside until you collapse ", he rants on in an authoritative tone.

" And you have to stop being a dick to Sarah when she tries to help you, she doesn't deserve it", he adds.

I agree with him and continue to apologize while he helps me dress and get into my chair.

" Is Charlotte coming back today", I hesitantly ask him.

" Yes, she will be back soon, but in the meantime, she asked me to make sure you eat and then have you ready in the gym for her", he replies.

I did what Nate said without giving him a hard time. I ate all my breakfast for once, and he chuckled at me. I just do not want to upset anyone any further. We got to the gym and he transferred me up onto the exercise table. I can sit on the side of the table using my right hand for support.

I can't help but smile when Charlotte walks in. I am relieved she came back, I started to convince myself that she would hand me off to someone else to do therapy with me.

She places my leg braces on the table next to me.

" Good morning Levi", she smiles at me. "When you finally fell asleep, I thought it was a good time to run home to shower".

I feel like a jerk, so I look down and say, " But you didn't get any sleep though... I am.... I'm sorry".

Charlotte places her fingers under my chin to lift my head up. She does not look upset with me at all. Her eyes a beautiful green shade today brought out by her forest green tank top. She focuses on my face and nonchalantly says, " I will get some sleep later, right now we have a lot of stuff to do", and grins.

She stands right in front of me and places her hand on both my sides to help me sit straight so I can practice balancing for a few minutes. She lets go of me but keeps her hands close to my body, so I do not fall. It is getting easier, but I can only hold myself up for a few seconds at a time. Charlotte beams at me the whole time letting me know I am doing good, I guess.

She lets me lean on my right arm again while she starts massaging my legs and moving my joints around.

" I'm sorry Charlotte", I whisper

"I am here for you every step of the way, you know, that right?", she asks me.

When I do not respond, she stands up to face me.

" Levi, please talk to me, tell me what you're feeling... please".

The only thing I can manage to say is, "I'm scared".

She nods while still looking at me and waits for me to continue. I am not good at this talking about my feelings or anything else, I have always had everything under control. But I think she might literally stand here looking at me until I spill.

I take a deep breath and nervously start rambling off every thought in my head.

" I'm scared of being in that chair the rest of my life, I'm scared that I will fail everyone, that my friends and family will always treat me different now, I'm afraid to go to that fucking gala and having everyone stare at me, I'm afraid that I'll never make another movie, and I can't help feeling that no one will ever want me this way and that I'll always be alone"

Dammit! Now my eyes are swelling. She is still standing in front of me, her hands on my knees now.

" I'm sorry you feel alone", she quietly says to me.

I pause a moment to compose myself before going on, " I'm scared that you'll get tired of trying to help me and you'll find someone else to do it".

She squeezes my knees with her hands and says without any hint of pity or doubt, but absolute certainty in her voice, " I'm not going anywhere".

Her words send a releasing sensation through my whole body and I feel my muscles letting go of all the built-up tension with just the way she looks at me.

Without delaying any further, she attaches my leg braces and locks them in place, so my legs are straight. She stands in front of me again and grabs both of my hands and wraps them around the back of her neck.

" Ready?", she asks.

" Ready for what?"

" You are going to stand up", she says without any worry.

I feel my body start shaking and she notices it too.

"Levi... what's wrong?"

"I'm afraid of what it will feel like, what if I fall?", I tell her.

" It will feel strange at first, and I promise I won't let you fall", she assures me.

She then wraps her arms around my body, gently pulling me towards her, sliding me off the table until I am standing.

Shit I'm standing! she's right it feels weird and I do not have any balance in my hips, but her embrace is keeping me from falling.

After a minute she releases her embrace and moves her hands to hold my hips.

" I've got you", she reminds me.

" Hold onto my shoulders", she instructs, and just stands there with me, keeping me steady while I soak in this moment.

She lets me know that we will be doing this a lot for the next week or so, along with a bunch of new exercises to get my lower core and hips stronger before I can take any steps.

Hell, I do not care what kind of work I will have to do. I start laughing a little, it is more of an excited nervous laugh, but a happy one too...

I am happy just to be standing.

Chapter 23

Pain

Levi's POV

Someone was always with me or had me in their sight for the next two weeks.

Everyone was still on edge, thinking I was going to lose it at any moment. So, Charlotte, Nate and Sarah rotated the night shift.

Normally this would annoy the hell out of me, but I don't blame them after what I put them through.

Nate and Charlotte acted the same as they did with me before the pool incident, but Sarah was a different story. She was no longer her bubbly carefree self. Whenever she was near me, she would only say a few words, never really making eye contact with me. I think she was still freaked out and blamed herself somehow.

I miss the Sarah who smiled about everything, talked too much, and occasionally made me laugh. So last night when it was her turn to be on *Levi duty,* I decided to confront her... well apologize really in hopes that she would return to her old self again.

"Sarah", I started. She briefly looked up at me then back down at her book.

" Yes", she softly answers.

"Please look at me", I sigh.

She closes her book and places it on her lap then slowly lifts her head to face me.

"It's not your fault Sarah", I assert.

A puzzled expression covers her face, "What?"

" I want you to know that what happened at the pool a few weeks ago was not your fault... It was all my fault, and I'm sorry", I tell her, praying she will stop blaming herself.

Her reaction was not what I expected. She practically leaped out of the recliner towards me, her hand rubbing her forehead and angrily fires back,

" I was the last one to leave the pool door unlocked and you could have DIED Levi!!"

I am a little shocked, I have never seen Sarah angry about anything before... she's a little scary!

"I know, I'm so sorry Sarah", I try to calm her.

After a few moments she sits back in the chair and reclines, opening her book back up to read it.

"I'm sorry too, I'm ... I'm just still mad at you right now", she admits.

"Fair enough, ... but I hope you can forgive me soon".

I know she will when I catch her smile before looking down at her book again.

The days have been long. I'm constantly moving from one therapy to the next, pausing only to eat. This is Charlotte's clever way of keeping me distracted from any irrational thought I might have I am sure.

I have made friends with another patient. His name is Jake, and he is 28, just a couple years older than me. We meet in the exercise room the same time every day. He was in a car accident leaving him paralyzed from the waist down, but he has all his upper body strength unlike me. I envy him for that and the fact that he can hold himself up on the parallel bars or with crutches to walk. He has only been here two months longer than me, but he makes it a point to show me his progress and encourages me to keep working.

Nate is in charge of working with me in the weight room, but Charlotte spends the most time with me trying to get me to stand for more than 5 seconds before my hips start swaying out of control.

My left arm and leg have not been progressing the way I want; the way Charlotte was expecting. My arm definitely can't hold up my body weight and the fact that I look like a complete idiot trying to take steps with my left leg infuriates me, and I end up acting like a jerk towards Charlotte. I cannot help it, I know it is not her fault either, she is trying everything she can think of to get me to take a few steps when only my right side is cooperating. She is tired and stressed out over it, I can see it on her face, and it makes me more discouraged. I cannot believe she has not given up on me yet. Whether I am a jerk or not, she stays, forcing me to keep going.

" How do you do this every day?", I ask her while she is holding me steady by my waist patiently waiting for me to drag my left leg forward.

" I want to be here every day, I never knew what I wanted to do in high school and I just picked some random college, changed my major four times, and still didn't know who I was or wanted to be. I saw my sister struggle after her accident and it bothered me, so I went back to school and figured out this is what I needed to do", she happily explains.

" Don't you get tired of being here all the time trying to help me? you're always here, when do you see your friends or boyfriend?"

I am curious as to why this beautiful selfless girl doesn't have multiple guys falling for her.

" First of all, I don't have a boyfriend, most guys can't handle the amount of time I work, but I guess I will find a guy who accepts me for who I am and what I do some day.... and I have a few friends, they just live far from here", she says to me then bites her bottom lip and stares off for a moment.

" And No, I don't get tired of being here helping you", she adds matter-of-factly.

I'm at a loss for words so I just give her a half

smile. I don't understand it, what guy wouldn't want

her? Or better yet, why would she give up any of her

free time to be here helping me?

The next morning starts off in a terrible way. I

woke up in pain from left arm and leg spasms. I could

not control them, and it took both Nate and Sarah's

help to get me dressed and in my chair. Thankfully, the

spasms and pain lessened by breakfast, but they were

still happening every twenty minutes or so and my

mood was turning grim.

To make matters worse, I happen to roll by a

table in the hall with this week's newspapers and

tabloids and catch a glance of Emma's face in the

upper right corner of a magazine. What the hell is this?

I pick up the magazine and sure enough it's Emma

standing with some guy, his arm around her waist and

the caption reads, "Emma Taylor finds new Love,

breaks up with fiancé Levi Dawson". What is this, a sick joke? I throw the magazine against the wall and roll straight back to my room. That did not take her long to forget about me and move on to the next guy. I slam my door shut and head over to the window.

The painful spasms return full force again! And why wouldn't they, I think to myself. I am just a hopeless cause anyway.

Moments later I hear Sarah talking to Charlotte outside my door.

" Did you see the tabloid", Sarah asks Charlotte

"Yes, I did" Charlotte answers with annoyance clear in her voice.

"Can you please have Nate bring my jeep around to the back door of the building" Charlotte asks her.

Charlotte knocks on my door and enters my room. I keep my focus out the window as I hear her come closer to me. She does not speak; she just walks over and sits down on the windowsill facing me. I am in pain and she sees it, my left arm constricting then spasming.

She gently holds my left hand with hers and starts massaging my fingers then my hand and up my arm, slowly bending and straightening my elbow, pausing momentarily when I wince. She stays quiet while she works her magic on my arm, looking up every few minutes so that our eyes fix on each other. Her softhearted multi-color eyes focusing on mine, her way of asking if I am alright.

After my arm calms and the pain goes away, she remains with me and places both of her hands on my knees then squeezes them slightly causing me to look at her.

Her thoughtful next words left me dumbstruck and I could not tear my eyes away from her face.

" If she couldn't accept you at your worst, then she didn't deserve you at your best".

What did that mean? Does Charlotte think I really deserve more?

Without further hesitation she gets up and softly places a kiss on my forehead, which catches me completely off guard then says,

" We are going for a ride, so let's get you into this chair", she points to the smaller mechanical wheelchair.

" Wait... what?", I choke out.

" I'm taking you out for the afternoon, it's time you get out of this place, a change of scenery", she says smiling.

Chapter 24

Road Trip

Charlotte's POV

I hand Levi off to Nate to help get him and the
wheelchair into the jeep while I packed a few
backpacks with food and other things we might need.

I am frantically rushing around trying to find
everything, a blanket, baseball cap & sunglasses for
disguise. I have a weird yet nervous sensation running
through me. Why did I kiss him on his forehead? I am

afraid to know what he thinks about that after I saw the surprised look on his face. I just felt like I had to, in that moment his guard was up, trying to shield his pain and I needed to do something. My head tells me that was not the right thing to do but my heart tells me otherwise. *Just get to the jeep Charlie, stop over thinking this ...*

Levi is sitting in the passenger side of the jeep, his chair in the back covered by a blanket. I hand him the hat and sunglasses which he gladly puts on. The last thing either of us want is for any photographers capturing any of this, it is the reason he hasn't left this building yet.

I hop in the driver's seat and look over at him. He is uneasy about this I can tell; his knuckles are turning white from gripping the door.

" Don't worry, as soon as we get around the corner, no one will assume you're out driving around in a jeep", I chuckle, trying to lighten his mood.

I sure hope I am right! I have only seen one or two photographers hanging around the front of the building lately, so the odds are in our favor.

We make it down the next street without anyone seeming to notice. It is a gorgeous summer day so the top and windows are down. Levi's arm is half over the door catching the wind with his hand and he looks content taking in all the sights.

He catches me smiling at him, so I quickly turn my eyes back to the road. I can feel my cheeks flush. *This is not good Charlie, just focus on the road, I remind myself.*

" Where are we going?", he curiously asks me.

" We are heading South of Boston to one of my favorite places", I gladly answer.

"Hmm", Is all I hear him respond before looking out the window again.

This city really is beautiful if you don't mind the traffic. Today is Sunday so the traffic is lighter than usual, and Levi's eyes are gazing, taking in everything around us. I knew he needed this.

Our silent ride to Hingham was comforting. The fresh air, the new sights, just the fact that he was going for a drive seemed to take him away to some peaceful place in his mind. At times he would lean his head back against the head rest and just close his eyes. *I wonder what he is thinking about.* I can't stop glancing over at him.

After about 30 minutes we arrived at the park entrance and pulled into a parking spot away from anyone. Lucky for us, there were not many cars here at all.

" We're here", I let him know, then grab the wheelchair from the back.

I help him swing his legs around and he grabs the back of my neck while I embrace his upper body, guiding him down into the wheelchair.

I grab the blanket from the back and stuff it into one of the backpacks then throw the pack over my shoulders. The other pack I hang on the back of his chair, and quickly turn him around to face the trail we are heading toward.

"World's End", he mumbles to himself as he reads the entrance sign.

He starts laughing, " You brought me to a place called World's End", laughing more now.

I let out a chuckle, "Yeah, I guess I did. Don't worry, this place is beautiful and relaxing, you'll love it".

" And you're going to push me down 4 miles of trails?", he asks in a more apprehensive tone while pointing at the sign.

"Is this your workout routine for today?", he adds.

"No, I'm not going to push you... I'm going to walk with you", I say to him, then grab to hold his left hand, pulling him to wheel along next to me.

He looks up at me with surprise and confusion.

" Well come on, we've got a long workout ahead of us", I giggle.

" Yeah, relaxing she says... I'll love it she says",
Levi sarcastically mocking me and laughs.

He squeezes my hand and lets me pull him next
to me while he pushes the right wheel, and we head
together down the carriage path.

Chapter 25

World's End

Levi's POV

Wow this place really is beautiful! Peaceful, and no one seems to bother with us, which makes it even better.

I can't believe Charlotte brought me here, she manages to surprise me with something new every day, usually I am too angry at the world to always notice. I have been stuck at rehab for months...of course Charlotte would do something like this for me... one of her many distractions she calls them. This is definitely her best idea of a distraction so far.

I look over to her, she looks so content walking next to me, holding my hand. I almost forget that I am not actually walking with her, but it almost feels like it. She is not standing in back pushing me, or walking ahead because she thinks I'm too slow, instead she's keeping with my pace gently squeezing my hand to let me know she's with me. She makes me feel somewhat normal. It's astonishing really.

The carriage paths are wide and flat, making it easy for us to enjoy. It doesn't feel like we are right outside the city. It is quiet here, we are surrounded by trees, marshes, and wildlife. It's incredible!

"Whoa!... look over there, there are two deer!", I nudge at Charlotte.

" Look at them, they don't even mind that we're here", I say with surprise.

I have never actually been up close to any deer before, I thought they'd run away as we got closer, but it appears we are no bother to them.

There are so many different birds I have never seen before either.

" That one looks sort of like you", I tease Charlotte.

" Hahaha.... well that one looks a lot like you", she laughs back, pointing to a bird who looks like it has a mohawk on top of its head.

I laugh back, " Touché "

Not much longer and we get to an open grassy area off the path. Charlotte grins ear to ear then says, " This is a perfect spot to have lunch".

"Wow! this is nice", I admit back.

From this spot we have an awesome view of Hingham harbor and the Boston skyline. It is almost like looking at a painting.

Charlotte places a blanket down on the grass and takes a few containers out of the backpack.

I look at the blanket on the ground, not sure if I like the idea of her trying get me to sit on it.

" What are you doing?", I ask her, my voice clearly disappointed.

" We are going to sit here and have lunch while enjoying this beautiful view", she confidently states.

"How are you going to get me back in the chair again after?", I ask, making it known that I am starting to feel on edge.

She walks over and stands directly in front of me. Facing me, she bends down, places her hands on my shoulders and tries to convince me that everything will be fine.

" We will figure that part out when it's time", she says with a smirk.

I just sit there frozen for a moment then look around to see if anyone is watching us.

"Levi are you ok", she asks me.

When I nod, she goes to my left side, takes my left arm, and wraps it around her shoulder then wraps her right arm around the back of my waist, supporting me. I help her by using my right arm and leg to push up from the chair and sit down onto the blanket.

" See that wasn't so bad", she remarks.

" I guess not", I say back.

I sit, leaning on my right arm for support and watch her take out a few sandwiches and drinks, placing them in front of us then feel her inching her body closer to me.

All the sudden a grape hit me square in the forehead.

" Earth to Levi!", she giggles.

She is holding a bag of grapes in her hand, preparing to throw another one at me.

Without any thought, she puts her right arm around my back, her hand gripping my side so I can sit up and eat. I quickly snatch the bag and toss a grape at her, but she catches it in her mouth.

" Oh, I see how it is now Charlie", I try joking around with her.

" Charlie huh? I though you only referred to me as Charlotte?", she smiles, and I just shrug my shoulders and laugh.

We continued bantering back and forth while we ate lunch. For the first time since my accident, I finally feel a bit like myself. Charlotte not even phased that she has had her arm around me the last hour, keeping me from losing my balance while we just sit here laughing about random stuff. The sound of her laugh amuses me. She is funny when she's not all stressed out trying to fix me.

I do not remember the last time I laughed like this with Emma. Emma would have never taken me to a place like this, nor let me joke around with her. She usually takes offense to everything.

"This view really is amazing", Charlotte says with all seriousness.

"Yes. it sure is", I reply.

I really want to tell her it is her who is amazing.

I can't tell her that though, I don't know what to make of any of this. Does she care about all her patients like she seems to care about me? Does she pull them out of the darkness and kiss them on the forehead when they are just about to fall apart? Who am I kidding, why would I think she could ever want someone who is paralyzed? She is surrounded by people like me every day, trying to fix us. I try to remind myself she is just my therapist, but I can't, to me she is so much more.

It's starting to get late she tells me. That is our cue to get back in the chair. Surprisingly, this time we manage to get me up into the chair without me panicking. *Ok, I can handle this, I think.*

We talked the entire way back that it felt like only seconds passed until we reached the jeep. I admit, my height and her lack of made it difficult to get up into the passenger seat, but we survived, and no one was around watching us.

Halfway through our journey back to Boston I feel a sharp pain shoot through my left arm, and it starts to spasm. I clench my jaw hoping to avert the pain and grasp my left arm with my right to massage it. I look out the window while trying to calmly massage my arm, praying Charlotte doesn't notice. *Why the fuck is this happening right now? Is my left side always going to do this?* I do not want her worrying about me again after the perfect afternoon we had.

Too late... she reaches over and grabs my left hand, pulling my arm over towards her and resting it on the middle console, then gently laces her fingers with mine.

" Just breathe", she says softly.

It doesn't make the spasm go away but her hand holding mine does relieve most of the pain. I can't help but stare at her and wonder.

" Charlotte, can I ask you something?"

" We're back to Charlotte now... this must be serious", she grins, trying to lighten my mood.

"Do you think it will ever get easier?... I know I will never be the same again, but will it get easier?", I ask her.

She takes a deep breath in before speaking, " It will get harder before it gets easier, but I promise it will get easier, you just have to make it through the hard stuff first", she peers over at me briefly and squeezes my hand.

I want to believe her, I really do. All I do know is that I will not be able to get through any of this without her.

Chapter 26

Unexpected

Charlotte's POV

I'm so delighted that Levi enjoyed the park today. I knew it was something he needed, but I didn't expect that it would go as well as it did.

He was smiling.... a lot! and laughing! I've seen him smile a few times since he's been here but never laugh, I mean belly aching, wanting to roll on the ground kind of laughing.

And he felt comfortable enough to joke around with me. I was amazed that he let me see that side of him, part of his true personality, the part he wasn't afraid of showing before the accident.

I wish I could get him to let go of all that anger and fear he's suppressing and help him realize all these obstacles are not what's holding him captive.

There is just something about him pulling me in closer, wanting to be here for him in a way that I've never felt before. Sure, his incredibly handsome face and perfectly sculpted body would attract anyone to him, but it's more than that. It's how natural it feels to hold his hand, how it upsets me when he's upset or how I feel happy when he is happy. The way his accent makes his voice sound softer when he talks with me and how his blue-green eyes have a way of telling me that he needs me. I'm starting to feel like I may need him too, it's hard to describe.

I know I shouldn't have any of these feelings at all. He is my patient, and he is here so I can help him walk out of this place and return to his famous life in London.

I need to stop drifting off into my own world, aimlessly walking the hall...*Wake up Charlie!... He's an actor for Christ's sake. Why would he see me for anything other than his therapist?*

I need a distraction, so I head to my office to finish some paperwork. This will keep me busy for a while. I sit down at my desk and open a drawer to look for a pen. Instead, I find an empty journal I bought a few weeks ago. I wonder if this journal could help Levi. He is so guarded all the time, maybe writing down his thoughts might help.

I open the first page and decide to jot down my favorite inspirational quote. I will leave the journal on his nightstand for him to find after he's done in the hot tub.

Not two minutes after, I'm startled by my phone ringing.

" Hello?"

" Charlie, it's mom", a hysterical voice cries out.

" Mom, what's wrong? Why are you crying?"

"You need to get down here, your father has had a heart attack! he's on his way into surgery now", she cries.

I hang up and immediately go online to find the quickest flight out of Logan. I make a few phone calls and rush out to find Nate.

"Nate!", I yell out to him, practically sprinting down the hall.

"Charlie? are you ok?", Nate nervously asks.

" I have an unexpected family emergency, I'm flying to North Carolina in forty-five minutes", I tell him.

Before I give him time to respond, I start spitting out instructions and let him know I've called Kelly to help him do all the therapy treatments this week.

He looks at me worried but then assures me he will hold the fort down while I'm gone.

"Great! I can always count on you", I say before turning towards the door.

"Oh ... one more thing... can you please give this to Levi for me?", handing him the journal.

"I'll call you when I get there", I tell him, then run out the door.

Chapter 27

Worst Nightmare

Levi's POV

I must have stayed in the hot tub for a good fifty minutes, it felt so serene.

I had Sarah bring me back to my room and help me get into bed. I'm exhausted and will probably have no trouble sleeping tonight. But not before I thank Charlotte for taking me out today.

The drive, the park, the way Charlotte held my hand to walk beside me made me feel important, everything was perfect. I didn't realize how much I needed that until I was sitting on the grassy field, overlooking the bay.

Somehow Charlotte knew though. She knew I needed one day away from everything, a day where I could forget for a few moments about all the obstacles in my way. I didn't want this day to end.

"Sarah, after you're finished with me, do you mind finding Charlotte? I need to thank her for today".

"No problem at all! I'm finished so I'll go find her for you", Sarah happily answers.

I think a half hour went by before Nate walked into my room.

" Oh sorry, were you sleeping?", Nate asks me.

I shift up in bed a little, rubbing my eyes so I can focus on him.

"Well Charlie asked me to give you this", he says, handing me what looks like a brown leather book.

"Oh?", I question.

Not liking how on edge Nate looks, rubbing his hand through his wavy hair and says, " Charlie had to leave in a hurry tonight, she's on a plane to North Carolina right now".

"Why?", I ask, a bit perplexed.

"She didn't have time to say much, only that she had a family emergency, and that she'll call when she gets there", Nate answers.

I know I come off a little selfish when I ask him, " Do you know when she will be back?".

He tells me he doesn't know how long she will be gone and makes it a point to show me that he's worried and hopes nothing terrible has happened. Then he quickly tells me Kelly, the "fill-in" therapist will be here to help this week.

"Great", I sarcastically reply.

I feel like such a jerk now. Of course, I am worried about Charlotte too, I was just to selfish to admit it. I let my insecurities rule my thoughts, so all I cared about was that she'll be gone for who knows how long, and I was going to be alone again.

There is no way I am going to sleep well tonight now. I'm too upset, I don't want anything bad to happen to Charlotte, but at the same time, I'm upset she is not here with me, that I didn't get to thank her for today, that she didn't even say goodbye before she left.

I'm such an idiot to believe that she could ever possibly think of me as anything more than a patient, that I was something more than just her job.

I lay in bed, sulking for a while. I just want to throw something, stupidly thinking that it will make me feel better. I grab the book next to me, preparing to take aim at something. Thankfully, I hesitate for a second, feeling the soft leather cover in my hand. And instead of throwing it, I open it.

Engraved on the inside cover, " *Penny for your thoughts*".

Hmm, ok I think to myself. The first page has a handwritten message, it's really a quote. It reads....

"Remember, you don't always need a plan. Sometimes you just need to breathe, to trust, to let go, and see what happens"
P.S.
Sometimes writing is the best therapy.
~ Charlotte

What does that even mean? Why did she give me this? I don't think I'm ready to write my feelings in a journal, I wouldn't even know how to start.

I put the journal on the nightstand, closed my eyes and forced myself to sleep. Hopefully, I will just dream of the great day that I had at the park and wake up to find out Charlotte has returned.

"Wait!" I yell out, waking myself up from the nightmare I was having. I'm shaking and sweating

profusely, it's 3am when I look at my phone. It takes

me a few minutes to realize where I am. In my dream I

had fallen on the floor not able to get up. Emma was

standing at the door, her arms folded, looking cross. I

was reaching for her, but she kept looking at me

shaking her head. Help me please I kept saying to her,

as she turned around and left.

I couldn't get back to sleep after that, I just
stared at the ceiling until Nate came in with my
breakfast four hours later.

The rest of the day I focused my energy on
getting my left side stronger. Nate attached me to the
weights, made me practice eating using only my left
hand...which was frustrating. He hooked me up to the
nerve stimulator then made me try to push myself
around in the manual wheelchair using both my arms. I
was willingly following along with endless therapy,

anything to keep my mind wondering to that horrible dream I had last night.

By evening I was sore, tired, and completely annoyed with my left side...it wasn't any stronger than it was from yesterday. But I did manage to hold onto my fork with my left hand to feed myself tonight.

A hot shower helped, but after that, I was alone in my room. Charlotte had called and left me a voicemail while I was in the shower. She called to say hi and check in on me she said.

Tomorrow, I was supposed to work with Kelly and wasn't looking forward to it. She's an older lady in her late 40's, she's nice enough, but everything is to-the-point, it's just not the same as when I'm doing therapy with Nate or Charlotte.

I decide to preoccupy my mind by watching TV until I fell asleep.

I can't seem to push my wheelchair down the hall. Why can't I feel my left arm? "Emma, can you please push me", I ask her. She's not moving, she's just leaning against the outside of my door with her hands crossed, shaking her head side to side. "I'm stuck Emma! Why aren't you helping me!" I start yelling at her.

I must have been holding my breath because I woke up gasping for air. What the fuck!! Another nightmare! I pick up my phone, it's 4:30am!

It's now Tuesday and I haven't slept well in two nights. Nate doesn't hesitate to comment on my bad mood when he helps me dress and into my chair.

Breakfast doesn't go over so well either. After I already tried protesting about having to use only my left hand, I lost the grip on my fork and food went flying. Kelly came in to get me for therapy as my plate hit the floor and I couldn't tell if she was disappointed or annoyed.

Jake is in the gym when we arrive. He's strapped into a harness that hangs from a ceiling track, and he's walking around the room using his metal forearm crutches. He makes it look so simple, I want to be happy for him and hate him at the same time. I'm such an asshole sometimes.

"Hey Levi", he greets me. "I'm going to watch the Premier League game in the lounge later if you want to join me? we can kick back, have a few beers", he says to me.

"Yeah, yeah... sounds good", I answer. I need a distraction anyway.

Kelly brings me over to the parallel bars and I immediately scowl at her.

"What are you doing", I grunt.

" You are working on the bars today", she says in a serious tone.

I start getting irritated with her, " And how do you suppose I'm going to do that with one arm?"

" We are going to see what we can do, Sarah's here to help", Kelly tries to encourage.

The parallel bars turned out to be a total fiasco. Kelly's failed attempt to support my left arm on the bar while Sarah held my hips steady was only slightly humiliating for me, until I realized an hour passed and I'd only taken five steps. It wasn't until I looked over at Jake who was easily walking around, guided by the ceiling track, that I felt completely defeated.

"Put me back in my chair", I angrily demand of Kelly and Sarah.

" I'm done with your therapy for the day", I add.

Kelly finally decides she's not going wait around for my foul mood to change and leaves.

"Come on Levi, I'll take you to the lounge", Sarah says.

" Ya, I'll meet you in the lounge in about thirty minutes", Jake yells out as I leave the gym.

Having a few beers while watching the game with Jake was a good interruption from my horrid day. I was still in a grim mood though after and refused any other therapy, didn't shower, and just went to bed. I surprisingly fell asleep quickly.

My dreams take me to the pool area. I feel like I'm up above looking over at someone, it's strangely eerie. There's no one around except for a body floating

on top of the water. As I get a closer look, I realize the
body is me. Someone help me! I hear myself saying.
The body remains still. Charlotte appears from
somewhere, but she doesn't jump in to save me, only
walks around the pool looking at the body and then she
disappears. Charlotte! Charlotte! come back! I want to
scream....

"Levi! Levi! wake up", I hear a voice say. I
open my eyes to find Sarah shaking me by my
shoulders.

"Levi, are you ok?", you were having a
nightmare", she tells me.

I sit up in bed, rubbing my eyes, my body
drenched in sweat.

"Do you want to talk about it", Sarah nervously
asks.

"No", is all I respond.

"Let's get you into a hot shower", she says while pulling the wet blankets off my bed.

" It's two in the morning", I groan.

" You're, up aren't you? And by the looks of you, I don't think you're going back to sleep any time soon", she points out.

" Fine", I acknowledge.

I sat in the shower for a while, letting the hot water run down my face. I don't know what's bothering me more, the dreams or the fact that Charlotte's been gone for 3 days and I keep thinking that she's not coming back. Out of all the nightmares I've had this week, that would be my worst one ... Charlotte leaving me here and having someone else take over. Maybe she really did need a break from me.

I told Sarah to leave me in my chair after my shower. She's right, there's no way I'm going back to sleep.

Sarah picks up the brown leather journal and tosses it into my lap. I give her a confused look, and before I can speak, she says, " I know you haven't slept all week, there is obviously something bothering you, and Charlotte didn't give you this journal so it can collect dust on your nightstand".

I look down at the journal for a while contemplating what I should do, then look up at Sarah, " But how do I start?"

She finishes putting fresh sheets and blankets on my bed and softly says, "How about you begin with how you feel right now and go from there".

Chapter 28

Small Steps

Levi's POV

I opened the journal and read the words
Charlotte wrote on the inside cover over and over
again....

*You don't always need a plan, sometimes you
just need to breathe...* Well Charlotte tells me that all

the time, whenever I start to panic about something, she tells me to breathe.

*To trust...to let go...*It's a bit difficult to trust, who do I trust? certainly not Emma. Do I trust Charlotte? Do I trust that I will eventually walk again?

I understand what she means by *let go.* That's easier said than done though. She already sees me as a cripple, she's already seen me panic on more than one occasion, she had to dive into the pool to save me from drowning myself for goodness sake! If I come out and tell her that I'm scared all the time, about everything, that I'm scared she's going to leave or give up on me, that I need her! Who am I then? What is left of me?

Without realizing it, my pen is at the top of the first page and I write, "*Small Steps",* as the title of my first entry.

After that, the words just kept flowing... *I'm afraid to let go, but I must try. One step at a time,* I write.

I continue writing until the sun comes up, filling up a good 10 pages of the journal. I could've gone on to fill another 10 pages, but Nate disrupted me by bringing in my breakfast.

I quickly shut the journal and put it back on the nightstand.

"wow, you look like shit", Nate reminds me and laughs a little.

"Same to you mate", I argue.

Nate and I have come to an understanding that when it comes to dealing with me, he's going to say it like it is. And that's fine with me. I have no problem giving him a hard time and he gives it right back; the way guys do. He can't fully understand what I'm going through, but he treats me the way he'd want to be treated I'm sure, if he was the one in my position.

" Eat your breakfast will you, god only knows what Kelly has planned for you today", he mocks.

" When is Charlotte coming back", I ask him.

" She's been gone all week and I don't think I can handle Kelly torturing me any longer", I try to joke, hoping he won't catch onto my desperation.

"Soon, maybe today", he says.

"Her father had a heart attack and needed emergency surgery", he lets me know.

Oh no!! I really feel like a jerk now, here I've been only worried about myself when I really should've been worrying about Charlotte.

"He is going to be ok?" I ask unsure.

"Yes, they put in some stents and he's going to make a full recovery, after some much-needed rest", Nate assures me.

" Now hurry up before Kelly has my head", he chuckles.

I arrive at the gym to see Kelly toying with the harness that hangs from the ceiling track. A pair of forearm crutches on the floor next to her.

She doesn't think I will actually be able to use those, does she? After my failure at the parallel bars yesterday, you'd think she'd realize by now that my left side isn't any help when it comes to figuring out how to walk.

I sit there, arms crossed waiting for her to finish what she's doing.

"Don't just sit there", she demands.

" Come over so I can get this harness strapped to you".

I roll over to her, slowly while showing her my disapproval. She gets the harness around me and locks my leg braces so that I can't bend my knees, then adjusts the harness so that I'm standing.

This feels so strange. My feet are on the ground, but I still feel like I'm dangling from the ceiling. My hips lose control and I start swaying side to side, back and forth until Kelly grabs a hold of both sides of the harness, keeping me still. She makes me stand there for a minute, continuing to securely grasp the harness so that I can gain my balance.

I'm still only able to stand and balance for a few minutes before my hips give way and I lose control again. She repeats this exercise with me over and over, letting me go when I'm balancing on my own, then lets the harness catch me when I can't.

After a half hour of doing this she finally speaks, "Do this every day, and you'll be able to balance yourself on your own a little longer each time".

Kelly then puts one of the forearm crutches to my right arm and instructs me to use it for support each time I take a step with my left leg.

What the fuck! I think to myself. This isn't going to be good.

She moves to my left side, grabbing onto my left arm by my arm pit, acting like my left crutch. " Now bring your crutch forward, putting some weight on it and take a step with your left", she instructs.

I do as she says, putting a lot more weight than I should on my right crutch. Since I can't bend my knee, I have to slightly swing my leg around to take a step forward which immediately causes me to lose my balance, so she jerks my left arm towards her to pull me straight again. I manage to take a step with my right and again with my left one more time before I feel a painful leg spasm.

Oh no! Not again! " This isn't going to work! I'm not ready for this yet", I start yelling at her.

My left arm and leg going into continuous spasms now. I'm going to lose my mind at any minute.

Just then I hear the gym door open and a familiar voice chip in, " Thank you for all of your help Kelly, I'll take over from here".

I'm stunned, my left side still shaking when Charlotte approaches. She gently glides her hand down my left arm until she meets my hand and places it on her shoulder. She's standing in front of me smiling and places my right hand on her other shoulder before bringing her hands to grasp my sides.

She looks up at me with her beautiful, caring multi color eyes, and says, " Did you miss me?".

I remain frozen, though my left side still shaking while she tries to keep me steady. I stare back at her, submerged in her eyes. I don't know what to say, what to think. I'm happy, relieved, scared all at the same time.

She keeps her eyes on me trying to read the expression on my face. Whatever it reads must have worried her because she moves my arms to wrap around her neck and then wraps her arms around my body, pulling me close to her, and hugs me.

As soon as she nuzzles her head into my chest, an overwhelmingly pleasant sensation takes over me and I hug her back.

" I did", I tell her, burying my face into her hair.

"What?", she asks softly.

" I did miss you", I say.

Chapter 29

Open Up

Charlotte's POV

I fixed my gaze on Levi, holding his hips steady while his body was shaking. He didn't try to move or say anything, he just looked back at me. The expression on his face was like staring at a blank slate, only peering into his blue-green eyes could I feel his despair.

Instinctively, I let go of his hips and folded my arms around his back, embracing him. Slowly I felt his body stop shaking, and I feel him let go of a little bit of uncertainty when he nestles his head into my neck and releases a sigh. I'm certain I let out a sigh too. Hugging him felt right, like something we both needed.

This week has been hell for me, and for Levi too from what Nate and Sarah have told me. After Hearing that he hasn't slept all week and that he's had terrible nightmares every night, I knew I had to get back here. So, after my father was released from the hospital and settled back at home, I jumped on the next available flight to Boston.

I wanted to get to the root of these nightmares he was having. He probably won't easily divulge about what's going on with him, but I must try.

I decide to be the first to break our hold and speak first, "Levi, I heard that you..."

"Wait! Charlotte...", he interrupts.

" I'm so sorry about your father and I'm happy that he is ok", he says concerned.

Scrambling for the right words I respond, " Thank you, I think he will be fine as long as he follows the doctor's orders".

I'm not going to succeed with getting him to talk any further, so I may as well try to lighten up the mood.

"Shall we walk a little?", I ask, gripping onto his hips again.

"Sure", he agrees, placing his hands back on my shoulders.

We carefully make our way across the room, guided by the ceiling track. After about 10 feet, his pace begins to slow, and I catch him wincing with each step he makes with his left.

"Levi, what is it?", I ask him.

"I keep getting a shooting pain up my leg when I shift my weight", he confirms.

"Alright, time to get out of this harness and take a rest", I tell him.

"Are you going to tell me about these dreams you've been having every night?", I nudge while pushing his wheelchair down the hall.

"No", he flatly states.

"Levi, you can talk to me if something is bothering you ", I push further.

"It's nothing... I'm fine now", he insists.

" Can we just go and eat? I'm starving", he adds, trying to divert our conversation.

After we make our way into the dining room, he tells me he's going over to eat with Jake.

I'm glad he's made friends with Jake. Jake is a great guy, always positive and works ridiculously hard. Jake is a good influence for Levi and Levi needs a friend here, someone who's in a similar situation.

I use this time to talk with the rest of the patients here. Marlo and Kenny, both in their 50's, both with low spinal cord injuries. Sometimes I feel like I don't spend enough time on their personal therapy treatments, but I have another therapist who solely works with them. Plus, their wives and children are here every day helping with therapy too. I just oversee everything.

Abby is our newest patient. She just turned 16 and is our first patient with quadriplegia. Kelly has agreed to be her main therapist and Abby's parents have been here around the clock.

That leaves Nate, Sarah, and I to focus on Jake and Levi. Although, I've put most of my focus on working with Levi lately, and Nate has taken over working with Jake.

My staff is wonderful, I couldn't ask for any better. I'm so grateful for all the work they did while I was gone this week, I'm going to surprise them by taking everyone out tomorrow.

Levi avoided me the rest of the afternoon and asked Sarah to help him with an early shower.

I'm worried about him. He's hugging me telling me his missed me one minute then ignoring me the next, and I need to figure out the reason for it soon.

While Levi was in the shower, I told everyone else that we are having popcorn and movie night in the lounge tonight. No one protested and Abby squealed with excitement.

" Great! I will meet you all in there with the popcorn, someone get in there and pick out a movie", I demand.

Everyone has a seat, waiting for me when I enter with all the popcorn and drinks. I hand everyone a bowl of popcorn, a beer for the guys and soda for Abby. Sarah takes Abby's to help her with it.

Levi is sitting at the end of the couch, his feet up on the ottoman when I hand him his popcorn.

He looks at me and smiles then pats the empty cushion next to him.

" Do you want to sit with me?", he asks.

I tilt my head giving him a confused look and reply, " Your mood swings are giving me whiplash".

"I'm sorry", he says patting the cushion again.

I take a seat next to him. We stay silent like everyone else, engaged in the movie. After about an hour into the film, Levi gently puts his hand on my thigh and leans over to my ear. Speaking so softly so no one else can hear.

" I'm sorry", he says.

" You have nothing to apologize for", I whisper back.

"Yes, I do!... the whole time you were gone I was angry with you when I shouldn't have been", he solemnly states.

I look at him anxious for his reasons, "Why?"

He puts his forehead down onto my shoulder to hide his features and slowly confesses,

" I was mad you left, and I was afraid you wouldn't come back... that you'd finally given up on me".

His words crush me, and I wait just a moment before putting my fingers under his chin, lifting his head to look at me and impulsively ask,

" Why would you think that?"

I instantly see hurt and confusion flash through his eyes. Of course, he would think that! I say to myself. While everyone else around him here has their family, wife or girlfriend by their side, Levi has no one.

He has his parents and manager who visit once a month, but that's not enough. He's been avoiding most of his friends who are back in London because he doesn't want them to treat him differently, and the girl he was going to marry... the girl who he thought loved him, left him here alone.

The only person he truly has here is me. He needs me and I just left last weekend without saying anything! I'm to blame for his recent nightmares.

"Levi, I'm so sorry, I shouldn't have left last Sunday without telling you why first".

" I'm just happy you finally told me what's been bothering you", I softly say.

He puts his head back on my shoulder and I speak to him in the most convincing tone...

"Please don't ever think I'm going to give up on you... not for any reason".

Chapter 30

Determined

Levi's POV

I finally got some sleep last night. I knew Charlotte would be back in the morning because she told everyone she has a surprise day planned for all of us.

Nate did my morning therapy session which consisted of stretching and core exercises in the gym. Nate had Jake join too so he could get both of our sessions done at the same time.

"You ready for our afternoon out in the city?",
Jake asks me.

"Not really, but it will be good to get out", I say
to him.

He's looking at me confused by my response.

"Why would you want to stay here all day
every day?", Jake asks with curiosity.

" Have you seen the reporters and
photographers waiting for me outside?" I point out.

" We will be kind of hard for them to miss, all
strolling around in our wheelchairs together", I add
trying not to offend him.

" Ya, I'm sorry, I didn't think of that", he
apologizes to me.

Of course, he would never think of that first. He's never had paparazzi following his every move. Jake is just excited to get out and enjoy someplace other than here. I know it's been almost six months, but I don't know if I'm ready for the whole world to see me as disabled. It's going to happen sooner or later anyway, so may as well be today.

Charlotte meets all of us in the lounge by 11:00 am. When she walks in wearing jeans and a Boston Red Sox t-shirt, everyone but me figured out where we were going.

" Hell yeah!", Jake shouts.

"We have box seats for the game today, so let's get going", she says with a big smile.

Everyone excitedly makes their way towards her, thanking her before heading out the door.

She looks over towards me sees that I'm still sitting by the couch after everyone has made their way out.

"Levi, if you're not comfortable with this, we can stay here?", she says while walking over to me.

"No, I'm going. I'm not comfortable with this, but I'm also not going to ruin everyone's day", I admit.

"You sure?", she asks again.

"No, I'm not sure, but I'm still going", I groan.

She holds her hand out to me and patiently waits for me to grab it.

"Come on then", she says. "We will try to have some fun!", she grins.

We get to the front door where the four other occupied wheelchairs and the staff are waiting for us. I immediately spot someone with a camera lurking around our small crowd and turn to Charlotte who's now giving me a worried stare.

" Well let's get this over with", I tell her.

We join the rest of our group and head down the sidewalk. I hear the constant clicking sound of a camera going off as the intruder pretends to keep his distance from us. I'm about to turn around and cuss him out until I feel Charlotte squeeze my hand, turning my focus to her. She's been holding my hand while walking by my side the whole way, helping me feel at ease, and I didn't think anything of it until now. Maybe she thinks she's helping me get around better, or maybe she's trying to protect me, I don't know. What I do know is that her hand in mine is comforting to me and I don't want her to let go.

Everyone in our group is laughing and talking about Fenway Park and the green monster. I obviously haven't the slightest idea of what that is, so I ask, "What's a green monster?"

Everyone halts to turn to me, hands over their mouths giggling, "It's the big green wall that surrounds the outfield", Jake answers.

"Oh", I say, embarrassed now.

"I thought you British knew everything about Boston?", Sarah chuckles.

"Ha...ha", I sarcastically return.

Having box seats was a brilliant idea. There was room for all of us, endless ballpark franks and drinks, and the Red Sox won. A much-needed day for everyone.

We waited for most of the crowd to leave before making our way out, but there were still a lot of people hanging around trying to push their way through like they owned the place. After the twentieth asshole bumped into my chair, I got angry and started calling them every rude name I could think of. Frankly, I'm Annoyed now that Charlotte was nowhere in sight. I can barely roll myself as it is, never mind through a crowd of morons with total disregard for the handicap.

My wheels stopped moving for a moment and I sat still, watching all the people walk by me. I was angry that they could easily move about... no one caring that I was down here, it made me feel worthless. *Is this what all people in a wheelchair feel like? Is this what I'm going to feel like the rest of my life?*

I felt someone grab onto the handles of my wheelchair, I was just about to scream at whoever it was until I felt Charlotte lean her face down next to my ear and ask, "Levi, are you alright?"

"I'm fine", I grunt. "Let's get out of here"

Thankfully, Charlotte and Nate bring us a round-about way back to rehab. It's shorter through the city, but it's more crowded. And although Boston is a beautiful city, it's also old and not easy for us wheelchair bound to get around.

Our group happily strolling along, still delighted about the game, laughing, and reminiscing about every great play.

I remain mute, letting Charlotte push my wheelchair, not even attempting to help her.

"Levi, you could at least help with the hills", she tries to joke with me, but I ignore her.

We return to the rehab center and Charlotte brings me to my room.

"Ok, well if you want a shower, I'll ask Sarah to come in", Charlotte says to me.

I wheel myself over to the window and see her through the reflection. She looks cross but I don't feel like explaining anything to her right now.

"I want to go to the pool", I more or less demand.

"What?", she asks, confused.

"I want to work on my balance and walking in the pool... without the leg braces", I tell her.

"If that's what you want, I'll go change and have Nate get you in the pool", she says then leaves my room.

Charlotte is already in the pool when I get there. Nate gets me into the pool lift and lowers me into the water. I wrap my arms around Charlotte, and she wraps hers around me, gliding me from the lift. She keeps a tight grip on me, knowing my legs will probably buckle from not wearing my braces.

"It's ok Charlotte, I need to try", I let her know.

She releases her tight grasp and moves her hands to my hips. Sure enough, my left leg gives out making her tighten her hands around me again.

My right hand clutches her shoulder and I pull myself upright. This is easier in the pool; the water makes me much lighter for her and for me. I'm surprised how strong my right leg feels, it's not giving out like my left.

"Hmm", I hum a little louder than I thought, and Charlotte gives me a little smile.

"You can ease your grip a little Charlotte, I've got this", I tell her, returning her smile.

She remains my crutch for the next hour, letting me almost fall over then pull myself back up, repeatedly, and she smiles at me when I manage to stand on both legs for more than 5 seconds.

" I'm proud of you", she finally speaks.

"Why", I ask her.

What is she proud of? I haven't done anything to be proud of, I think to myself.

"You've gone at this for an hour, falling and getting back up every time, you haven't given up", she states.

"I don't like being in the chair.... I want to walk again, whatever it takes!", I tell her.

"I like this newfound determination", she beams at me.

"Yeah, yeah... don't make such a big deal of it", I smirk.

Before I have a chance to say anything else, she pulls me close and wraps her arms around me, hugging me.

"Charlie! I said it's not a big deal", softly laughing into her hair, hugging her back.

Chapter 31

Surprise

Levi's POV

The next few days went by fast. Charlotte obliged, helping me with endless therapy throughout the day. She brought me to the pool, to the gym, lifting weights then walking with the ceiling harness. She knew I was tired and needed more rest, but I refused to stop.

My left side was still week and uncooperative, jumping into spasms whenever I pushed too hard. I was getting angry with myself and I knew that if I took a break, even for a moment, that I would end up giving up.

Charlotte sensed my conflict and tried to reassure me, but it only made me take out my frustrations on her. I know I was being a dick, but she was there and that's the only way I know how to deal.

Friday morning arrived and I impatiently waited for Charlotte to take me to the gym. I was sitting in my chair facing the door with my arms crossed when she walked in.

Not phased at all by my discourteous appearance, she says," I see someone is in a foul mood this morning".

"Can we just get to the gym", I rudely ask.

I know I haven't been the nicest all week, and she has put up with my sour behavior, but it's my birthday and I haven't even heard from my parents this morning. It's like six hours ahead of Boston time, so there's no excuse for them not calling.

"Actually, Nate is going to work with you this morning, I have a lot of things to catch up on", she says.

"Great", I slow and sarcastically respond.

" I will see you this afternoon", she says and walks out the door.

What was that all about? Maybe she's finally had enough of my attitude this week. She didn't even wish me a happy birthday! How does she not know, I thought she's looked up everything about me? This is just like any other day here, it's not like I can really go out and celebrate.

Nate takes Jake and I into the gym for strength training. The two of them act oddly strange the entire time. I've probably made them angry this week too. I better figure out how to lighten up before everyone hates me.

Rolling out of the gym after my workout, I'm startled by someone grabbing my wheelchair handles and pushing me.

"Hey, how was your workout?", Charlotte asks.

I shift my body and head around to look at her. She looks happy... that's a relief from our earlier encounter.

"Umm, it was good", I answer her.

She starts to push me faster and turns me into the door of the lounge.

"SURPRISE! Happy Birthday!", I hear everyone shout.

I catch my mouth in my palm before it almost drops to the floor. Nate, Sarah, and all the other patients are there as well as my parents, Mark and three of my mates from back home. I'm speechless!

"How...What... are you all doing here?", I stutter.

"We're here to celebrate! you wanker!", my mate Andy teases.

My other mate Landon chimes in, " You may be avoiding all of our phone calls, but you can't avoid your birthday", he laughs.

"It's really good to see you", Josh says to me, punching my shoulder.

" Charlotte told us that if we didn't get our asses here, she was going to come to London and beat some sense into us", Andy confesses, everyone laughing now.

I turn around to look at Charlotte. She's leaning against the wall, arms crossed, smiling.

"You did this for me?", I ask, my voice filled with gratitude.

Charlotte smiles at me and shrugs her shoulders like it is no big deal.

We all chat for a while and enjoy some pizza and cake. My mum smothering me with too many hugs and telling me how proud she is of the progress I've made.

My mates tell me about everything going on back at home. Andy has been living at my flat, taking care of everything there. I didn't know how they would act around me now that I'm in a wheelchair, I didn't want them to pity me. I can see now that they are the same lads I knew and loved before my accident. It's me who is different. It's me who can't be back home hanging out and doing what we used to together, I'm afraid of not being the same person anymore so I tried to push them away.

" Get ready mate! we're taking you out for drinks tonight", Mark states.

" What? no! I can't ", I protest.

"Oh yes you can! we didn't come all this way to watch you sit here... we're going out to celebrate", Landon adds in.

"Charlotte has given us permission, so go get your ass ready", Andy jokes.

I wheel over to Charlotte, " Do you mind helping me", I ask her.

She follows me to my room, and I stop near my bed, staying silent for a few seconds.

" I can't believe you got them all here", I say softly.

"They wanted to be here Levi, they missed you!"

I stay quiet, looking down towards the floor, trying to hide my fears about going to the bars tonight.

Charlotte sits on the edge of the bed, close to me and puts her hand on my knee.

" You need your friends Levi, and they need you", she says.

Her face is so pure, I can't help but stare back at her, mesmerized by her solicitous multi- colored eyes.

"How am I going to get around stairs and such?", I nervously ask.

"There's five of you, I'm sure you'll all figure it out, and none of them will let anything happen to you", she assures me.

"It's your birthday, now go have some fun", she reminds me, and pushes my chair towards everyone waiting for me.

Josh claimed a low table at the first semi-crowded pub we went to and Mark bought a few rounds of shots. Apparently the first pub was too boring for them, so after we swallowed down our last shot, they maneuvered my chair along the cobblestone walkway to the next pub.

Charlotte was right, my mates had no problem pushing, pulling, and lifting me over any steps. It felt like old times, the only difference was that I'm not standing and walking, I'm being pushed around.

The next pub was much more entertaining. A live band, people were dancing and drinking.

"This is the place ", Landon is pleased to announce.

I don't remember much after the fourth drink I was handed. I remember being coerced onto the dance floor, people spinning my chair around to make it look like I was dancing.

It was extremely late when they strolled me back through the doors of the rehab center.

I hear Charlotte say something that sounded like, " What did you guys do to him?".

Then one of the lads jokingly says, " We only promised to get him back here in one piece".

I must have passed out shortly after because I woke up at 10:00am the next day with a splitting headache. I looked over towards my nightstand to see someone left me orange juice and aspirin.

Charlotte knocked on my door a few minutes later, "How are you feeling?", she chuckles.

"Hahaha", I smirk back.

"Time to get up", she demands.

"Everyone's waiting to have breakfast with you, and apparently they all want to participate in the gym workout", chuckling again.

"Fuck No!", I blurt out.

"They are here for a few days and they insist on torturing you they said".

Everyone enjoyed mocking me at breakfast, except my parents, they were just pleased to be enjoying a meal with me.

The lads acted like fools in the gym, playing wheelchair bumper cars and swinging on the parallel bars while I was trying to walk with the ceiling harness. Jake and Nate were in hysterics following along with them of course.

I'm glad they came now. I was thoroughly amused by their behavior in the gym. All was right until Landon picked up a pile of tabloids from the table in the hall and shouts, "Oh shit! Did you guys see this?".

Multiple pictures of me on the cover from the pubs last night. A random girl wearing a half shirt and mini skirt sitting across my lap and kissing my neck. Ridiculous headings flash across the top of the page... " Levi breaks out of rehab", " Levi finds new love interest".

"What the hell!... throw that shit away", I demand.

I look over towards Nate, "Did Charlotte see these?", I nervously ask him.

"Yes, I think so, as she's the one who took them from the delivery guy", his voice shaky when he answers me.

Oh no! I didn't want her to see these pictures. I don't even know who that girl is. I don't even remember her on my lap. I know I'm not with Charlotte, but I can't shake this guilty feeling I have inside, I need to apologize to her or something.

"Where is she?", I ask Nate.

When he tells me she's in the lounge I head straight there. I'm not sure what to say. I just need to know if she is upset with me or not.

Charlotte is sitting on a chair in the corner of the room. She's reading one of those stupid magazines with my picture all over it and has a blank look on her face which worries me even more.

"Charlotte?", I speak softly as I slowly approach her.

She quickly looks up, places the magazine on the table, her expression still unreadable, but her voice light and simply says, " Oh Hi Levi". She then gets up and turns like she's headed for the door, and I grab her arm to stop her.

" Charlotte, please don't believe any of that garbage those people write in there, they will say and do anything to make headlines from a picture of me... I don't even remember most of last night", I try to assure her...or myself, I don't know.

"I know Levi, no worries, you were having a good time", she blankly states. Then before she leaves the room, she tells me that Nate will be doing the rest of my therapy today and she'll see me at dinner.

Crap! I knew having a good time this weekend would be short lived. Nothing ever goes right.

The lads sensed my troubled mood, so continued to banter with me during the rest of my therapy, hoping I'll snap back to my usual self.

Charlotte showed up to dinner and sat with all of us. I was so relieved to see her and glanced at her every few minutes wishing to catch her glancing at me.

"So, we're leaving tomorrow but we will see you again in two weeks in London for the gala", Mark says.

"No, I'm not going", I protest, my body tensing up.

"Yes, you are going, even if I have to drag you on that damn plane", Mark argues.

"Charlotte can come with you", he points out.

Charlotte accidentally drops her fork, surprised by Marks suggestion.

"What? me go to the gala in London... with all the other movie stars?", she nervously shrieks.

" Well why not? it's no different than hanging out with Levi or with me", Mark tries convincing her.

"Except for the fact that it is different…
everyone else can walk", I angrily remind him.

"You're going Levi, end of story", Mark orders.

Everyone had to leave after dinner. Their flight
was early in the morning and no one got much sleep
this weekend. We said our goodbyes and thanked
everyone for coming to visit me. I promised Landon
that I would answer my phone when any of them call
me from now on, and they seemed happy with that.

Charlotte was waiting in my room after I was
done my shower. She didn't say anything, she just
walked over to me and helped me get onto the bed. I
kept looking at her trying to figure out what she was
thinking.

"So, do you want to talk about your reason for
not wanting to go to England for the gala?", she asks
with a serious tone.

"No, I don't want to talk about it", I firmly answer her.

"She looks defeated and starts to walk towards my door saying, "ok, I guess I'll see you in the morning then?"

"Wait!... I'm sorry... don't leave please", I'm feeling frantic now.

I scoot over in the bed and pat the space next to me.

"Can you please stay a little while? we can watch the tele?", I anxiously plead with her.

Feeling I could have a panic attack if she decides to go, she surprises me instead, slowly making her way over, climbs up and sits next to me on the bed.

" Thank you for this weekend Charlotte", I whisper while clicking the remote, searching for any good show we could watch.

I'm surprised again when she reaches over to hold my hand, gently linking her soft fingers with mine, sending a shiver through my body. I don't know what it is about the way she takes my hand in hers, but it always makes me comfortable enough to unveil my thoughts and say things I normally wouldn't.

"I'll go to the gala if you come with me", I quietly say to her.

"I can't, why would you want me to go to that type of important event with you"? she curiously asks me.

I take a deep breath before pouring all my emotions into what I say next.

" I need you there with me, I'm terrified of what might happen there... I can't be there without you Charlotte".

My heart feels like its pounding out of my chest at a rapid speed. This momentary pause is too long. She probably thinks I'm crazy or desperate. I'm definitely feeling like a little bit of both, and the way I'm staring at her waiting for her response proves it.

"Ok I will go", she grins, squeezing my hand with hers again.

Chapter 32

Someone to You

Levi's POV

So far, I've managed not to make anyone angry this week. Everyone here has been in a good mood and I have been fully cooperating for once, it's nice!

The only person who seems preoccupied and anxious this week is Charlotte.

Ever since I asked her to accompany me to England for the gala, she's been in a rare mood. I've never seen her get upset or impatient with anyone until this week.

It's not that she doesn't want to talk about the gala, it's more like she asks questions about it and when I answer them, she gets all worked up.

She goes on and on about how everyone that will be there is famous... how all the women will be in gorgeous dresses that she can't even afford...

I chuckle at her when she says those things, but she glares at me and walks away. I don't like that she feels that way, that she feels so inferior to people whose jobs are acting on film. Because of the media and paparazzi, movie stars are portrayed as perfect, beautiful, flawless beings, who people like Charlotte only dream of meeting. Never mind attending a gala with!

Charlotte has nothing to worry about though. She's as beautiful as any other actress who will be there. Everyone gravitates to her uniquely caring personality, and Mark and I will be there to keep her company. Hopefully by next weekend I can convince her that everything will be fine. I'm the one who's nervous about being the movie star in a wheelchair, nervous about how hard it will be to travel in a chair, how I'm not looking forward to facing Emma again.

Most of my therapy was in the pool this week. Charlotte thought it would be a good idea for me to walk without braces in the pool instead of in the gym. It has been frustrating getting my left leg to take any successful steps without collapsing, even with the water surrounding me. Since Charlotte was already in a bad mood, I refrained from showing any of my emotions.

"We are going to walk at least 10 steps today, even if it takes all day in here", she tells me.

"That's not a very reasonable expectation", I sarcastically respond.

I'm holding onto her shoulders to support part of my weight...well really just my right arm is supporting my weight, my left hand is only resting on her shoulder and she's holding my hips. My balance is much better when I'm in the pool that she only tightens her grip on me when I take a step.

I've tried stepping with my right leg first and I've tried stepping with my left leg first, either way it doesn't make any difference, I have to put my weight on my left and my leg always gives out. Luckily, my right leg is quite strong now and I'm able to place all my weight on that leg without falling over when I'm in the pool.

Charlotte looks just as frustrated as I do, and I hear her sighing when I fall towards my left.

She looks embarrassed when she notices I hear her sigh and quickly says, "I'm sorry. I'm not frustrated with you Levi, I'm upset that I haven't figured out a successful way to help you with your left side yet", she admits.

"It's not your fault Charlotte, we are both trying here... maybe my left side will never work the way we want it to", my voice heavy as I come to terms with this possibility.

"I don't believe that", she retorts.

She then slowly reaches up and grabs my left hand, slowly moves herself to stand by my left side and wraps my left arm around the back of her neck and over her left shoulder, keeping hold of my hand with hers. Her right arm now firmly wrapped around my lower back and her hand grasping my right side. We are attached to each other side by side now, her supporting my left side like a crutch.

I look at her with curiosity, "What are you doing", I ask.

"I'm not sure yet, but let's give it a try", she says.

"Take a step with your left when I step", she instructs.

I start doing like she says, and we start walking together. My left leg still giving out but I'm not losing my balance and falling over while we are holding on to each other like this.

She lets out a "Hmm", and then smiles, so we continue walking this way until we make it all the way across to the other side of the pool.

"This doesn't fix your left side, but while we keep working on getting that side stronger, we can keep practicing walking this way... if you're ok with this?", she asks me.

"Yeah of course", I happily answer.

"This way does feel much easier", I add.

After lunch Charlotte meets me back in my room. I'm sitting on the side of my bed when she arrives, carrying one of my leg braces and one forearm crutch.

I look at her curious as to what her next plan is.

"So, I thought we could try walking together but with your left leg brace on to keep your leg straight, and we can try having you use the crutch with your right arm for extra support", she says to me.

"Ok, yeah", is all I say.

She attaches my leg brace to my left leg and then sits down beside me on the bed. Suddenly she takes in a deep breath and lets out a long sigh before putting her head down and whispering, " I don't belong at the gala... I'm not famous or important, I'm nobody compared to everyone who will be there".

This time I'm the one placing my fingers under her chin, lifting her head up to look at me. Her beautiful eyes glassy like she's holding back tears.

It's my turn to comfort her and let her know how important she is to me. I place my palms gently on both sides of her face so she can't turn away from me and I say with the most soothing tone," You are someone to me".

She blinks her eyes shut then opens them again to look at me one more time before she leans her head onto my shoulder. The only thing I can think to do in this moment is lean my head down and give her a small kiss on her head.

I'm falling for this remarkable girl and it's killing me inside trying to refrain from grabbing her into my arms and holding her.

This mutual uncharted territory we've entered abruptly ends when she wraps my left arm around her shoulder and her right arm around my waist then stands me up.

It's not as easy to balance as it is when I'm in the pool, but Charlotte's grip around the back of my waist keeps me steady.

" Use the right crutch to put some of your weight on as we walk", she tells me.

With my left leg brace on keeping my leg from giving out when I step, using the right crutch and the way I'm connected to Charlotte, makes it so much easier to walk. For the first time in a long time, I feel like this will all work out.

We walk together at a steady pace towards the front lobby.

"Should we head out the door so the paparazzi can take pictures of this and write stories about us?", I joke with her.

She starts laughing back at me then goes silent, abruptly stopping us in our tracks. I turn to her, wondering what's wrong. Her eyes are wide staring straight ahead and her mouth open like she's in shock. Before I turn my head again to see what she's looking at, I hear a familiar voice say, " Hello Levi! I've missed you".

I whip my head around, my eyes focused on the tall blonde walking through the door. I swear Charlotte and I are wearing matching expressions and I start coughing as I try to speak,

"Emma!"

Chapter 33

Confused

Charlotte's POV

"Emma, what are you doing here?", Levi belligerently asks her.

"You're walking!", she says with surprise and excitement in her voice.

"Sort of.... you didn't answer my question", he growls.

"I wanted to see you, I missed you", her voice becoming high pitched.

Levi squeezes my neck in his arm to wake me up.

"Unlikely", he says to her.

This feels like a dream. If Levi hadn't grabbed onto me tighter, my eyes would still be fixed on her, dumbstruck.

"Charlotte, please bring me back to my chair", he whispers into my ear.

I turn us around so we can walk back to his room. I can almost feel Emma walking behind us, watching closely. I quickly glance back at her, her head slightly tilted, and lips pursed together. She's studying the way we are walking.

I help Levi into his chair and unlock his leg brace so he can bend his knee.

"I thought we could go out and get a cup of coffee, catch up on things?", I hear Emma ask.

"No, I'm good", Levi retorts.

Emma crosses her arms and frowns at him.

" Come on Levi, Mark told me you went out with the guys last weekend, so I'm sure you can go out for a cup of coffee with me", she argues with him.

"Fine, there's a coffee shop two blocks down from here", he finally gives in.

Levi maneuvers his chair through the door.

" You don't want to walk with me?", Emma asks.

"No, I'm fine in the chair... let's go", he commands her.

A small crowd of flashing cameras follow them as they make their way down the sidewalk together.

This is not going to end well; I think to myself. What is she really doing here anyway? She heard he went out with his friends last weekend, so that justifies her visiting him now, after five months!

"Why the sour looks on your face?", Nate asks while walking by me.

" Emma just showed up and they are out having coffee together", I answer.

"Oh...... umm, Jake is waiting for you in the gym", he says, concern clear in his voice.

Jake is sitting on the floor mat when I enter the gym. His head jolts back as he gives me a wide- eyed stare. Before he has a chance to ask me about my foul mood, I proceed to tell him everything.

" I wouldn't worry too much about Emma anymore", Jake tells me.

"I'm worried about her hurting Levi again", I point out.

"You shouldn't worry about that either, it's you that he cares about, not her", Jake informs me.

"What makes you think that? Jake"

"Haven't you seen the way he looks at you and how he acts around you... it's love!", Jake exaggerates.

"You mean his constant mood swings?... he needs me to help him, it's not love he's feeling it's gratitude!", I try to convince him.

Jake shakes his head, giving me a disappointing look and continues trying to persuade me.

" Charlotte, I feel overwhelming gratitude for you too, but I'm also in love with my girlfriend, there is a difference between the two".

I shrug my shoulders and he realizes I still don't believe him, so he continues.

" His mood swings are from feeling confused and frustrated. Gratitude doesn't relieve his panic attacks or calm his spasms or make him fight to be better... love does"

"Having my girlfriend here every day by my side, helping me and supporting me through it all, shows me how much she loves me. She is the reason why I don't give up. It's Love that makes me want to get better, for us... and that is who you are to Levi!", he divulges.

I stay quiet, holding Jakes feet firm to the mat while he completes his sit ups and ponder everything, he has just told me.

Maybe Levi does feel something other than gratitude for me? I know I have feelings for him, the way my body shivers when he squeezes my hand, how I'm always thinking about him even when I'm not near him. He makes me laugh, and cry, he gives me purpose and makes me feel needed. These are things I have never experienced before with any other guy. I want more of him, but I can't. I wish there could be more, but I'm not naive. As soon as his treatment is complete and he can live on his own again, he will go back to

England, go back to his famous life, probably go back to Emma too or any other beautiful famous actress.

I help Jake get up to stand, hand him his crutches, and thank him for the talk.

"Charlotte, please think about what I told you. I think it's you who has to figure out what you really want now", he says to me on his way out of the gym.

Dammit Jake, why do you have to be right!

Just as I enter the hall, I catch Levi rolling toward his room from the lobby, Emma following behind. They are both arguing about something, but I'm not close enough to make out what they're saying.

By the time I reach Levi's room, I see him sitting on the edge of his bed. I was about to knock and enter his room until Emma gets up onto the bed and straddles her legs around Levi's, aggressively kissing his mouth then his neck. I'm frozen by the door, once again in shock by Emma's actions. I see Levi pull his head away, trying to avoid her lips and harshly tells her to get off him. She ignores him and continues to invade his neck.

" Get the fuck off me Emma!", he shouts.

Emma climbs off Levi, and slowly backs away, startled by his rejection. Levi looks over at me which causes Emma to turn around too.

Emma's face turns red, her eyebrows crease as she angrily glares at me.

"It's her isn't it?", she hysterically asks Levi while pointing at me.

"You're a fucking movie star, you deserve someone like me, not some therapist!", she adds with equal hysteria.

"Just leave Emma! I don't want you here", Levi tells her.

Emma grabs her purse and walks through the door, gives me a smug look and gloats, " See you two next weekend".

My head is spinning. What the hell just happened? This day has brought nothing but torment. I need to take a walk, clear my head.

Levi quickly gets himself into his wheelchair and starts after me.

"Charlotte, wait, where are you going?", he frantically asks while I jog down the hall.

All the sudden he grabs my left hand with his right to turn me, then pulls me down towards him and crushes his lips onto mine. A jolt of electricity surges through my body, my lips moving slowly in sync with his until my mind regains control of itself and I pull away.

I focus my gaze on Levi's perfect face. I'm so confused right now, and the way Levi is looking back at me shows my feelings are reciprocated.

" I'm sorry, I didn't mean to pull away like that... I'm confused", I quickly say to him.

He's looking at me like he's hurt now, so I just start spitting out what's going through my mind.

" You spent the day out with Emma, then she's climbing all over you sucking at your neck, then she leaves, and you pull me down and kiss me! I'm upset, confused and I want to kiss you again", I blurt out.

His eyes change from worry to glowing after he realizes what I just said.

I grab his hand and give it a slight squeeze letting him know I acknowledge what he feels.

"Can we just talk?", he softly asks me.

We both head into the empty lounge and sit down on the couch together. He proceeds to tell me that he thinks Emma only came because someone told her he was walking. He told Emma about his progress and all the ways I've helped him, but that she just seemed angry and disappointed in him, and when she saw how we walked together, she was jealous.

I thanked him for telling me then brought him back to his room and helped him to his bed.

" I have to go to California for 3 days this week", I nervously say to him.

"Why?", he asks, his tone angry.

I tell him about my new opportunity to expand my rehab center.

"There's a new building my partners want me to look at before making any renovations."

"It will only be 3 days and when I return, we can get ready for our trip to England", I promise. " I will see you in the morning before I leave", I tell him, but he just gives me a half smile and turns his face towards the window.

Chapter 34

The Gala

Levi's POV

"Hey man, it's already been two days, are you going to continue to be an ass until she gets back tomorrow?", Jake jokes with me.

"Just focus on your own workout and I will focus on mine", I smirk back at him.

"I don't know what you're sour about? she's called you like four times a day since she left, she's obviously thinking about you...a lot!", Jake reminds me.

"She's only calling that many times to make sure I'm not doing anything stupid like I did last time she was gone".

"Do you honestly think that mate?", he asks me in a more serious tone.

"I don't know what to think! I kissed her then she pulled away", I confess to him.

Why am I so stupid to think that she would feel the same way I do? I think to myself. How could we even have a relationship? What if I can never walk again or go back to acting again... what then? She pushes me around in a wheelchair spending all her time trying to fix me. I can't even take one step without her holding on to me...

"Fuck!", I accidentally blurt out and throw my crutch to the floor.

"Calm down man! you're thinking about this all wrong", Jake points out.

"Enlighten me please", I sarcastically plead.

Jake shakes his head at me then explains with complete confidence in his voice,

" I've known Charlie a bit longer than you, the way she is with you is different than how she is with me or anyone else. She is the most kindhearted person I know, and she never gives up on any of us, she wants all of us to succeed. But when it comes to you, it's more than that. You make her go crazy with worry, you make her laugh and cry, she smiles every time she's with you.... she brings out the best in you when no one else can".

"She feels something for you... and it's not pity, I know that's what you're thinking", Jake tries to convince me one last time.

The rest of my day was really a blur and I found myself in bed early for the night. I didn't get much sleep though. My mind awake most of the night trying to rationalize everything Jake said to me today.

Charlotte returned the next afternoon. She was smiling when she found me in the gym, but I could read the worry in her eyes when she looked at me.

" I'm ok Charlotte, I was actually nicer than usual to everyone while you were gone", I try to amuse her.

"Oh, that's good to hear! I thought I'd come back to hear that you made Sarah cry again from your cruel behavior", she chuckles.

I'm relieved to see that we are still acting like our normal selves, bantering back and forth, and laughing. I was worried things would be awkward between us.

" I should help you get packed since we're leaving tomorrow", Charlotte reminds me.

She quickly goes from one bureau to the next then to the bathroom collecting things I might need. She hasn't let me do anything, so I just sit on my bed and watch her run her fingers through her hair, looking around one more time to make sure she didn't forget anything.

" Is this how stressful packing is supposed to look like?", I tease her, but she just hisses back at me.

"What's wrong Charlotte?"

"I'm nervous, that's all", she tells me.

I grab her wrist when she tries to walk past me.

"Stop, you didn't forget anything, you packed everything I'm sure, now sit down and relax for a minute", I command her.

She sits down next to me then takes a deep breath in followed by a long sigh.

"Sorry, I'm worried about not finding a dress when we get there", she says softly.

I can't help but start laughing, " That's what you're worried about? a dress?"

Charlotte scowls and hits me on the shoulder.

" Not every girl is lucky enough to have their dress tailored to them by a famous designer", she snips at me.

"Charlotte, you will look perfect in any dress",
I try to convince her.

She gets up off the bed, looks through my bag
one more time then tells me she must go home and
pack her things. This time things did feel awkward
between us when we both paused and looked at each
other, contemplating our next move. Charlotte acted
first and decided to just say goodbye and she'll see me
in the morning. *Wow, I really screwed up that moment!
I think to myself.*

The next morning, Nate brought his car around
the back side of the building, hoping the photographers
out front won't spot us when he brings us to the airport.
Charlotte gives me a baseball cap to wear, hoping it
will help hide my face. She puts both leg braces on my
legs but only locks the left one straight. I wish the cap
would hide my face better because Charlotte catches

me wince in pain and instinctively reach towards my left leg.

I've learned that my left side spasms become more frequent when I work those muscles too much or when I'm overly anxious. This morning I'm extremely anxious. How is she going to get all our luggage and me around the airport? I know we are flying first class, but It's still going to be difficult for me to get onto the plane, and anyone who recognizes me will be snapping photos of it all.

"Hey, everything will be fine, remember?", she says to me as she unlocks my leg brace and starts moving my leg around, massaging my muscles, before locking my brace again.

Nate already has my wheelchair in the car, so Charlotte puts my left arm around her shoulder, wraps her arm around my waist and stands me up with her. I wince again and exhale when I stand causing her to look up at me with concern.

" I'll be fine, let's just walk it off", I reassure her, then grab my right crutch so we can walk to the car.

Logan Airport is crowded when we arrive. Nate checks in our bags curb side while Charlotte helps me out of the car and into my chair. I hang on to my crutch as Charlotte pushes me to the security check in. We get priority check in but since I'm in a wheelchair, security pulls me aside and searches every part me and my chair like I'm a terrorist. It was completely embarrassing and attracted too much attention for my identity to go unnoticed by strangers claiming to be my fans.

"Let's just get to our gate", I groan at Charlotte who looks just as embarrassed for me.

Charlotte grabs my left hand and pulls me to wheel next to her as we make our way to the gate. I don't want to make the boarding process more of a problem so I ask Charlotte if we can have the flight attendant check in my wheelchair and we can walk onto the plane together. She happily agreed with my suggestion and the flight attendant allowed us to be the first ones to board.

Our 6-hour flight to London went by quick. We both watched a few movies, listened to music, and took a short nap.

My mate Andy picked us up when we landed and took us to my flat.

" Andy's girlfriend Kate is going to bring you out dress shopping while I stay here with Andy", I inform Charlotte.

"What about your tux? when are you going to get that?", she asks me.

"Oh, Mark already has my tux, he's bringing it over later", I tell her.

"Of course, he is!", she says slightly annoyed.

The gala was being held at the Waldorf, so Mark had a car pick us up. When we arrived, Charlotte and I checked into our adjoining rooms. I still need help, so I made sure our rooms are connected.

Charlotte helps me get into my tux and has me stand in front of her, holding on to her shoulders while she buttons my shirt.

When she reaches the top button, she pauses for a moment and looks up at me.

" Have you seen or spoken to anyone here besides Mark", she quietly asks me.

"No, I'd rather wait for everyone to stare at me all at one time... get the humiliation over with in one shot", I try to joke with her, so she doesn't notice how much it bothers me.

She reaches up and cups my face in her hands and says, "Levi, people only stare because they're afraid of what's different or unknown to them. And if that's all they want to do is stare, then stare back, make them feel uncomfortable. The ones who look at you just for a second are the ones who are fascinated with you... I mean, that's why I'm always staring at you", she smiles.

"You stare because you're fascinated with me?", I smirk at her.

" Of course, I am! you were just balancing with only one hand on my shoulder and you didn't even realize it", she beams at me.

"Shit! I was!", I chuckle, a little too soon to celebrate as my left leg gives out and Charlotte quickly has her arms around my waist.

She finishes straightening out my tux and helps me in my chair before going to her room to dress.

Women take so long to get ready I complain to myself. But it's worth the wait because as soon as Charlotte walked back into my room wearing a long silky blue dress that accentuated every part of her perfectly toned body, my mouth nearly dropped to the floor. I was breathless, she was beautiful!

"So how do I look", she asks with a high-pitched voice, clearly nervous.

"You look stunning!" I tell her. It's true, I don't want to look away. Maybe I will just stare at her all night and won't worry about who's staring at me.

" Ready for this?", I ask her, holding out my left hand for her to grab.

" No, I'm not ready for this", she says.

" I'm not either", I laugh as we head out towards the gala.

We arrived at the vast room, large glass chandeliers hanging from the ceiling. Every round table covered by silky white cloth and decorated with gold silverware, red and white roses for the centerpiece. A large dance floor situated under the balcony which holds the live orchestra band.

Charlotte gasps in awe, like she's never seen anything like this before. I squeeze her hand to try and ease her anxious thoughts.

"Levi!", Mark yells from across the room.

All eyes turn to look at me. The entire cast from my last movie is here along with their significant others, the director, producer, and everyone else who's important. They are all staring at me like I was afraid they would. I feel Charlotte squeeze my hand because she knows how I'm feeling at this moment. So, I do what Charlotte said and make my way over to the people who didn't look at me like I was some alien and start up a conversation with them.

Turns out Charlotte was right. Mark, my producer and anyone who I was close to on the set treated me like I was me, they were curious and wanted to know how I was doing....and the others, well, I did my best to ignore them.

"Emma! Liam!" someone shouts.

I look over and see Emma and Liam walk through the door, arms linked together at the elbow. *Of course, she's with fucking Liam!*

Everyone sat at the round tables for dinner. Mark and his girlfriend sat with us and he proceeded to inform everyone at our table about how wonderful Charlotte's rehab center is and all the stuff they have there for me. Charlotte looks uncomfortably shy when all attention is focused on her, so I reached under the table and put my hand on her leg letting her know she's doing fine.

Mark then changes the subject and starts talking about the movie and its release date. All the guys engage in Mark's conversation. Thankfully, some of my co-stars' girlfriends include Charlotte in a different conversation, otherwise she would just be sitting there feeling totally out of place.

After dinner everyone was dancing. Charlotte was up standing near the bar getting another glass of wine, and I was sitting alone at the table while everyone else hit the dance floor with their partner. A few songs later I was still alone watching everyone, and I felt myself getting angry the more I gazed at them all, gliding along the floor, me stuck in this stupid chair. Emma made sure to look my way every so often trying to provoke me with her body draped around Liam. I don't know where Charlotte went, she wasn't near the bar and I need her here with me before I lose my mind.

Just then I feel her face next to my ear, she's in back of me, leans down and wraps her arms lightly around the front of my neck and whispers, " Will you have this dance with me?".

Before I can answer, she moves in front of me and grabs both of my hands, pulling my wheelchair with her towards the dance floor.

"What are you doing?", I growl at her.

"I don't want to dance in my chair, it looks ridiculous ", I tell her.

"You're going to stand and dance with me", she says.

I pull my hands away from her and cross my arms when we stop at the edge of the dance floor and glare at her.

"I can't, I will fall in front of everyone, I'm not wearing my braces", I angrily whisper to her.

She leans down and takes my arms and wraps them around the back of her neck then looks straight into my eyes and asks, " Do you trust me?

"Yes of course I do", I say.

"Then dance with me! we got this", she tells me.

My arms are tight around the back of her neck and her arms are tightly around my lower back as she stands me up. I hear a few loud gasps and look up to see that all eyes are on me.

" Everyone's staring at us ", I inform Charlotte.

"Let them stare ", she says back.

We are still holding onto each other in a tight embrace.

" Step when I step", she instructs me until we've made it a couple feet onto the dance floor.

She tightens her grip around my waist then takes my left arm off from her neck and brings it down so she can hold my hand in hers. My right arm holds tighter to the back of her shoulder, we are wrapped around each other carefully swaying our hips side to side.

"See we're dancing", she says softly and smiles up at me.

I don't say anything, I just see everyone looking at me, and picture myself falling.

"Just Breathe", Charlotte whispers to me when she notices I'm holding my breath and beginning to shake a little.

"Levi, don't look at them, only focus on me", she says softly and holds me tighter.

We are in a dancing hold, and we are very slightly moving side to side, so I wouldn't call this dancing, but it's close enough. I put all my focus on Charlotte, forget about everyone else in the room and lean my head down to softly plant a small kiss on her neck then bury my face in her hair as we dance.

"You have no Idea what you do to me Charlotte", I say so low into her hair, I'm not sure if she heard me.

Halfway through the second song I feel my legs start to shake.

"Charlotte!", I frantically murmur.

She senses my worry and sits me back down into my chair. All eyes focused on me again like they are waiting for something bad to happen. Charlotte puts her hand on my cheek and moves my face so I can only see her.

"Let's go back to the room", she leans down and speaks into my ear.

She grabs my hand and leads us back to my room.

"I'm going to find you something to change into", she says as she darts for my suitcase. When she starts to walk past me, I grab her arm and pull her down onto my lap, hold her face in my palm and crash my lips onto hers.

At first, she hesitates, but I press my lips harder to hers and she gives in, her lips taste sweet, and she caresses her tongue with mine. I brush my lips across her jawline then down to the base of her neck. I want her so badly it hurts.

She lifts my head, and her mouth catches mine again until she pulls away to catch her breath. When her green-blue eyes meet mine, I can't look away.

She starts unbuttoning my shirt then gets off my lap and pushes me back towards the bed. I wrap my arms around the back of her neck so I can stand, and she quickly detaches my belt and tugs my pants down to the floor. I sit down on the bed and pull her close so she's standing between my legs and I unzip the back of her dress, letting it slowly slide off, revealing her perfect body.

Damn she's so hot, standing so close to me wearing only her black lace panties! She's seen me fully exposed before, but this is the first time I've seen her. Her flawless skin, her smooth flat stomach, the perfect shape of her breasts.

I drag myself up onto the bed, so my back is leaning up against the headboard and watch her slowly climb on top of me, straddling her legs over mine. My right-hand steadies myself up, while my other hand grabs the back of her neck, pulling her closer to me to kiss her. The way her lips feel as she kisses me back, arouses a feeling deep inside me, making my need for her undeniable.

She pushes me back to lean on the headboard again, then leans her body into mine and slowly nips at my ear then softly kisses my neck. A shiver runs through my whole body as she moves her lips down to my collarbone. I caress her back with my fingers while she grazes hers down my stomach and stops just above my boxers. My whole body is shaking now, and my paranoia takes over.

I grab her hand before she pulls my briefs down.

"Charlotte, what if I can't .... you know", I say to her, my voice cracking.

She puts her finger on my lips, preventing me from saying any more then pulls off my boxers and takes me into her mouth. Her slow movements send a spark through my groin, I feel the flick of her tongue and the muscles in my thighs tighten.

"Fuck!", I gasp. My craving for her is getting physically painful.

I can't wait any longer, so I reach down, pull her back up and roll her over so that I'm half on top of her now. I bring my right leg up and drape it over her hip, squeezing her closer to me and slide myself into her. She feels so soft, so warm as I move in and out of her, it's intoxicating.

"If you only knew how you make me feel", I moan.

We lay in bed after, her head resting on my chest and my arm around her back.

" Everything's going to change now", she says.

" Not everything, but some things", I remind her.

For the first time in a long time, I feel like I can breathe again.

Chapter 35

My Place

Charlotte's POV

We spent the next day at Levi's flat so we could kill some time before our evening flight back to Boston.

His friends Andy and Landon hung out with us. Andy's been living there taking care of the place while

Levi's been away, and I could tell by the way he slowly wheeled himself around through each room, that Levi now felt out of place in his own home.

I sat next to Levi on his couch listening to him talk and joke around with his friends, but he was not acting like himself. He held my hand the whole time and sometimes he would stare off into the distance while Landon and Andy bickered about who knows what. When I would nudge him back from wherever his mind wondered off to, he would squeeze my hand and give me a little smile.

I caught Andy glaring at our locked hands with disapproval more than once, but I could not figure out what he didn't like about it. Am I not good enough for his best friend, or does he just think this is an odd relationship for us to start... like I am sure most people will think?

Things will be different when we get back to Boston. I will have to figure out how to balance professional with personal. Just because Levi and I might seem strange or different to Andy and whoever else, does not mean it is a bad thing.

"Can you help me into my chair?", Levi whispers in my ear.

"Sure", I gladly say, I then bring his chair close to him and guide his left arm, making him do most of the transfer on his own. He thanks me then rolls himself out onto his balcony and closes the glass door behind him.

Andy gets up and follows him out there, leaving Landon and I in the living room. We both look out towards Andy and Levi arguing about something then we look back at each other, both awkwardly trying to avert our eyes elsewhere.

"So, you and Levi huh?", Landon breaks the discomfort in the room.

"I was waiting for you two to finally realize how you feel about each other", he smirks.

"Is that a good thing or a bad one? because Andy seems to disapprove", I point over at the two arguing outside.

"You seem like you really care about Levi, and lately Levi only seems happy when he is with you, so that's good enough for me. Andy is just worried that's all. When Emma left Levi it nearly destroyed him, then he didn't talk to Andy and me for almost 4 months!", Landon reminds me.

He continues on... "Andy always hated Emma and how she only cared about herself. Andy told Levi she was only with him for status, but Levi did not listen to him. And when Levi ignored our calls after, Andy was really upset".

I clear my throat thinking of how to defend Levi before responding to all that information.

"Levi was hurt when Emma left, he thought he was worthless because he was confined to a chair and needed everyone to help him with normal everyday things. He didn't want his best friends to see him that way and he was afraid you would treat him differently, so he tried pushing you away before you had the chance to give up on him first", I confess to Landon.

Landon sits back against the couch and crosses his arms. I can see that he is thinking about what I said. I look back at Levi and Andy and I am relieved to see Andy sitting on a patio chair, that their arguing has stopped.

I turn to Landon again, who is still sitting there quiet and I continue to tell him,

" Levi felt like he didn't deserve anyone, I think he still feels that way, and I will do whatever it takes so he doesn't feel like that anymore".

"And that's why I think you two will be perfect together", Landon chirps, then taps my knee as he gets up to join Andy and Levi on the balcony.

The sounds of laughter coming from the three of them makes me less anxious, so I let them be and make my way to the kitchen to get a glass of water. As I go to grab some ice from the freezer, I notice the fridge door has a picture of Levi and his friends toasting together at some party. Looking at them all together happy like that makes me smile, until I go to close the freezer door and notice a picture of Levi with Emma. They are standing together, Levi's arm around her shoulders while he is kissing her on the cheek. I must have been staring at that picture a little too long because the three guys startled me by strolling into the kitchen laughing and I frantically try to hide my face while I catch the lone tear rolling down my cheek.

"What's wrong?", Levi asks me.

"Nothing… I… I had something in my eye", I stuttered.

"Well, let us go then! I've got to get you two to the airport before you miss your flight", Landon blurts out.

Thank goodness it is Landon taking us and not Andy! I think to myself. Knowing that Andy is not too keen about all of this makes me feel a little weird around him now.

As we head out to the car, me following behind Landon, I look back to catch Andy stop Levi.

"This isn't going to end well", I hear Andy say slightly louder than a whisper so that I can hear him.

I just keep walking, pretending I don't know what they are talking about when Levi surprises me by responding, " Well I think you're wrong".

Levi stays unexpectedly quiet the entire ride to the airport, throughout the humiliating security search, and all the way to our gate. Only when I left him sitting in the waiting area so I could check in his chair and come back, did he simply say, "Thank you".

Once again, we were the first ones onto the plane. The flight attendant gave us enough time to walk down the ramp so we could sit in the front row before the other passengers made their way down. Right after I helped him into the aisle seat, he grabbed the arm rest and his body stiffened, "Ow! Dammit!",

he yells out, trying to reach for his left leg now in full

spasm. I quickly unlock his leg brace and apply

pressure to his thigh and knee with my hands,

massaging his muscles until the spasm stops. I look up

at him, his expression a mix of pain and anxiety. His

breathing picks up, he is about to panic, and I know it

is because he is afraid the other passengers will start to

board and witness this ordeal. I press my hand down

firmer onto his leg with one hand, step my leg over

him so I am standing in front of him and lean towards

his face, planting my lips onto his. He tries to speak,

but I stop him, kissing him again.

I pull away just as passengers start to enter the

plane and he keeps his gaze on me. His lips slightly

parted, his eyes wide, he is calmer now so I carefully

move his left leg to where it should be and climb over

him to the window seat.

Levi keeps his gaze on me, trying to ignore all the passengers walking by us. His breathing has slowed but not back to the normal rhythm it should be.

"Are you okay?", I softly ask him.

"Um, yes I think so, I don't know ", he says back.

"Do you want to talk about what you and Andy were arguing about earlier today", I nervously ask him.

Levi's been way too quiet this evening and after the leg spasm he just had, I know it is because something is really bothering him, probably something Andy said to him.

"I don't want to talk about it", he groans.

I try a few more times to persuade him into talking, but he shut me down every time. He was content just holding my hand while I leaned my head on his shoulder.

Three hours into the flight, he finally speaks, " Thank you for coming on this trip with me, I wouldn't have gotten through it without you", he softly says, then leans his head on mine and falls asleep.

Everyone at rehab was happy to see us when we got back. Nate informed me that I looked like crap and probably needed some sleep. He told me he would cover the rest of the day and instructed me to go home and come back tomorrow. I thanked him for running things while I was gone, then followed Levi to his room to drop off his luggage.

As soon as we entered Levi's room, he shut the door and locked it behind me. Before I could ask him what he was doing, he grabbed my waist and pulled me onto his lap. He then brushed his finger softly down my cheek and his thumb across my bottom lip, triggering a fluttery feeling in my stomach.

"You're so beautiful", he says to me before tucking a strand of my hair behind my ear and pulling me towards his heavenly lips.

"Come rest in bed with me for a while", he says.

"Levi, we can't do this here, believe me, I want to.... but not here, I must be professional here", I grudgingly say.

"Bring me with you to your place then, just for today?", he shyly asks.

"You haven't had any therapy in the last 24 hours", I remind him.

"We can do some at your place, then you can take a nap because Nate says you look like crap", Levi giggles.

"Fine, you can come", I tell him.

His moods change so quickly so seeing him happy and joking around with me makes it hard to deny him.

" I don't want to take my wheelchair", he sternly says.

" I want to walk with you".

"Okay", I say, a little confused.

We get to my place and I am thankful now that I picked to live in the apartment building with an elevator. Levi asks me to walk him around on a tour of my apartment. It isn't too fancy, but I have plenty of room for myself, a big kitchen, living room area with a huge couch and flat screen TV, hardwood floors throughout and two bedrooms... one I use as my office.

" I like your place", he says to me while I walk him over to sit on the couch.

"Glad you like it", I tell him.

" Will you be alright here for a bit while I take a quick shower and change?"

"Yes sure, hurry back", he smiles.

I hurry into the shower and let the hot water pour over my tired muscles. I feel like my stomach is doing flips and my heart races every time I think about the way he touches my skin. I want to be close to him all the time. I have never felt this urge with anyone else before. I could stay enjoying the hot shower for another hour, but I just want to get back to Levi.

I put on a light pair of sweats and a t-shirt then make my way back to the living room. Levi is lying on his side, fast asleep on the couch. I grab a blanket and start to cover him with it when I feel him tug on my pants and pull me down to him. He shifts himself closer to the back of the couch so I can lay down. He wraps his arm around my stomach and squishes me into his chest and rests his face in my neck. I feel his lips gently brush the base of my neck and it sends a shiver down my spine.

"The things you do to me Charlie", he breathes into my neck then gently kisses me.

Our bodies were aching for more, but our minds were exhausted from the complete lack of sleep in the last two days, and jet lag on top of it. So, we just snuggled together on the couch, his arm and leg nestled tightly around me, holding me close against his chest until we happily fell asleep.

Chapter 36

Inconvenience

Charlotte's POV

I gently unwrap Levi's arm from me to sneak away from the couch. It is 5:30am so I decide to use this time to shower and pack some clothes before I wake him up. My neck hurts from sleeping in the crook of Levi's arm all night, but I am not going to complain too much, I love the comfort of his body holding mine. It is the first time I have gotten a full night's rest without having any worry invading my mind.

"Levi, wake up!", I tap on his shoulder.

He rubs his eyes and stretches while trying to focus on me.

"What time is it?", his voice groggy.

"It's 6:30", I tell him.

"6:30 at night? come back and lay down with me", he pats the couch.

I pull on his arm, making him sit up.

" It is 6:30 in the morning, now come on I have to get to work", I laugh and wrap his arm around the back of my shoulder to help him stand.

I bring him into the bathroom to use the toilet and so he can brush his teeth. We are awkwardly standing together at the sink while he maneuvers his toothbrush with one hand, his left arm around my neck and my right arm holding around his waist so I can support his weight. I am a little annoyed that he does not think anything of it, he just goes about doing what he has to do at the sink while I hold him up.

"You know this would be a lot easier if you sat in your wheelchair to do this".

"No, this is fine", he says nonchalantly.

"Ok, let's get going then", I say as I lead him around with me to my room to grab my bag, then to the kitchen to grab my keys and out the door to my jeep. I guess I cannot be too annoyed, I am the one who didn't force him to take his chair with us yesterday.

We grabbed some Starbucks coffee and breakfast on the way to the rehab center. When we get there, I lead him to his room and towards his wheelchair.

"I'll sit on the bed for now", he says.

"Alright", I exaggerate.

"I have a ton of work to catch up on, so you'll have to meet Nate in the gym", I let him know, and then lean towards him and plant a quick kiss onto his lips.

"I'll bring your chair next to you so you can transfer when you want", I try to say, but he cuts me off and says with a stern voice,

" No chair, Sarah can walk me to the gym".

I give him a weird look even though he is the one acting weird today. I turn to walk out the door, let out a small sigh of confusion, and simply say, "Fine... I will come find you this afternoon".

Why is he acting so strange about his wheelchair? I ask myself. Is it something I did or said, or worse, is it something Andy said to him yesterday causing this newfound persistence to not use his chair? As much as I want to be with him every minute, our arms wrapped around each other, walking together... I can't. I cannot walk him around everywhere and get my work done. I need to get his stubborn ass back to using his chair.

I found him sitting on the couch in the lounge after I finished all my other work. No wheelchair in sight, only Levi. I walked over to him and he looks up at me smiling, then pulls me down onto his lap to kiss me.

" I missed you all day", he cheerfully says.

I'm glad he's in a good mood so I quickly blurt out, " let's get to the gym, we are going to tackle your fear of the parallel bars", hoping he doesn't switch his mood to angry.

Too late! He pushes me off his lap and glares at me.

"What? No, absolutely not", he grunts.

"Levi, you have to work on this and I'm going to be the one helping you this time", I try to deter him from thinking about his first horrible experience with the bars.

He sighs while I lock his left leg brace, then puts his arm around me so we can walk to the gym. I stop with him right at the edge of the piece of equipment he's so scared of and move myself to stand in front of him, in between the bars. I tightly grab both of his hips. He does not move and keeps both of his arms firmly holding my shoulders.

"Levi, you have to let go and grab the bars", I tell him.

"No!... I can't", his accent accentuating his shaky voice.

"You're not going to fall, your leg brace is locked and I'm holding you... you just need to grab the bars and practice using your arms to help you balance while you walk", I let him know.

He slowly releases his grip from my shoulders and places both hands down onto each bar. As soon as he takes a step forward his left arm gives out and he huffs loudly at me. He does not fall though because I am holding his hips steady. He pauses to peer into my eyes and all I can see is frustration all over his face.

So, I glide my grip up his left side to help straighten his stance while he tries to make his left hand hold the bar again. His arm continues to give out every time he tries to support his weight with each step, and he is staring at me like he wants to strangle me, but I ignore it. We almost reach the end of the bars when all of the sudden his left hand lets go and he yells, " Ow! Fuck". He winces in pain at his left arm going into spasm.

I quickly reach my left arm to wrap around the back of him, bring his spasming arm up to rest against his chest then bring myself close and embrace him.

"I'm sorry, we should've stopped after a few steps, I made you work too hard", I apologize.

I keep hold of him, putting pressure on his left arm while it is embraced between us. It seems like he has been holding his breath forever, waiting for the

pain to stop. When it finally does, he exhales and says,
" I'm fine now, can you bring me back to my room?".

I get him back to his room and he lays down
onto his bed, grabs the remote and starts flipping
through channels, all while keeping his eyes from
looking at me.

I sit down beside him on the bed, put my hand
on his thigh and speak softly hoping that he will at
least acknowledge me,

" I'm very proud of you for trying so hard on
the bars, it will get better if we keep working at it". He
does not look at me, he just keeps his eyes focused on
the screen and says,

"Hmm".

Not sure what I should do or say now. I feel
terrible that the parallel bars ended with a painful

spasm and he is upset right now. So, I force myself to leave him alone in his room since he does not want to talk to me anyway.

I went home to try to get some sleep but of course I just ended up lying in bed worried about Levi. In the morning I made sure I got back to the facility before he woke up.

"Where did you go last night?", I hear his tired voice ask me when I entered his room. I thought he would still be sleeping, but instead he tells me that he was up all night wondering why I left.

"I know you were upset with me, so I wanted to give you some space", I tell him.

"I don't need space... I just hate using the parallel bars", he looks at me hoping that I believe him.

"I know ... I'm sorry...that's why we can take a break from the bars and try something else", I say to him.

He is only in his boxers, so I throw a pair of sweatpants and a t-shirt at him and tell him to get dressed.

He looks at me surprised and asks, "You are not going to help me?".

"No, you can dress yourself, I will be back in a few minutes,", I smirk, pushing his wheelchair next to his bed before heading out of the room.

When I get back, he's dressed and sitting up on the edge of the bed.

"Why aren't you in your chair", I ask him.

He narrows his eyes at me and growls, " I'm not using the wheelchair so stop asking me".

"Fine", and I lean down next to him so we can grab hold of each other like usual and walk to the weight room. I bring him to the weight chair and strap in his left arm and leg. I set the weight at 5lbs and he begins alternating his arm and leg, pulling, and pushing the weight. After the first set of ten, I see him wince and hold his breath. He can barely move 5lbs now and his arm is twitching under the straps.

"Ok, take a break before you try it again, I'll lower the weight this time", I say.

"No! do not lower the weight", he demands in a harsh voice.

He struggles through another set until I see both his leg and arm shaking.

"Levi, you need to stop now so that you still have strength to work on something else today", I persist.

He reluctantly lets me detach him from the weights and I pull him up to stand in front of me. When he wraps his arms around the back of my neck, I pull him into me and hug him for a quick moment. He does not seem to want to hug me back, so I let go and reach up to put my hands on both sides of his face, look into his worried blue eyes and say,

" You are doing great".

He doesn't respond, instead he looks at me and gives me a fake smile.

We went from weights to stretching to working in the pool the remainder of the day. I could see he was exhausted, dark circles forming under his eyes from lack of sleep. His stubbornness kept him going and he worked through his painful spasms. I kept praising him and rewarding him with small kisses and hugs, but he did not want to reciprocate my affection and I was afraid of finding out why.

The same went on for the rest of the week and then the next. Still stubborn, working himself too hard and refusing to even look at the wheelchair. I slept alone at my place each night while he was alone in his room. Somehow, even though I was also getting frustrated, I managed to keep acting the same around him, showing him affection and showing him that I cared. He is not going to push me away that easily.

It was now the day before Thanksgiving, and I had had enough of Levi's behavior. If he no longer wanted me to be more than just his therapist, then he needs to tell me that.

Again, he was dressed and sitting on the edge of his bed when I arrived. This time he smiled at me when he saw me walk in.

"Good morning Love!", he greets me.

I am in shock of course, not expecting this mood at all.

"Good morning", I slowly stretch the words out from my mouth.

"Come here", he beckons, stretching his arms out towards me.

I hesitate to make my way towards him. He pulls me into him and hugs me.

"I'm sorry for the way I have been acting", he says with his head on my chest.

"You have been mad at me for the past two weeks! I want to know why", I say to him.

He lifts his head from my chest and discloses,

" I was not mad at you; I was mad at myself... I just took it out on you, I shouldn't have... I'm sorry".

"Why are you so mad at yourself?", I ask him.

"Because we have tried everything to make my left side stronger and nothing is working. I am sorry if it bothers you to always have you walk with me, but I hate being dependent on a wheelchair, I do not want to use it.... I want my left side to work and I want to walk!", his eyes tearing up as he confesses this to me.

I place a soft kiss onto his lips then he lays his head on my chest and hugs me again.

"I know Levi, that is why I'm going to California on Friday", I tell him.

He quickly pushes back,

"What?".

"My new rehab facility in LA is open and I need to go there and make sure all my new programs are up and running", I tell him.

I can see he is nervous, and I know he hates when I leave, so I quickly assure him,

" It is a very short trip, I'll be back Sunday night, I promise".

"Ok", he solemnly says and looks down at the floor.

I grab both of his hands and he looks at me.

" Will you please come to my place for Thanksgiving tomorrow?", I ask him.

His face lights up, "Sure I would love to".

Thankfully, he stays in a good mood the rest of the morning and does not give me a hard time when I tell him I am leaving early to go food shopping.

"I am picking up my brother and parents from the airport tonight, and I'll be back to get you in the morning", I smile and kiss him goodbye.

Thanksgiving morning Levi was waiting in the Lobby for me when I arrived. I had to catch my breath at the mesmerizing sight of him. His hair was smoothed up and out of his face. His black jeans and light blue button-down shirt accentuated his blue eyes and his perfectly sculpted upper body. I am not sure what his firsts thoughts are when he looks at me, I am only dressed in a dark grey knee length dress with long laced sleeves. My long black coat covering most of me.

"Hey beautiful", he grins widely.

"Hey!", I smile then lean down to kiss him.

" You look really nice", I whisper into his ear before we head out to the car.

Levi sat quietly and held my hand the whole drive to my apartment, only looking anxious and squeezing my hand when we finally get there.

" Don't worry it will be fun!", I try and convince him and kiss him on his cheek before helping him out of the car.

I have already filled in my parents and brother about Levi and his accident, so they will not be surprised to see me holding onto him as we walk in.

My parents are usually disappointed in my choice of guys. My dad has always wanted me to find some smart doctor, but that would never work out with our jobs and schedules. My brother does not understand why I would want to date one of my patients, he says it's like taking my work home with me all the time. I obviously do not agree with him, I know he is just looking out for me.

Everyone greets us when I walk in with Levi. My dad and brother shake Levi's hand and ask him if he wants to watch the football game with them. I bring Levi to the couch and sit him down so he can lean on the arm rest. This is my chance to help my mom in the kitchen and get all the food out onto the table.

"Dinner is ready", my mom shouts to the guys.

My dad heads right to the table but my brother takes his time watching Levi put his arm around me while I stand him up. I look over at my brother and he rolls his eyes at me to prove his earlier point. It would be better for Levi if he used his wheelchair here, he would not have to wait for me every time he wants to move somewhere.

Dinner tastes great and everyone is engaged in constant chatter. A few times I feel Levi reach under the table and squeeze my leg which makes me smile.

The three guys get back to watching football while I help mom clean up.

" Sorry I have to leave tomorrow mom, you can stay here while I'm gone and we can spend some time together when I get back", I tell her.

She gladly takes me up on my offer and says they have a hotel for tonight but will stay at my place the rest of the weekend. I got my brother and father tickets to the Bruins game this weekend, so they are psyched about that.

After everyone left, I walked Levi to the bedroom, and he sat on the bed while I looked for comfortable clothes to sleep in. He changed into some cotton shorts but did not want a shirt. I certainly didn't mind that.

He pulled me onto the bed with him.

"Come lay down next to me, you've done enough today", he smirks.

I gladly lay next to him and pull the covers over us. He immediately turns on his side to face me while I lie on my back and he starts tracing my ear with his finger. Slowly and lightly, he brushes his fingers down my neck. He reaches under my shirt, making small circles around my breasts with his fingertips, then glides one finger down my stomach until he reaches my panty line.

"You should take these off", he says, his accent makes his voice more seductive.

"Yes, that's a good idea", I breathe out.

My breathing is getting heavy as he continues to gently brush my skin with his fingers, causing goose bumps to form all over my body. He reaches his hand down and gently glides his finger into me and slowly pumps it in and out, my body tenses with pleasure and I grab down on the sheets.

" You are so ready for me", he says.

I roll onto my side so that we are face to face, our bodies touching and move my hand down between his thighs and see that he is ready too.

" I need you Charlotte", he moans, while sliding himself into me.

" It feels so good", I say to him.

He catches my words with his mouth, pressing his lips hard onto mine while our bodies move together in a sensual rhythm.

We fell asleep after, encased in each other's arms, both too tired to speak.

The next morning, I got Levi back to the rehab center, checked on all the patients, then talked with Nate to make sure he was all set for the weekend.

I went back to Levi's room to say goodbye and found him still sitting on his bed where I left him.

" Are you going to stay in this spot until someone comes and walks with you?", I joke with him.

He laughs, " Yeah probably".

" I don't want you to go", he looks down and says to me in a low voice.

I walk over to him and stand in between his knees and he grabs my hips to bring me closer. I grasp his face in my hands then lean down and kiss him.

"I have to go... there's a new treatment that I have to make sure is up and running", I say.

He pulls me in close and hugs me and I lean my chin on the top of his silky brown hair.

"Everything I'm doing over in L.A. is for you Levi, you will soon see".

Chapter 37

Am I Broken?

Levi's POV

I woke up early Saturday morning and spent most of the day in the gym. If Charlotte was going to be gone all weekend, I may as well keep myself busy to pass the time.

I let Sarah hook me up to the ceiling harness so I could practice balancing without anyone having to hold on to me. Nate got me working on the weight machine then doing some floor stretches and sit-ups.

"You're being unusually cooperative today", Jake jokingly points out as he is doing his stretches on the mat next to me.

" I promised Charlotte that I would be on my best behavior while she is away ", I smirk.

Jake laughs, "And when Kelly comes to work with you this afternoon, you will still be this cheerful I assume?", he is mocking me now.

" If she doesn't try to get me to use those damn parallel bars, then everything should be fine", I chuckle.

We both stay silent after, continuing with our stretches. A few minutes go by and Jake stops his workout and sits down on the mat facing me. He looks at me and begins speaking to me in a serious tone.

" You know, you should be nice and cooperative like this more often, especially to those who are here to help you, and even more towards the one person who stays by you even when you are acting your worst... the one person who will do anything for you".

"I know", I agree with him.

"Then why? Why do you always close yourself off so that all is left is anger? Why does it seem like you are always trying to push her away?", Jake presses me.

I stop my stretches so I can focus on our conversation. I drag myself back so I can sit and lean against the wall. Jake is patiently sitting on his mat waiting for me to respond.

"Honestly, I don't know why. I do not want to act that way with her. I just keep thinking that my twelve months will be up, and I will be left with only my right-side functioning. I don't want this to be all I can do, just the thought of it makes me angry all the time", I confess.

"Well, if that's the fate you are dealt with, then it is up to you to choose how you are going to live with it, and who you want by your side", he plainly tells me.

I don't want to accept that this will be my fate though. But each day that goes by that I cannot stand on my left leg or use my left arm to support my weight, reminds me that this might be the rest of my life, that I will be dependent on a wheelchair and someone assisting me the rest of my life.

"Why don't you tell Charlotte how you feel instead of holding it all in and then taking it out on her?", Jake asks me.

"She already spends enough time trying to fix me. I want to be the one who is there for her, doing things for her, but I can't. I do not want her to have to be the one always taking care of me. Her brother already doesn't like me and thinks I am a burden to her", I put my head down feeling ashamed while I explain how I feel to Jake.

He grabs his forearm crutches and stands up to walk out of the room. Just before he leaves, he throws one more reminder at me.

"Please try and talk to her more, you two are good together and I would hate to see you drift apart just because you are too scared of what you don't know".

Everything Jake said is right. I know I need to work on a lot of things, I don't want to lose her.

Sunday came and went without a hitch, and before I knew it, it was almost half past eleven. Charlotte isn't supposed to be back until after midnight, so I get in my wheelchair, grab my journal and head to the lounge. I would stay in my room, but I do not want to fall asleep before Charlotte gets here, and it is too late to ask Sarah to walk with me, so I dismally resort to using the chair.

Venting my thoughts into my journal will be good for me, while I sit on the couch waiting for her.

Some time passes and I must have dozed off while I was writing because I open my eyes and realize I am lying on the couch with a blanket covering me. My phone says it is three in the morning. Oh no, did I miss her? did she even come back yet?

Right before I allow myself to get upset, I see my journal set on the seat of my wheelchair with a note attached to it.

The note reads....

I'm sorry I got in so late. You looked so peaceful sleeping; I didn't want to wake you. I will see you when the sun comes up.

~Charlotte

P.S. I am glad to see you used your chair again and your journal.

There are still a few more hours left before sunrise, so I make my way back to my room, hop onto my bed and force myself to fall asleep again.

Morning comes and Charlotte wakes me up by climbing into my bed next to me and wrapping her arm around me. I wouldn't mind waking up to this beautiful girl next to me every morning, I smile to myself.

I roll over and plant a kiss on her soft lips.

"Good morning beautiful", I smile and kiss her again.

"Good morning, I missed you", she says which makes me grin wider.

She gets up off the bed and grabs my hand, pulling me to sit up on the edge of the bed.

"Get up, we have a lot to talk about", she says.

I am puzzled, did Jake tell her about what we talked about yesterday? All kinds of random thoughts start flooding my mind and I can feel my heart beating faster. I cannot let myself get worked up when I don't even know what she wants to talk about. So, I take a deep breath and reach for her hands and hold them in mine as she stands in front of me.

"What is it you want to talk about", I slowly ask her.

"About next week's trip to L.A. This time we will have to stay there for two weeks", she says.

I stopped listening after she said the words, "next week's trip" and my mind immediately went into fight mode.

"You just got back and you're leaving again for two weeks? my voice loud and harsh.

My gut has been telling me this would happen. Andy warned me that this would happen, that she would find ways to escape and turn her attention to her other facility far away from Boston, far away from me. I do not give her any chance to speak, instead I ramble out every insecure thought I have.

"Is it because of the chair? I will use the stupid chair! Fuck, I will use the parallel bars too. I am a burden to you, aren't I? You are finally tired of trying to fix me...."

She grabs my face with both of her hands and crashes her mouth onto mine, to shut me up.

I want to push her away so I can continue my ranting, but she presses her lips harder and I cave. Her mouth tastes like mint and our lips move together as she caresses her tongue with mine.

She pulls away but still holds my face in her hands, her smile is stretched ear to ear, and she lets out a tiny laugh.

"What are you laughing about?", I growl.

"I said WE will have to stay there for two weeks! I want you to come with me Levi", she says.

I remain still, staring at her with utter confusion. I feel like such a fool for getting upset with her. It is Jake who was right this time.

She notices my confused expression while I continue sitting here like a statue, so she proceeds to tell me that the facility in California does stem-cell therapy treatments. She thinks the treatment might help me gain more strength in my hips and left arm and leg if I want to go through with it.

She throws her arms around me and tightly embraces me. She nuzzles her face into my neck and asks, " Levi, all those things you said... is that really how you think of me?"

"What? No, I shouldn't have said any of that", I finally speak.

She hugs me tighter and says,

"I don't want you to ever feel like you are a burden to me because that is not what you are. And you are not broken Levi, there is nothing I need to fix, I am only trying to help you. You know that, right?"

Her words flood my soul with a sudden and striking realization that I have been blinded by hopelessness and that she is my fortitude.

Chapter 38

A Perfect Date

Levi's POV

I try my best to stay in a good mood the rest of the week. I feel like I am treading water, making sure I do not say or do the wrong thing. I wish I could take back all those things I confessed to her, but I can't, so instead I keep apologizing to her every chance I get.

Since Charlotte is the most understanding person that I know, she just repeatedly reminds me of how proud she is of me for telling her how I feel.

How can anyone be lucky enough to deserve someone like her, especially someone like me? I am grateful that I have Jake to talk to about everything with. He helps put things in perspective for me and tries to make me realize that I can be with her if I just let go of my fear. I need to stop being such a jerk all the time and start treating her the way she deserves to be treated.

Charlotte comes to get me from the gym after Nate finishes with my therapy. We walk together back to my room and she tells me that we need to pack since we are leaving tomorrow.

" I would like to take you out to dinner tonight ... well you would be physically taking me out, but I would like for us to go on a date", I beam at her.

My hands fidgeting, nervously waiting for her to answer me. I hope she says yes, I really need to show her that we can go out and do things like a normal couple, not just her taking care of me all the time.

She smiles at me with those captivating multi-colored eyes of hers and speaks in the most endearing tone, "I would love that".

I open my arms to her and pull her into me. I kiss her sweet lips before she breaks away and starts walking me towards the bathroom.

"Take a shower while I pack your bag, then we will bring your stuff to my place so that I can take a shower before we go out", she instructs.

I pause to look at her for a moment.

" We will stay at my place and get a ride to the airport from there tomorrow", she explains.

" And please do not be mad, but we need to take your wheelchair on the trip with us tomorrow, so we need to bring it with us tonight.... you don't have to use it on our date though if you don't want to", she timidly states.

"No, it's fine, I will take you out in my wheelchair tonight", I say which completely surprises her.

She kisses me on my cheek and leaves me to shower.

I ask her if I can take my wheelchair up to her apartment when we get there. She gives me another surprised look, then smiles and agrees. I do not want her to have to walk me around everywhere or worry about me being stuck sitting in one place while she gets ready. This is my chance to show her I can do things for her.

"Make yourself at home while I get ready", she says to me, leaving me in the living room as she heads for the shower.

Usually, I am stranded on the couch waiting for her to help me walk to a different room, but this time I'm glad I took my chair, I move about freely and get a better look at her home. It is simply decorated; I see she likes candles too. There is a small corner table in the living room with pictures of her family and a picture of her with two of her friends. Besides furniture, she really does not have much else to clutter her place with. She probably feels she doesn't need much because she spends all her time at the rehab center, which makes me a little sad for her. I hope I can be the one to make her happy outside of work.

"Ready?" I hear her voice.

I turn around to face her. She is wearing dark tight-fitting jeans that hug her curves and a pale blue blouse. Her long wavy dirty blonde hair hanging down over her shoulders.

"You look beautiful!", I tell her.

"I'm only in jeans and a shirt", she smirks.

"I know, but you are still beautiful", I reassure her.

She grabs my hand and leads me outside.

"Burr, it's cold", she says and rubs her arms.

"Do you want my jacket?", I offer her.

"No, it's fine, the restaurant is just around the block", she says and then grabs my hand again.

I roll along beside her, grabbing her hand tighter as she

shivers. Why didn't she take her jacket, I should have

reminded her.

We quickly arrive at a small Italian place

hidden between two large brick buildings. Inside is

warm, only a few small tables with burgundy

tablecloths. Murals of Little Italy across the walls. I

like it, it's quaint.

"Do you want to stay in your wheelchair or sit

in a regular seat at the table?", she looks down and

asks me.

Not sure what I should do, I am trying not to

make her do any work for me, but I would really like

to sit in a regular seat.

"Could you walk with me to a regular seat?", I

ask her with a shaky voice.

"Of course!" she smiles, then unexpectedly leans down, and kisses my lips before helping me to stand.

Our arms wrap around each other's side, and I pull her closer into me so I can kiss her cheek.

We sit at a small table in the corner. There are only two other couples here which makes me feel more comfortable.

Dinner was excellent and we talked the entire time. We mostly talked about her though, which was my intent. There was a lot about her I did not know. I learned that she played sports in college, her friend Jen taught her how to drive a stick in a cemetery when she was fourteen, she is afraid of swimming in the ocean, and she has never had a best friend because she likes being friends with everyone.... I can totally picture that. I got a buzz off watching her face light up as she spoke about every fond memory she has. Getting to know more of her tonight made me realize how self-absorbed I have been.

When we talked about me, I made sure it had nothing to do with my accident or disability. I told her about all the trouble my friends and I got into when we were kids, told her how I grew up hanging around with my cousins since I was an only child, and how I first got into acting.

We laughed and joked around with each other while we ate our food. For a moment we were a normal couple enjoying a normal date.

When it was time to leave, I gave her my jacket, insisting she wear it on our walk back.

We hung out the rest of the night on her couch, watching comedies, eating popcorn, and laughing some more. I am addicted to hearing her laugh now.

She has been happy and carefree all night. I love this side of her! I love every side of her, but this one reminds me how absolutely perfect she really is and how lucky I am that she wants me here with her. This has been a perfect date.

I use my chair to get to the bathroom and get ready for bed. My mouth almost drops to the floor when I wheel into the bedroom and see her standing there wearing only a long grey t-shirt.

My heart starts racing as I quickly get myself to sit on the edge of the bed. Charlotte doesn't hesitate and climbs on top of me, her knees on the bed, her thighs straddling mine. I grab her hips, holding her close to me and she combs her fingers through my hair. I can feel the heat from her body and see the fire in her eyes. Her touch sends a quivering sensation throughout my body.

I cannot hold it in any longer. I need her. I want her... all of her. I want her laughing, her crying, her smiles, her caring, her stubbornness, the way she believes in me... all of it!

I take hold of her face with my hands and kiss her soft lips with fervency. She digs her fingers into my back and I almost lose control. A magnetic force keeps our lips moving together. I never want to let her go.

" I love you Charlotte", I profess, in between breaths as I continue to capture her lips.

"I love you Levi", she whispers back.

We lay back on the bed, our bodies entwined by lust and she gives herself to me. Our passion is strong, and it feels like we are making love for the first time.

Chapter 39

If There's a Chance

Levi's POV

I woke the next morning, Charlotte's head burrowed into my chest. She looks so beautiful even in her sleep. I lightly kiss the top of her head and whisper "I love you".

Now that I have confessed my love for her, I can't stop saying those three words to her every chance I get. There is no going back. She is mine and I am hers and I know I must do whatever it takes to walk again, to be the man she needs, to make her happy always.

"Good morning!" she looks up at me smiling.

"Good Morning, Love" I kiss her lips this time.

"Are you ready for today?" she asks, looking slightly worried for me.

Honestly, I am not sure I am ready for this trip to California. I have come to despise the process of getting onto a plane. I am excited and apprehensive about the stem-cell procedure. There is nothing I want more than to get back the strength I need in my hips and left side, but there is also the chance this treatment may not work and that is the part that really scares me. I know Charlotte is worried about that too, she knows how badly I want this, and knowing her; the most conscientious person I know, will feel like she has let me down if this doesn't work. I will not let her feel that way, I promise myself this. Whatever happens, I need to remind her that she is doing everything she can to help me.

"Levi!", she snaps me out of my thoughts.

"Sorry, yes I am ready for today", I smile.

We get to the airport and I numbly undergo the same degrading security procedure. Charlotte is patiently waiting for me nearby looking at me with her beautiful doting eyes, so I keep my gaze fixed on her while security invades my space.

She holds her hand out for me after and I happily grab it, our fingers intertwined as we make our way to our gate.

"I am sorry you have to go through that every time", she says to me.

"I am getting used to it", I try to convince her.

We check in my chair and walk together onto the plane and get into our seats without any problems. Halfway into our flight Charlotte notices that I am bouncing my leg up and down out of nervousness and I accidently squeeze her hand tight enough to cause her concern. I can't hold it in any longer and the thought of what comes next vexes me.

"Levi, what's wrong?"

"I have to piss", I huff.

I hear her breathe in deep and let out a sigh. She is dredging this as much as I am, but she does her best not to show it for my sake.

"Okay, let's go then", she says in the most confident manner.

"How are we going to do this?", panic clear in my voice.

"The bathroom is three feet away, we can do this, I will just squeeze into there with you", she half laughs.

"This isn't funny, everyone will be staring at us", I remind her.

"What? Don't tell me you haven't made any movies where you meet a nice girl on an airplane and have sex with her in the tiny bathroom", she laughs again.

"Um, no I haven't", laughing with her this time.

She helps me stand and locks my left leg brace while I hold on to the back of my seat. There isn't any room in the aisle for us to walk side by side, so she stands behind me, her body close to mine and holds my hips steady as we take a few steps to the bathroom. We get inside the cramped space and she shuts the door.

"This is humiliating you know", I mutter.

"Well, I can always start moaning loudly then let everyone know that we just had the most amazing sex when they stare at us walking back to our seats", she giggles.

"Charlotte!"

"I'm kidding Levi, but I am sure the onlookers will be the ones humiliated If I blurted that out, not us".

"You're killing me Charlie! I'm done, let's get back to our seats", I smirk.

We sit back in our seats and decide to watch a movie. I can see her peering at me every so often and gripping my hand a little firmer.

"I can feel you looking at me", I smile.

"Your handsome face makes it hard not to…I love you", she utters.

Her eyes look as if they are peering right through my soul. Her touch and the way she tells me she loves me, causes that butterfly feeling in my stomach. I gape at her as if she weren't real. The butterfly feeling turns into fear and trepidation with just the thought of what will happen if this treatment doesn't work.

"Charlotte, will you still love me if it doesn't work? If I never get my strength back or ever walk again", my voice trembling when I ask her.

She grabs hold of the front of my shirt and pulls me towards her and kisses my lips, slowly and passionately. She runs her fingers through the back of my hair before grasping onto the strands and leaning our foreheads together. She releases her lips from mine and says, "No matter what happens, I will always love you, I am not going anywhere".

"Good", I smirk.

Somehow, we finagle our luggage and my wheelchair into an uber and head over to her new rehab facility. The building is more expansive than the one in Boston. She says it holds double the patients and offers more invasive treatments right on site, so no one needs to have anything done at the hospital. I can have the stem-cell injections done here along with my therapy afterwards.

She brings me to meet Dr. Lee, who will be performing my procedures. We watch a small presentation on stem-cells and how they work with the body. I will be having four procedures, two this week and two next week where they will inject the cells directly into my spinal canal. After each injection, I will undergo extensive physical therapy. Dr. Lee goes on to say that there are risks with every procedure, I could get an infection, or my body may reject the cells. And there is always the grim realization of the 50/50 chance it may or may not work. He gives me hope though and tells me that there has been a lot of success with other patients and he is confident that I will also have some success.

Charlotte shows me to my room then tells me to feel free to tour around place while she gets some work done in her office.

"Can I see your office?", I ask her.

I don't want to be alone in this strange place, the size of this building is intimidating, and she is the only person I know here.

"Of course! you can come, as long as you do not mind hanging out while I do boring paperwork?", she says.

"You do not have to worry about me as long as I am with you", I attest.

"Great, and afterwards I can give you a tour and we can grab something to eat. Your first procedure is at eight tonight", she reminds me.

Even with the six-hour flight, it is still early in the day here because of the time difference. Charlotte had enough time to get some work done and bring me around the facility.

"So, this is where you run off to every time you leave me alone in Boston, huh?" I josh.

"Yup, this is the place".

"This place is amazing! You are amazing", I praise her which causes her to smile ear to ear.

The cafeteria is massive, and it offers every kind of food imaginable. She reminds me to pick something light to eat because of my upcoming procedure. She watches me with concern as I pick at my food, but she doesn't say anything. My nerves are getting to me and I do not have much of an appetite.

"How about I help you get into the shower? The hot water will feel good after our long flight and will help ease some of your stress", she suggests.

"How about you take a shower with me? That will surely relieve my stress", I tease.

"Don't tempt me Levi".

We hurry back to my room and she runs the water until it turns hot, then helps me get undressed and onto the shower chair.

"Are you all set?", she asks me.

But I don't respond, instead I quickly grab her arm before she walks away and pull her into the shower with me. Her clothes are still on and she lets out a yelp when the water touches her.

"Levi, what are you doing", she shrieks with excitement.

I still do not answer, I just start taking off her clothes and throwing them onto the shower floor. Her flawless naked body standing in front of me while the hot water pours over her. All worry flushed away from my mind at this moment and I reach around her waist and pull her onto straddle my lap. Her skin feels so soft against mine. I grab some soap and start massaging her back while she runs her fingers through and tugs at my hair. My body aches for her touch, her sublime lips softly caressing mine as she takes me into herself.

"I love you so much", I moan as I release all of myself to her.

Our perfect moment comes to an end and she helps me get into some boxers and a hospital gown for the procedure. I walk with her so that we are both sitting on the edge of the bed, waiting for the doctor to come and take me away. She starts gently rubbing her soft hand up and down my back in a comforting gesture, then looks at me and asks, "How are you feeling about all this?

"I am eager and scared at the same time", I admit.

"Yes, I am too. I am also extremely proud of you for going through with this", she says.

"I would not be able to do this without you", I say to her just as the doctor enters my room.

Charlotte helps me into my wheelchair then gives me one last kiss before she whispers into my ear, "I love you, and I will be right here waiting for you when you get back".

"I love you too Charlotte"

She gives my hand a squeeze and I bring her hand up to my lips to kiss the back of her palm.

"See you shortly", I smile while Dr. Lee takes me away.

Chapter 40

A Long Week

Charlotte's POV

I sat in the recliner next to Levi's bed while I held his hand and read a book, waiting for him to fully wake from the anesthesia. He woke briefly after the procedure was over, but he was groggy, so I told him to sleep it off. Dr. Lee told me the procedure went well and Levi should start physical therapy in the morning.

He slept for another three hours. It was half past one in the morning when he finally squeezed my hand and looked over at me. I had dozed off, so when he grabbed my hand, it startled me, and my book went flying off my lap.

"Sorry I woke you", he mumbled.

"It's ok, how are you feeling? I ask him.

"Tired. Thirsty. Hot", sighs.

I lean over and plant a kiss on his lips. His lips feel much warmer than usual, so I kiss his forehead too. He is extremely warm.

"I am going to get you some ice water, I will be right back", I quickly spout.

Moments later I return with water and a thermometer.

"What is that for?", he asks, pointing to the thermometer.

"You feel warm, I just want to check your temperature".

I scan the thermometer over his forehead and sure enough, it reads 103.2 degrees.

"Crap!", I unintentionally blurt out.

"What is it?", he looks at me with concern.

I kiss him again then head out of the room to call and inform Dr. Lee.

"Where did you go? Don't just leave me like that with no explanation!", Levi vents out with an angry voice when I return.

I give him a couple Tylenols to take then start rambling off.

"I am sorry I walked out of the room like that! I just got nervous when I saw your high temp and went to call Dr. Lee. I know that getting a fever or infection is a possible side effect, but seeing it happen to you just caused me to panic...I do not want anything bad to happen to you"

He starts to struggle, trying to move his body closer to the side of the bed. My body feels tenuous and shaky because of the anxiety taking over me. I hate seeing him struggle and now he is sick with a fever.

"I am having a hard time moving, please come lay with me", he softly says while patting the mattress.

I climb in to lay next to him, rest my head in the crook of his arm and place my hand on his chest.

"No more panicking and no more running off, I will be fine", he whispers before leaning over to kiss my head.

I do not try to carry on any type of conversation, I just let him sleep and pray that the fever will be gone by the time the sun rises.

I did not get any sleep at all. I was so worried that I checked his temperature without waking him every half hour. The Tylenol helped some, only bringing his temp down to 101 degrees by the time he woke up.

I was already up, showered, and changed when Levi opened his eyes searching for me.

"Morning! I am right here", I lean over the bed and run my fingers through his messy hair causing him to smile.

"Here, please take these meds, you still have a fever", I tell him.

"We need to get you up for breakfast then to therapy", I inform him.

Again, he struggles to move. He can barely get himself to sit up, and when he finally does, I rush over to catch him from falling over.

I sit next to him on the edge of the bed with my arm around the back of his waist waiting for him to secure his balance.

"Will you be ok if I let go to put your leg brace on?"

"Yes, I think so", he says.

I quickly attach his brace and sit back down next to him. He puts his left arm around my shoulder, and I hold around his back so we can stand together. As soon as I help him up off the bed, his right leg gives out and I swiftly sit him back down.

He puts his head down in defeat, not sure what to say or do at this point.

I press his body against mine to gesture that I am here for him.

"Levi, describe to me what your body feels like?"

He keeps his head down and speaks so low I can hardly hear him say, " I don't know, my whole body just feels weak".

"Can I help you into your wheelchair? Maybe getting some food into you will help?", I ask him, but he just nods.

I push him down to the cafeteria. I know he doesn't feel well or much like eating, so I get him a hot tea and some toast and fruit. He eats as much as he can before we head to the gym.

Even his arms are too weak to be able to do anything that requires using any of his weight and getting out of and back into his chair again takes too much out of him. I know he is discouraged, and I try to remind him that his body is just reacting to the stem-cells and it is going to take a little longer to adjust.

He is so quiet and keeps his focus down towards the floor while I massage and manipulate his limbs.

Without hurrying I move my body to stand in front of him and reach down to hold his face in my hands. His skin is hot to the touch, his eyes full of anguish when he looks at me that I instinctively kiss his warm lips, then peer into his eyes while giving him an encouraging smile.

" I love you so much, and I know how hard you are trying right now, but you need to rest today so your fever will subside.... tomorrow we can try again", I express to him.

He agrees to let me help him back to his room and help him take a shower before getting into bed.

It is only noon time, but he is exhausted, and his temp is holding steady at 101.1 degrees. I sit up next to him in his bed and flick through the channels until we find something interesting to watch on TV. Neither of us can seem to find a good program and all I can focus on is him and how to get his fever down.

" I am going to get you some lunch and more Tylenol", I tell him before placing my lips on to his then walking out the door.

I don't want to leave him for even a second, yet a small amount of relief comes over me when I leave his room. Is this what love is supposed to feel like? This lightheaded, shaky, and worrisome feeling consuming my whole being. I am not sure if all these intense emotions from being in love are a blessing or a curse.

Levi takes the meds I bring him and eats half of his soup and sandwich.

"Why don't you take a nap, maybe a good rest will help you feel better", I suggest to him.

"What are you going to do?" he asks, clearly worried about me.

"I have some paperwork to catch up on in my office", I tell him.

He averts his eyes from me, and I know it is because he does not want me to leave.

"I can grab my papers and laptop and do my work in here while you sleep?"

He instantly smiles at me, and his voice perks up.

" Really? I mean if you don't mind, I would like that", he beams.

I rush to and back from my office with all the work I need to finish. His eyes are closed, so I give him a gentle peck on his cheek and whisper into his ear that I am here so he can sleep.

Again, he ate little of his dinner in the evening and went back to sleep for the night. I was so tired from my lack of sleep, that I had no trouble resting in the recliner, only waking up periodically to check his temp.

Morning arrives and Levi's temp has thankfully returned to normal.

"Good morning beautiful", he pipes up. "I am feeling much better", he smiles.

A rush of calm floods my veins and I exhale loudly, "Thank goodness!"

He was able to eat all his meals and participate in most of his therapy today. His body was still weak, but not nearly as weak as yesterday. He got strong enough to make it through every therapy session with each passing day and he was happy, which made me happy. There was no visible improvement in his left side yet, but that was expected after only one injection.

His next injection procedure is scheduled for tomorrow morning. With the reaction his body had to the first injection, Dr. Lee and I were hesitant to let him continue the treatments, but Levi insisted on going through with them no matter what.

"I am a little scared of what will happen after your injection tomorrow", I confess to him while we are lying in his bed together.

"I survived the last one and I will survive this one too", he affirms. "Now stop worrying about me so much, I know you haven't slept all week!", he points out.

" I cannot help it", I convey.

"I know, if this was happening to you, I would not be able to stop worrying about you either", he softly says as he kisses me.

" Have I told you how proud I am of you", I proclaim.

"All the time!", he kisses me again then wraps his arms around me so we can fall asleep.

Chapter 41

Something is Working

Levi's POV

The second and third injections also caused my
body to react with high fevers, but they subsided after
a day or two and I was able to continue with physical
therapy.

I could not tell if my left side was getting any
better or not because my body always felt weak after
each procedure and I spent the following days working

my way back to my previous strength, what I had before I started this treatment.

Charlotte was a nervous wreck this whole trip, constantly taking my temperature, not getting any valuable sleep at all. I felt horrible when my temp would get too high and scare her. The fact is, I was scared too but I could not show it because it would worry her even more. I need to be the one supporting her in this relationship as much as she supports me. I know I could never live up to the level of selflessness she has shown me, but I can do my best to try.

Tomorrow is my last injection, so I made sure to work extra hard during PT this morning. Charlotte refused to accept any help all week and insisted she did all my therapy sessions with me. She needs a break, not from me, but in general, before she makes herself sick.

It is nearly noon when Charlotte comes to find me in my room after getting a bit of work done in her office. I know she is expecting to get me to the cafeteria to eat and then to my next therapy session. She has been relentless, but I plan to change that.

"You ready for some lunch and more exercise?", she poses.

"Nope! We are taking the afternoon off, and before you object, I already got permission from Dr. Lee", I declare.

She retorts with multiple different expressions on her face. The fact that she is speechless at the moment makes me laugh and she looks at me and shrugs her shoulders.

"Well, if Dr. Lee said it is ok, then we shall listen to him", she smirks.

"Great, I have looked up a few places and thought we should try Palisades Park? We can grab something to eat and walk around and look at the ocean!", I suggest to her.

"Sounds good", she says as she brings over my wheelchair.

"I am walking with you today, no chair… consider it my afternoon therapy", I chuckle.

Fortunately, she doesn't mind that I want to walk with her, holding on to me the rest of the day.

We take an Uber to Santa Monica and when we get there, we spot a few food trucks and order some food. There are some benches in the park that overlook the ocean, so we head towards the only empty one left.

The weather is beautiful here in California. Besides the smog that everyone speaks of, it has been

70 degrees and sunny every day. Charlotte is loving the sunny weather too. She leans her head onto the back of the bench and closes her eyes. I hear her take in a deep breath and let out a long sigh, her eyes still closed, letting her face soak in all the sun. I am so glad we did this, she needed this.

"Thank you, Levi for taking me here, this is nice and relaxing", she says while pulling herself up to rest her head on my shoulder. I think she might fall asleep.

I won't mind if she slept here leaning on my shoulder, Lord knows she hasn't had much sleep since we have been here. Sitting here with her head on my shoulder as I look out at the ocean is pleasantly comforting.

An hour goes by with us sitting here. I listen to her slow and peaceful breathing and know that she is surely sleeping. Her peaceful nap doesn't last much longer though when clumsy me accidently knocks over my crutch and Charlotte springs up from my shoulder wiping her eyes at the same time.

"Oh my God! I am sorry, I fell asleep", she tries to apologize.

"It's alright Love, I enjoyed listening to you snore on my shoulder", I joke with her.

"Shut up", she playfully slaps my arm.

"We should head back before it gets dark", she suggests.

She wraps her arm firmly around my back to support my balance while I wrap my arm around her shoulder to support my left side and we walk embraced together towards our ride. I look at her beautiful face and appreciate the happiness she expresses the whole walk back.

"I cannot wait until the two of us can walk hand in hand together", I divulge to her.

She doesn't respond, she just acknowledges me by kissing me on the cheek. She does that when I say things that I want to be able to do in the future, like walk on my own only holding her hand. She does not want to say the wrong thing and get my hopes up I am sure, yet she always reminds me in subtle ways like a with a peck on my cheek or a squeeze of my hand, that she is here with me no matter what. Little things like that make my love for her grow stronger each day.

We make it back to my room and she runs a hot shower for me. I want to take her into the shower with me. We have not had an intimate moment with each other since our first night here and I am not sure if tonight would be the right time either. I yearn to feel her supple skin close to mine, to feel her fingers trace my back while I inhale her sweet scent and caress her majestic lips.

Tonight, does not pose the most opportune circumstance though. Charlotte is acting strangely subdued, keeping her demeanor discreet the entire ride back here. Her unspoken language tells me something is bothering her, or maybe she is over tired, I can't put a finger on it. All I can do is ask her, so I get into my wheelchair and roll myself in front to face her. I reach for her hands and gently trace the palms of her hands with my thumbs while looking up at her.

"Charlotte, please tell me what's wrong, I know something is bothering you".

"I am concerned about your procedure tomorrow, I hate how it makes you sick after every time...I am just worried for you that is all", she confides.

"I hate that I cause all of this worry for you Charlotte, but tomorrow will be different...I can already feel it!", I say, trying to lighten her mood.

She nods and smiles at my statement then tells me to get into the shower before the hot water runs out. I kiss her hand and do as she tells me. She does not follow me or try to help me, which further proves my speculations that tonight is not the night to fulfill any sexual desire.

After my shower, I open the curtain to find that Charlotte brought in a towel and my night clothes and left them for me on my wheelchair. Usually, she helps me transfer from the shower chair to my other chair and helps me stand to get dressed, but tonight I am doing it on my own, which I am fully capable of now, but I still love when Charlotte is near me making sure I do not fall.

When I finally finish struggling with my pajama shorts and head back into the bedroom, I find Charlotte fast asleep in the recliner. I do not have the heart to wake her even though I want her lying next to me in bed, so I carefully place a blanket over her and softly kiss her forehead.

Morning hastily arrives and I am anxious for today. I did not get much sleep last night without feeling Charlotte's body nestled against mine. But knowing that she slept soundly all night for the first time in two weeks, puts my mind at ease.

"Morning Love! I greet her when she opens her eyes and starts stretching her limbs.

"Good morning! Are you okay? I am sorry I fell asleep in this chair", she quickly sputters out.

"I am fine Love! and don't apologize for finally getting some rest", I smile at her.

"Today is going to be a good day!" I remind her.

Charlotte helps me get into the ugly and uncomfortable hospital gown I need to wear for my procedure and sits with me while we wait for Dr. Lee to arrive.

I touch her chin and turn her face towards me so I can kiss her. She slowly and nervously moves her lips against mine, so I press my mouth firmer to hers trying to force her worries away.

"Please don't worry, I love you", I breathe into her mouth, kissing her again before the Dr. whisks me away for my last procedure.

The anesthesia always takes a while to wear off and after I wake up, I always seem to need another few hours of recovery sleep. Charlotte is sitting in the chair next to my bed like she always does, waiting for me to open my eyes.

"How are you feeling", she asks me, her voice sounds so sweet and full of concern.

"Fine, just tired", I let her know.

"Go back to sleep, I'll wake you up for lunch, I will be right here if you need me", she says and softly kisses my lips right before I close my eyes again.

My body needed the extra sleep, but I am relieved when Charlotte runs her fingers through my hair, and whispers for me to wake up. I feel surprisingly rejuvenated. Charlotte places her hand on my forehead, and I see her face light up.

"No fever!", she squeaks with excitement.

"See, I told you today would be a good day", I squeak back.

Charlotte helps me up and dress, a smile fixed to her face the entire time. This is the Charlotte I have missed lately; the carefree and confident Charlotte whose unconditional love for me reminds me that all hope is not lost.

My body feels stronger than it usually does after a procedure. I am able to walk with Charlotte to the cafeteria for lunch and then to the gym for therapy. After the gym she gets me into the pool without my left leg brace. I am a little warry about what she wants me to try, I do not want either of us to be let down when my left leg gives out on me.

She keeps her grip tight around me while she glides me off the pool chair and into a standing position.

"Charlotte, I don't know about this", I huff.

"It is better that we try in the pool, the water will help you balance", she tries to convince me.

Her hands are secured to my hips waiting for me to keep a steady balance. Once my hips remain still, she lets go of me and grabs both of my hands. She is facing me while I face her.

"You're still standing!", she joyfully points out, then I realize both of my legs are holding strong and I look at her, letting her know I am scared and thrilled at the same time.

"You are doing great!", she beams at me. "Now take a step with your left", she instructs.

I hesitate out of nervousness and take my first step. Both of our eyes go wide with anticipation and I take another step with my right. She is holding my hands and stepping backwards while I step forward, it's working! I take a third step and this time my left leg gives out and Charlotte lunges forward to quickly wrap her arms around my body to catch me from falling.

"Oh my God! you did it!", her tone is full of praise as she embraces me.

"I am so happy for you, let's try it again", she spouts out.

We practiced this for another hour. Each time my leg giving out with the third or fourth step and each time Charlotte catching me at the right moment and applauding me. I know we are in the pool, but this is the first time I can stand without my leg brace, let alone take a few steps. The stem-cell treatment is working!

"I think we are ready to get back to Boston and see what other surprises are instore for you!", she exclaims.

I am happy with my new progress, but I do not want to get my hopes too high. Charlotte is so thrilled with my small accomplishment, I hope it continues, it would kill me if I let her down.

Chapter 42

The Sweetest Gift

Levi's POV

We got back to Boston with two weeks left until Christmas. Charlotte and Sarah got right to work shopping and decorating the whole place. Everyone helped put the ornaments up on the tree which was fun. The place looked amazing with all the lights and garland everywhere. It felt like home to everyone in a way.

Charlotte took it upon herself to invite my parents, Landon, Andy, Josh, and Mark over to her apartment to spend the holiday with me, but only my parents could make it for Christmas, Mark and my friends promised to make it over for New Years.

I don't understand how Charlotte finds time to do everything. She checks on every patient here daily, manages how their treatments are progressing, decorates for Christmas, all while constantly making sure I am okay and getting through all my therapy sessions. No wonder why she looks so tired lately. The only time she has taken a break in the last two nights since we have been back, is when we go to her house for the night, and even then, I find her fast asleep on the couch when I leave her alone for a few minutes to use the bathroom.

I don't know how I can help her. She does not want to revert to having Sarah and Nate take over some of my therapy sessions, which is mostly my fault since I practically begged her in the beginning not to leave me in someone else's hands. I am a stronger person now because of her and I am ready to get through some of my challenges without her holding my hand.

We arrive at rehab early in the morning with ten days left until Christmas now. I want to give her something special, but I am not sure what, so I decide that I am going to ask Sarah to bring me shopping.

Charlotte brings me into the gym, then tells me she is going to bring her things to her office before starting therapy.

"Is it alright if Sarah does my morning therapy with me?" I ask Charlotte who stops dead in her tracks and turns to me looking utterly confused.

She is not angry or sad with my request though and shrugs her shoulders at me.

"Sure, if that is what you want", she says back to me.

"Yeah, I mean I haven't spent any time with them in a few weeks, so it will be nice to catch up. Go get whatever work you need to get done. I will be fine, and you know where to find me", I persuade her.

Charlotte reluctantly leaves me in the gym with Sarah so she can tend to her other responsibilities.

"Sarah, I need to do or get something special for Charlotte for a Christmas gift", I blurt out.

Sarah presses her finger to her pursed lips like she's thinking.

"Well from my experience with Charlotte and gifts, she would rather be the one giving not receiving", she tells me.

"Of course, she would", I chuckle.

"I have an idea! How about you and I focus on one thing to work on in therapy every morning, that way by Christmas you can surprise her by showing her something new you have accomplished, like doing something with your left arm that you have not been able to do before?", Sarah suggests.

"That sounds great, but what if we put in all that work and my arm just stays as it is now?" I say to her with slight anticipation of defeat in my tone.

"Charlotte will take your determination in trying as a gift Levi, trust me".

"You are probably right, okay let's do this, but I still want you to take me shopping so I can get her something nice", I warn Sarah.

Sarah and I got right to work. Whatever type of exercise that involved using my arms I did, even girl-style push-ups which were exceedingly difficult to perform.

Sarah worked with me for my first session every morning and Nate took over the sessions right after, making me use the weights. Sarah and I let Nate and Jake in on our little secret, so every day he added a little more weight for my left arm to lift, push, and pull while Jake cheered me on.

Charlotte met back up with me every afternoon for lunch then took me to the pool to practice walking without my leg brace.

I could feel my arm getting physically stronger. It has gotten easier to get myself out of bed and transfer to my chair on my own. Even Charlotte noticed while we were in the pool one afternoon.

"Your grip on my hand with your left is much stronger!", Charlotte expresses while walking backwards in the pool holding my hands as I take a few steps forward.

"Yes, I can feel that it is", I give her a huge grin.

My left leg improved right after my last stem-cell procedure, but it has remained the same since. I am still only able to take two or three steps before my leg buckles from under me. My balance has not improved much either, I can only balance on my own for a few seconds, although when I first got into the pool today Charlotte squealed with excitement after she purposely let go of me and I unknowingly stood on my own for thirty seconds.

"You are doing so great! I am so proud of you", she shrieks. This is something she has continued to say to me daily, more times than I can count. The way her beautiful soulful eyes look at me when she tells me how proud she is, let me know she truly means every word.

I love this girl so much I don't know what I would do without her.

"How about you and I have an evening off to spend some quality time together?", she asks me.

Oh my God! Yes please! I think to myself. I have been waiting for the past four weeks for us to have a night just her and I together, hanging out, talking, I will do anything. Charlotte seems to have more energy lately and she has been staying awake later at night ever since I made Nate & Sarah do all my morning therapies with me. I am glad my plan is working.

" How about we order out, watch some funny movies, and eat popcorn tonight?", she asks me.

"Brilliant!", I yelp.

We ate the Chinese food Charlotte had delivered then snuggled on the couch together eating popcorn and laughing. By the time we started watching our second movie, Charlotte looked like she was getting tired. I noticed her squinting at the screen more than once and rubbing her eyes often trying to clear them. I was getting concerned.

" Are you alright, Love?", I ask her.

"Yes, the screen appears blurry to me sometimes, maybe my eyes are tired", she affirms.

"Do you want to go lay in bed? Tomorrow is Christmas Eve, and we have a lot to do, so maybe getting to sleep early will be good", I try and convince her.

"That is a good idea! We need to get to rehab early tomorrow to fit some therapy in before we pick your parents up from the airport", she reminds me.

We both happily go to bed and she lays her head on my chest while I wrap my arms around her, listening to her soft breathing as she falls asleep.

Tomorrow is the big day. Sarah has helped me prepare my big surprise for Charlotte; I cannot wait to show her.

In the morning I make sure I am up and ready before Charlotte even wakes up. I am eager to finally be able to do something special for my girl and I can't stop smiling.

"Wow! you are up early and looking cheerful this morning", Charlotte says in a surprised voice.

"I am just excited for the Holiday!" I exclaim. "Now let's get going sleepy head", I chuckle.

I am so anxious that I practically rush her to rehab.

"Please come meet me in the gym in ten minutes, I need your help with something", I tell her, hoping she will agree without asking any questions.

"Umm, okay", she shrugs.

I meet Sarah in the gym, and she helps me prepare by attaching my left leg brace and putting a gait belt around my waist as a precaution.

Charlotte walks into the gym and looks at us with curiosity when she notices us at one end of the parallel bars.

"What is this?", she questions, her voice sounds perplexed as she points at us and then the bars.

" I have something to show you", I grin. "Now please stand at the other end of the bars", I instruct her.

Her eyes go wide, so does her smile when she realizes what I am about to do and brings herself to stand at the other end of the bars, facing me.

I can feel the jitters, but the anticipation of watching the expression on her face when I get through this will be all worth it.

I tell Sarah I am ready, so she stands behind me holding my gait belt as I place both of my hands on the bars and she helps me pull myself to stand. I take a moment to adjust my stance between the bars and make sure my left arm is cooperating. I cannot balance on my own, so it is up to my arms to support me with each step.

" I am ready Sarah, you can let go now", I inform her.

Sarah releases her hold of me but stays close behind me just in case.

Charlotte is still wide eyed with anticipation when I look up at her. I take a deep breath and exhale then carefully move my left hand forward on the bar, then my right hand, followed by my left leg and right.

I hear Charlotte gasp, but I don't want to see her expression yet, so I continue slowly moving both arms forward on the bars followed by taking a step with each foot.

So far so good! my inner voice assures me. I have taken two steps with each leg, only four more to go. I can do this; I talk myself up.

Another two steps down before I feel my left arm shake a little.

"Levi?", Sarah softly questioning if I need her support.

"I've got this, just give me a second", I convince her.

After I take another deep breath and exhale to try and calm my nerves; I succeed with my last two steps and stop a few inches in front of Charlotte and look up at her.

Tears are flowing down her cheeks, but the way her watery multi-color eyes are looking at me is pure admiration. Her body is noticeably fidgety, and I can guess that she wants to throw her arms around me, but I stop her.

"I have one more thing to give you", I force her to wait just a little longer.

Sarah hands me a four by two-inch box. I shift my wait to my right arm so I can let go of the bar and hand Charlotte the box.

"Go ahead, open it", I smile.

Charlotte opens the box and pulls out a silver heart shaped pendant attached to a silver chain. She holds the pendant in her hand and brushes her thumb over the single diamond in the middle, then flips the pendant over and reads the engraving on the back...

My Love, My Hero

"Merry Christmas Charlotte!", I softly say and help her clasp the necklace around her neck.

She is still crying, and I am hoping it is because she is happy, so I ask, "Do you like your gift?"

Just as I imagined, she throws her arms around me and embraces me.

"Oh Levi, it is so sweet! I love it! and what you accomplished just now walking across the bars... is the best gift I could ever receive", she sniffs, and I can feel her tears soaking my t-shirt.

" Those better be tears of joy", I smirk.

"Definitely tears of joy", she replies, hugging me again.

She releases her grip and looks at Sarah and then me and inquests, " This is why you insisted I get other work done every morning? So, you two could work on this?"

I can't stop smiling at her and confess, " Yes, I wanted to do something special for you, to surprise you".

" Yes, Nate and Jake were in on it too", Sarah chirps.

" I can't believe you guys! Thank you! This is amazing! Not just for me but for you, Levi!", her voice ecstatic, and she grabs my face and kisses me.

"I love you!" she breathes as she kisses me again.

"Now I have a surprise for all of you", she boasts.

" Can you two round everyone up and meet me at the door to the lounge?", she asks us, then gives me one more peck on the lips before bolting out the door.

Sarah and I do as she requests, we find Jake, Marlo, Kenny, and Abby and all wait together for Charlotte by the lounge.

Charlotte pops her head out of the lounge, holding the door almost shut behind her.

" Are you all ready?", she squeaks with excitement.

We all smile and nod and she flings open the lounge door.

"Surprise! Merry Christmas everyone! she blurts out.

We all slowly make our way into the room, our eyes soaking in the magnificence, our jaws hanging from shock and amazement.

My parents, Charlotte's parents and everyone else's parents or wife, girlfriend, and other family members are all here for us. Christmas decorations adorn the room, food tables line the back wall, and a massive pile of presents engulf the lighted tree.

"How and when did you do all this?" I pull her down towards me and whisper in her ear.

"You are not the only one who can secretly plan something special", she laughs.

"You're incredible!", I express to her.

"What you did for me earlier was incredible ", she smiles and presses her soft lips to mine.

"Any more secret plans in the making?" she jokes with me.

I laugh along with her playful banter before I spill out, "Why yes my love, I do have something I would like to work on next, but only if you will help me this time"

Chapter 43

$\mathcal{A}$ New Year

Charlotte's POV

This was probably the best Christmas I have ever had. Levi and I had a quiet Christmas Day dinner with just his parents and mine. We took the entire day off from any therapy and any work. I felt guilty about it, but we both deserved a day off after everything we accomplished over the last few weeks, we were drained.

Levi was eager to get back to rehab the next day so we could get started on his next plan. When we got there, he dragged me into the gym, but not before requesting I bring both forearm crutches with us.

"I want to start walking with my crutches", he insists.

"Hook me up to the ceiling harness and let me try the crutches", he impatiently demands.

He is getting ahead of himself, I think he needs to gain more strength in his hips so he can better balance himself when he steps, but he is adamant about using the crutches, so I do as he wants and attach him to the harness and watch him grip the crutch handles.

He does fine standing there, leaning his weight forward on the crutches. Taking a step is a whole other obstacle though. Apparently, he wants to try this himself with only the harness holding him.

I stand behind him, waiting for him to ask for my help but he doesn't, instead he stubbornly tries to move his crutch forward and takes a step.

"What the hell", he huffs.

He loses his balance, and his hips sway out of control each time he moves one of his crutches or takes a step. If it weren't for the harness holding him up, he would be falling on his face.

I refuse to watch him do this to himself any longer and grab hold of his hips, steadying him while he regains his composure. Neither of us move or say anything, and after about a minute, he releases a loud sigh and puts his head down in defeat.

"Thank you", he mumbles. "I must have looked like a fool to you just now", he sighs again.

"Of course not, Levi! Do not ever think that! I commend you for trying this on your own, but you do need to let me help you succeed at this", my voice stern so he takes me seriously.

I keep a firm hold on his hips while I teach him how to use the crutches properly for the first time.

"Just like you did on the bars, move one crutch forward then the other, followed by moving one leg forward and then the other while I support your balance", I instruct him.

He follows my instructions and we slowly make our way around the room guided by the ceiling track.

"This is harder than I expected", he admits.

"Yes, it is, but we can work on this every day and walk in the pool more too", I reassure him.

"Ok but promise me that you will let Sarah and Nate work with me too, I do not want to be the reason why you are so tired every night", he pleads with me.

I find it easy to agree with him. I have been unusually tired over the past month. I am sure it is because of our trip to California and worrying about the holidays. Having Sarah and Nate work with Levi part of the day will give me a pleasant little break.

Levi worked hard the rest of the week leading up to New Year's Eve. Every morning he had Sarah attach him to the ceiling harness and help him walk with his crutches. Afterwards, Nate worked with him and Jake in the weight room, and after lunch I would work with Levi in the pool. When evening came, I would help him use his crutches again. By nighttime, he was so worn out that he would fall asleep in his room here, so I let him sleep and met him for lunch the following day.

I miss him lately, the only quality time we have had together all week was in the pool. Levi agreed to meet me in the gym this morning so that I could do his only therapy session for today with him. Tonight, is New Year's Eve, and his friends couldn't make the trip so, I made reservations for him and I at a fancy club where we can sit and eat, listen to music, and maybe slow dance if he is up for it.

"Hey beautiful! His cheerful voice greets me as he rolls into the gym.

"Hey", I smile back at him then then quickly kiss him when he reaches me.

"What do you think about using your crutches without the harness today? I will stand behind you and hold your hips like I have been doing, you just won't be attached to anything", I ask him.

He thinks about it for a minute and then nods. I know he is apprehensive, but he has progressed quickly this week, so I think he is ready.

I stand beside him and help him to stand, then hand him each crutch before moving behind him to grip his hips. He still needs his left leg brace locked to keep his leg straight, but his left arm is so much stronger now, he has been handling his crutches well.

He hesitates for a moment and I can feel him shaking a little.

"I've got you babe! You can do this! I encourage him.

I hear him chuckle and he smiles when he hears me call him babe and he takes a courageous step forward. He easily brings his crutches forward followed by his legs, like when he is attached to the harness. I keep his hips steady as we make it across the room. I am so happy for him. Learning to walk with crutches is a big achievement in his recovery. Only if we could get his left leg stronger and his balance better, he would be able to do this without me holding onto him.

We get to the exercise table at the end of the room and I leave him sitting on the edge of it so that I can get his wheelchair. While I'm walking to get his chair, I get a stabbing pain in my forehead just above my eyes and accidently blurt out, "ouch!" and squeeze the inside of my eyes near the bridge of my nose with my fingers to get the pain to stop.

"Charlotte, what's wrong?" I hear Levi's worried voice.

The pain subsides to a dull ache and I roll the chair to Levi who is anxiously waiting to see if I am alright.

"It was weird, I felt a sharp pain but now it only feels like a regular headache", I explain to him.

He doesn't look convinced, so he pulls me to stand in front of him and gently rubs his thumb over my eyes and across my forehead and then kisses me.

"Let's get you some headache medicine and go back to your place to shower and change for tonight", he says.

My headache is only causing minimal discomfort by the time we reach my apartment. Dinner reservations are in about an hour and I suggest to Levi that we should probably shower together to save some time.

Levi's face instantly lights up when I say "together", and I can't help but laugh a little. He swiftly pushes himself to the bathroom and turns on the shower.

"I'm waiting!", he playfully shouts through the bathroom door.

When I enter the bathroom, the room is steamy, and he is already in the shower.

"Come in Love, the water feels fantastic! He allures me.

I remove my clothes and join him in the shower, he grabs my waist and pulls me onto his lap and brushes my hair behind my ear with his finger before taking my face in his hand and crashing his full lips to mine. He kisses me softly at first then nibbles my bottom lip causing my body to shiver and my heart to pulsate.

"I have missed you this week", I moan between our passionate kisses.

"I missed you too, I do not sleep well when you are not lying in bed next to me", he breathes heavily into my ear and begins kissing my neck.

His lips slowly caress my skin, and he slides himself inside me, lifting my hips up and down in a steady motion until the sensation causes my body to arch back and I let myself go. He captures my moans with his lips and presses my body against his again and I feel his release.

We cannot get enough of each other. Our lips stay locked together until he lifts me from him and transfers himself to his wheelchair. He pulls me back onto his lap again and whisks me into the bedroom, arousing me again with his feverish lips and motions me to lay onto the bed. He lays his succulent body on top of mine and captivates me with the touch of his skin.

"Let's skip dinner, I only want you, right here", he pants, as I run my fingers down his back while he moves himself inside me again.

We make love until our bodies can't handle any more, then blissfully nestle ourselves together while we lay in bed.

"Happy New year", I softly say.

"I cannot wait to see all the great things that will happen for you this new year", I smile.

"Happy New Year my Love! There is no one I would rather share all those great things with than you", he smiles back.

Chapter 44

Round Two

Levi's POV

So far January has been uneventful. We have developed a good routine though. Sarah helps me work with my crutches every morning for an hour, then Nate takes over and does core exercises and weight training with Jake and I, and after lunch I am with Charlotte for the afternoon.

I cannot stand on my left leg without my brace locked, even when I am in the pool, so Charlotte decided it is best I keep my brace on while I focus on my balance. She also doesn't want me walking with my crutches all the time because she says it discourages my natural walking posture and leaning over on my crutches when I walk hinders my progress of keeping my stance upright and balancing.

At first, I would get upset with her when she refused to let me use the crutches in the afternoon or even at night at her apartment, but when I pushed my stubborn pride aside and realized she would have to constantly hold onto me if I used my crutches, I decided it would be in my best interest follow her advice.

Charlotte mostly worked with me in the pool. She now had me wear my left leg brace and when we walked, I would stand straight up and we would face each other, she would walk backwards when I would take a step forward while gripping onto each other's outstretched arms.

Walking this way was much easier with the surrounding water and my leg brace helping to keep me upright. When I felt my hips sway, I would grab onto her arms tighter and she would pull me back into the direction of my normal stance.

After the pool she would take me to the gym to work on standing. Keeping my left brace on, I would either practice standing with Charlotte facing me with my hands on her shoulders for support, or she would stand with her hands by my hips while I support myself on the parallel bars. And that is all she had me practice, standing on my own until my hips gave way, then do it all over again.

I made it through the entire month doing the same therapy each day and I wasn't gaining any more control of my left leg or hip movement. My previous mood swings were coming back, and they also proved to be hard for me to control. Charlotte was also getting frequent headaches in the evenings which could only be from the same stress and frustration I was feeling.

"I spoke with Dr. Lee this morning and he thinks you should try another round of stem-cell treatments", she informs me while we are practicing standing together in the gym.

"Oh? What do you think I should do?" I question her.

"Well, even though you nearly worried me to death the first time around, I think it is your best chance of gaining more balance and strength", she confidently tells me.

"Jake and his girlfriend are coming this time too, he is also going through with the treatment as well", she surprises me.

She notices me half smiling, half in my thoughts with my head down. She places her hands on the side of my face and lifts my head to face hers and rubs her thumbs across my cheeks. Her expression is so calm, and her eyes are so hopeful for me.

"What do you think about this?" she cautiously asks me.

I grab the back of her neck with my right hand and pull her lips to mine before I tell her, "I will do it again if it will give me any chance of getting better, and only if Jake decides not to react like I did with high fevers and take all or your attention away from me", I laugh with her.

"That is why his girlfriend is coming along", she laughs again and then informs me that we are leaving tomorrow.

I am not as nervous for this trip to California; I know what to expect and I have Jake to share with in my humiliation as we are both practically strip searched at security. The horrified and embarrassing look on Jake's girlfriends face makes be burst out laughing. I remember those looks on Charlotte's face my first experience through security with a wheelchair, but now her and I joke about it.

"You are loving this right now aren't you?", Charlotte chuckles, pointing at Jake and his girlfriend.

"You know it!", I gloat.

I am used to this whole traveling with a wheelchair process now, but Jake is not, and I do my best to try and lighten his mood, remembering how I felt my first time taking a plane as a disabled person.

We arrive at the L.A. facility and I gladly take Jake and his girlfriend around on a tour while Charlotte heads to a few meetings with the staff.

"This place is amazing! It has everything!" Jake blurts out with excitement.

"I still like our place in Boston better, it is smaller and has more of a homelike feeling", Jake says, and I agree with him.

Charlotte warned us we would be having our first procedures tonight and to meet her in the café for dinner. I don't mind her going off all day to get her work done. Even though I am the third wheel, Jake and his girlfriend keep me company while we wait to meet up with Charlotte again.

After dinner, Charlotte helps Jake and his girlfriend prepare for his procedure, then comes back to my room to help me. I have already changed into my hospital gown when she enters my room, so she smiles at me and joins me on the edge of the bed.

She starts rubbing her forehead, something she has been doing a lot of lately, and I voice my concern, "You have a headache again?"

"It's from stress, I have had one all day", she tells me.

I instantly put my head down and clasp my hands together, rolling one thumb over the other while I let my bad thoughts invade my mind. Am I the one causing all her stress? Am I too much work for her to handle anymore?

She catches me lost in my head and reaches for my hand.

"Levi, look at me, I know what you are thinking", she says, holding my hand in hers. "You are not the cause of my stress; you are the reason I make it through each day... I just have so much other work to do between this place and in Boston...knowing I have you keeps me going", she softly kisses my lips.

"I will admit that I am worried about your procedure tonight and any kind of reaction you might encounter", she groans.

"I will be fine, I promise...knowing I have you is what keeps me going", I smile at her, repeating her own words.

I remember waking up a few hours later in my bed, Charlotte next to me.

"Do I have a temp?", I nervously ask her.

"Only a mild one, 99.9 degrees", she smiles.

"How is Jake doing?" I ask her, I am worried for him too.

"He is doing great! No reaction so far", she informs me.

"Good! Now promise me you will get some sleep and refrain from checking my temperature every thirty minutes" I press her.

Charlotte was ecstatic in the morning when I woke up without a fever. I didn't feel weak either like last time and that made me ecstatic too. She took Jake and I to the gym for our first therapy session and designated a different therapist for the rest of our sessions. Jake and I kept busy with our exercises while Charlotte kept busy with her other work. We all met up for dinner in the café that night. Jake's girlfriend found us a table while we waited for Charlotte to show up.

"Surprise!", I hear her familiar excited voice say from across the café. When I look up, I see her walking towards our table with Landon and Andy following closely behind.

"What are you lads doing here?", I gasp in shock.

"We are here to cause some trouble mate! Landon retorts.

Charlotte is beaming, obviously thrilled with my surprised reaction. I don't understand how she can always find ways to astound me like this, what makes me so deserving of this brilliant woman, I constantly ask myself.

"I think these two will be a perfect comical distraction for you and Jake this week as you get through your treatments", she laughs causing us all to laugh along with her.

"Thanks Love, you are amazing!" I remind her.

It was great having my friends here. Charlotte let us explore L.A. as long as we finished our therapy sessions. My mates kept Jake and I laughing all week, to the point of annoying our therapists at times which made it even more fun.

For some reason Charlotte stayed away from Andy when she could, but her and Landon got along fine. Sometimes I would disturb one of her and Landon's serious conversations, and other times I would catch them in hysterics about something. It makes me happy knowing that we both have a mutual friend, it makes my relationship with Charlotte seem more real, outside of therapy.

I managed to sneak a few minutes alone with Landon before their flight back to London. Him and Charlotte have become close friends lately and I need his advice and his help with something I have been worried about.

Before I run out of time, or someone disrupts our conversation, I decide to just blurt out, "Hey Landon, I'm concerned about Charlotte and all these headaches she's been having. She says they are from stress, but I cannot help thinking I am causing her some of this stress. What should I do?" I plead.

"Listen Mate, that girl loves you unconditionally, whether these treatments work or not or whether you ever walk again or not, will not change the way she feels about you. She may worry about you because she loves you, but she is not stressed out because of you, trust me on this", Landon asserts.

"How do I help her then?

"Continue to treat her and love her the way she does you! People like her are hard to find, so don't screw it up!", he laughs and punches my shoulder.

"Good luck with the rest of your treatment and I will be back for another visit as soon as I can", Landon slaps me on the back before leaving.

Jake and I survived our remaining stem-cell procedures without any adverse reactions. Charlotte decided to make dinner reservations for the four of us to celebrate, and because it just so happens to be Valentine's Day.

"I am sorry I don't have a Valentine's gift for you", I say as we are getting ready for dinner.

"Levi, you pulling through these last two weeks without any reaction or infection is better than anything you could buy me for a gift", she smiles before planting her sweet lips to mine.

The restaurant Charlotte picked was busy, but they were able to seat us right away because of our reservations. So far, we were all enjoying our double date. Jake and his girlfriend are good company, and we all have something to celebrate together tonight.

"Charlotte, what is wrong? Do you have another headache?" I lean over and whisper to her when I notice her squint at the menu then blink multiple times.

"No, the menu is a little blurry to me, maybe I need reading glasses or something", she shrugs.

"I am worried about you, at least go have your eyes checked", I pressure her.

She places her hand on top of mine, attempting to ease my mind and says, "I promise I will make an appointment as soon as we get back to Boston"

Chapter 45

This Can't be Happening

Charlotte's POV

"Miss Charlotte Thomas! The doctor is ready to see you now", the young medical assistant announces into the waiting room.

I feel like I have been sitting in this waiting room for hours. I do not have time for this, there is too much going on at the rehab center for me to bother with having my eyes checked.

I walk into the exam room and take a seat in the chair closest to the doctor's stool. Moments later, the tall slender optometrist enters the room and offers to shake my hand.

"What brings you into my office today, Miss Thomas?", he asks me, his tiny spectacles inching their way down the bridge of his nose until he pushes them back up with his finger.

"I think I may need some reading glasses", I tell him.

He starts typing on his laptop and says, "Tell me what has been going on for you to assume you need reading glasses?"

I don't know where to begin and notice him reading over my questionnaire and symptoms checklist I had to fill out when I arrived.

"You wrote that you have been tired and sometimes things appear blurry to you but not all the time?", he questions.

I still don't respond so he continues, "And you have had frequent headaches with dizziness at times?"

"Yes, that is correct. Does that mean I need glasses?" I finally speak.

"I would like to give you a complete eye exam and run a few tests", he informs me.

I do not have time for a full exam, I wish he would just prescribe me the glasses so I can get back to work.

First his assistant sits me in front of a machine that I press my forehead against. A forceful puff of air shoots into my eye making me blink rapidly. Just when I think I am prepared for the next eye; I am shot in the eye again making both my eyes water uncontrollably.

My next test consists of me staring at a beam of light for fifteen seconds without blinking while they capture images of behind my eyes.

After those tests are completed, I am instructed to sit in the exam chair so the doctor can test my sight using different lenses. I can easily read all the letters on the board in front of me and the doctor confirms I am not nearsighted.

He then brings what looks like a pen with a square tip close to my face then slowly pulls the pen away from me until I read the letters on the square tip. He then tells me to let him know when the letters become blurry. As soon as I focus on the pen moving closer to my face, I become dizzy and nauseous.

"Miss Thomas, I am going to prescribe you some reading glasses, but I am concerned about some of your tests and I had my secretary make you an appointment with a neurologist for tomorrow", he says in a serious tone.

"Should I be worried?" I ask him with a shaky voice.

"I would rather you speak with the neurologist tomorrow, my secretary will help you check out and give you your appointment information", he lets me know before jetting out of the room.

I slowly drive back to rehab; I feel sick to my stomach wondering what is wrong with me that I must see a neurologist. I can't tell Levi about my appointment tomorrow; he will just freak out, like I feel like doing. Levi has been rapidly improving since we have been back from California, and he is so happy about it.

Shit! Levi is sitting in the lobby waiting for me when I walk through the door.

"Hi Love, how was your appointment?", he shyly asks.

"It was ok I guess, I have new reading glasses", I show him the blue framed specks.

Levi doesn't seem to notice my nervous tension, so I ask him if he wants to practice walking with the ceiling track. Lucky for me he does not ask any other questions about my appointment and is content with working out in the gym.

The distraction of watching Levi try to walk on his own with only the ceiling harness is enough to keep my mind from worrying about myself. Since his last stem-cell treatment, he has gained a tremendous amount of strength in his hips and can take up to five steps on his own without crutches before he loses his balance and sways in the harness. I can't help but smile and cheer for him when he takes his steps. He still requires the left leg brace and needs me to hold him steady so he can regain his balance after the harness catches him, but the progress he is making is astounding!

"You are doing fantastic Levi! I shriek, forgetting about all my future troubles.

"Thanks! I am so glad you brought me back to California for my last treatment, it was so worth it", he beams.

During the last three weeks, we have been able to put the wheelchair away and he uses his crutches to walk around now. Under one condition though, he must wear a gait belt and he must have someone near him when he walks because he has a tendency of miss stepping and faceplants. At least with a gait belt, someone can easily grab onto it before he falls. After bumping his head and bruising his knee during his last tumble, I put a squash to him walking around unsupervised. He doesn't like it, but as soon as I threaten to take his wheelchair back out, he obliges.

Jake has made significant improvements since his stem-cell treatment as well. Tomorrow marks the end of his twelve-month program here and him and his girlfriend have decided to continue his therapy at my California facility. They found an apartment to live in together and he plans on another round of stem-cell treatments.

Jake's injury was more severe than Levi's, so he has come to terms with needing his crutches for possibly the rest of his life. He has been walking with his crutches for a few months now, but since the treatment in L.A. his legs have become much stronger.

With the help of his crutches, he can now walk up and down stairs without anyone holding on to him.

We have a big going away party planned for him tomorrow, just like I have with everyone who has graduated from my program. I am so happy for him and his girlfriend.

Back at my apartment, Levi points out that I am acting weirdly quiet, so I quickly force my behavior into my usual happy self. I am so nervous for tomorrow's appointment. I wish the doctor gave me a hint of what to expect instead of keeping me in the dark. This is torture!

I keep my cool around Levi for the rest of the night. Forcing myself to smile and joke around like we

515

normally do. Only after Levi falls asleep, nuzzled up next to me do I let my fears sink in and silent tears roll down my cheek.

Morning fast approaches and I arrange for Nate to pick up Levi on the way to rehab. When Levi asks me what I am doing this morning, I tell him I have a meeting at Mass General, which isn't a lie, I am meeting with my neurologist at Mass General. I just denied Levi the important details.

Here I am waiting in another waiting room, the clock ticking in slow motion, my nerves on high gear. A nurse directs me to the doctor's office, and I take a seat on the couch in front of his desk. The doctor strolls in holding my file and proceeds to show me pictures of the back of my eyes, and other test results from the eye doctor yesterday.

I feel completely numb, like my body in in the room but my mind is not. I can see Dr. Sulls lips moving but I am imagining myself listening to the teacher in a Charlie Brown episode. I only focus on a few words like biopsy, and smaller and surgery. Even though I feel like my spirit has left my body sitting on this couch while this doctor rambles on…. I am not an idiot; I know exactly what he is trying to explain to me. My mind does not want to accept it.

The doctor must be waiting for me to respond to one of his questions or something because my mind finds its way back to my body and I hear him say, "Charlotte did you hear what I just said?", he's giving me a weird look.

"Yes, I heard you", I respond without any emotion in my voice.

"When do I start?", I ask him, not wanting to believe anything he is saying to me.

"Right away! You can schedule your first appointment with the front desk", I think is what he just said.

The receptionist hands me my appointment card and instructions and I walk out the door in a robot-like fashion to my jeep.

I slide into the driver's seat and begin sobbing. This can't be happening to me right now, not when Levi is on the verge of walking on his own.

Chapter 46

The Unknown

Levi's POV

Charlotte hasn't been acting like herself today. I know she is busy getting everything ready for Jake's party this evening, but I feel like she's avoiding me.

We are alone in the gym, just her and I, hand in hand while I work on my balance. Her mind is noticeably elsewhere even though she smiles at me when I can stand longer than the last time.

"That's it, if you don't want to tell me why you are in a glum mood...", I yank her into my chest and hug her tightly.

She tries to pull away after a few seconds, but I hold her even tighter and say, "I am not letting go until you either cheer up or reveal what is bothering you".

"I am sorry I am in my own world today; I will perk up, I promise", she still doesn't convince me.

"I have just the thing that will lighten your spirits! will you please walk with me to the parallel bars?" I ask her.

We get to the bars and I instruct her to stand in the middle of them, facing me about two feet away.

"Levi, what are you doing?", she drags out my name.

"Wait for it! I tease her.

She is in position to catch me, but I shoo her hands away.

I hear her suck in a deep breath and hold it when she watches me stand up straight and let go of the bars. She instinctively moves her body closer to me, it's her protective nature.

"Freeze! young lady", I tease again. "I am coming to you", I disclose.

Keeping my hands close to the bars without touching them, I shift my weight to my right and swing my left leg forward, taking a step.

Charlotte is bug-eyed and still holding her breath, so I quickly steady myself before she passes out. Carefully, I disperse my weight to the middle and take a step forward with my right leg.

Her smile widens and I reach for her face with both of my hands and capture her mouth with mine. She kisses me back and finally breathes again, " That was amazing! You just made my whole day!", she declares, wrapping her arms around my waist, embracing me again.

" I thought you might like that! Sometimes I can take two steps before I need to grab the bars", I say with glee.

She hands me my crutches. Her mood is different now, she looks happy again and says, " How about we help get Jake's party started?".

Once again, the lounge is full of people, music, and great food. Sarah put together a slide show on the big screen reminding us of all Jake's milestones. Seeing picture and videos of when he first arrived here, in pain, not able to do much on his own, brings back memories of when I first arrived. I wanted to forget about those days all together yet looking at these pictures on screen reminds me how hard Jake worked... how hard I have worked and all the challenges we have overcome.

I most enjoy the pictures of the two of us goofing around in the gym together and racing our wheelchairs down the hallway. Jake has been a great friend; he has helped me through everything while I have been here. I hope he can say that I have helped him too. I'm going to miss not having him around every day.

Charlotte dances around from person to person, engaging in endless conversations while I talk with Jake. My eyes drift in her direction every few minutes, making me smile when she catches me staring.

Nate suggests that some of us stick around a little longer after the crowd leaves to have some drinks and reminisce. Only Nate, Jake, his girlfriend, Charlotte, and I stay. We spent the next two hours laughing and talking, all of us were buzzing at this point, except for Charlotte, she didn't have a single sip of alcohol tonight. I was curious as to why Charlotte refused to drink tonight, but I was too off my trolley to ask her. All I heard her say was, "Someone has to make sure you make it to your bed without falling on the floor".

The next morning, I woke up on the couch with Charlotte squeezed in next to me. Looking around I notice that we all passed out on a couch or a chair in the lounge. We must have been inebriated!

We all swallow a couple headache pills and head for breakfast. Charlotte realizes I am still a little tipsy and places my arm around her shoulder, hers around my waist and walks me to the dining room.

"I'm sorry", I grin at her.

"Don't be! Everyone had fun!" she returns my grin.

"Don't you look like a sorry bunch", Charlotte giggles as she walks over to our table with a pot of coffee. I think we all drank two or three cups worth hoping it would dissolve our hang over.

After breakfast I headed to the gym with Sarah while Charlotte took Jake and his girlfriend to her office to go over his discharge paperwork, and everything else they would need for California.

I said my goodbyes to Jake and promised I would visit him in the summer. Jake of course couldn't leave without giving me some advice. He told me not to let fear or anger get the best of me and to remember, that when life brings me down, having someone who loves me by my side will always make it better.

Damn Jake! He should be some kind of inspirational speaker or something of the sort.

In the gym, Sarah helped me work with the parallel bars. This time I convinced her to remove my leg brace.

My left leg isn't very strong, even after two rounds of stem-cell treatments, but I have been able to add an extra pound to the weight machine every other day; so luckily my leg is improving but at a slow and steady rate.

Sarah attached the gait belt to my waist and stood behind me, her hands firmly gripping the belt.

My left leg feels funny whenever I bend my knee to pick it up. I need to be extra cautious when I place my foot back down because I don't have complete control of my ankle, my foot is usually set in the brace. Charlotte says it's good to start using the bars without my leg brace so that I can get used to walking with a more natural hip movement instead of swinging my leg around to take a step, like I do when I am wearing the brace.

This is not so hard. I have mastered the bars with my leg brace on. With no brace, I have Sarah holding me steady with the gait belt and my arms carrying most of my weight.

When I was all done in the gym, I met with Nate in the weight room. Nate added the extra pound to the leg press, and I worked my way through multiple sets until I had no energy left.

Charlotte met me for lunch in the afternoon and instantly noticed I was in pain.

"Levi, you cannot work your muscles that hard in one day", she scolds me.

"I know...", I grunt back in pain from the constant leg spasms I am having.

The spasms are coming one right after the other. I am trying to breathe and put pressure on my leg at the same time and nothing is helping. I can't even get up to walk anywhere so Charlotte has Sarah bring a wheelchair over.

"Come on, we are getting into the hot tub", Charlotte angrily mumbles as both her and Sarah help me into the chair.

I am already wearing gym shorts, so Charlotte doesn't bother having me change into swim trunks.

The hot water combined with the jets pulsating against my legs helped calm my spasms. The hot tub was a good idea even with Charlotte sitting in the water with me, looking at me with a scowl on her face.

"I am sorry Love", I say, giving her my best puppy dog eyes.

"I just hate it when you are in pain, it makes me sick to my stomach when I know you are in pain", she confesses.

"Awe... that is because you love me so much", I say, pulling her close so I can give her a smooch.

Charlotte massages my leg until she feels no further spasm.

"I walked all the way across the bars today without my brace!" I brag, changing the subject.

" I heard! That's awesome", she finally smiles at me.

"Do you feel like you can walk with me now, back to your room?", she asks.

" I think you should rest the remainder of the afternoon, and we can stop for dinner somewhere on the way to my place", she adds.

She helps me out of the tub, hands me a towel to dry off, then we slowly walk back to my room. She has her arm tightly around me while we walk. My muscles are extremely sore and not just my leg, but my back and arms too.

After a snail's pace, we make it to my room, and I lay down on the bed.

"I think I have learned my lesson", I joke with her.

" Oh, have you now", she hums in return.

She bends down to pick up my wet towel from the floor and when she goes to stand back up straight, I see her wobble and grab onto the bureau for support.

"What just happened?", I blurt out.

"Nothing! I am just dizzy, I think I stayed in the hot tub too long, maybe I need some water", she looks away from me while she speaks.

"Get some water then", I demand.

I don't like what just happened, she is making me nervous.

Some time goes by before Charlotte returns to my room. She appears to have more energy and she is smiling.

"Where shall we eat tonight?", she asks all chirpy.

"Are you feeling better?", my voice serious when I ask her.

"Yes! much! I must have been dehydrated", she attests.

Thankfully, I did not catch her having any other dizzy spells the rest of the week, which led me to believe she really was dehydrated.

The following weeks after told me differently though. It was difficult for me to pinpoint what it was exactly. She acted like her normal self around me, praising all my progress, continuing with my afternoon pool sessions, showering me with love every chance she could. Everything seemed fine except for when she disappeared for a few hours every other morning. I didn't mind because I had therapy with Sarah and Nate, but I was curious. When I would bring it up to her, she would tell me that she was getting stuff taken care of at the hospitals.

It all made sense, it is part of her job, spending time at the hospitals, going to conferences and finding new patients who would benefit from her program.

What has gotten me the most concerned lately was when she ran off to the bathroom because she was sick last week. She blamed it on the stomach flu. This week she is blaming it on food poisoning. I took care of her the best I could, making her tea, rubbing her back when she got sick, checking her temp like she would do for me.

Today she seems to be feeling much better. She is back to her old happy self this afternoon, working with me in the gym.

I am on my eleventh month now of this program. I have gained back strength in my hips, both arms and my right leg. If it weren't for my stubborn left leg, I would be walking on my own by now. My right crutch and my left leg brace are all I need to help me when I walk around. Charlotte is so happy for me, and so am I.

So far this week, I have taken five or six steps without my leg brace on. My ankle isn't sturdy, so Charlotte had a new brace made that forms around my foot, ankle and up my calf. The brace easily fits into my shoe and keeps my ankle locked in place when I step.

"What you have accomplished is remarkable Levi", Charlotte happily reminds me.

Both my hands are on her shoulders while hers grip my waist. We are walking around the gym

together, her moving backwards while I move forward.
I am wearing only my new ankle brace as I practice
walking, Charlotte catching me with her strength the
few times my knee buckles.

Her eyes are so inviting and the way she gazes
into mine shows me how proud of me she is. I would
not be able to do what I am doing now without her.

"So, Mark tells me you have an audition for a
new role back in London at the end of next month?",
an inquisitive tone to her voice.

" Only if I can walk on my own by then... and
even then, I don't know if I want to jump right back
into acting", I admit.

"You should go and try it anyway, maybe you
will realize you have missed it...missed home", she
points out.

"Yeah, maybe, but I do not want to leave you here", I give her a half smile.

"I promised you I would help you to walk again so you could get back to your prior life and your career. I am not going to be the one to hold you back", her tone serious.

Is she trying to make me go back to London, I wonder? I am not even sure if that is what I want to do anymore. What I want is to be with her. She is right though; she didn't do all of this for me so I could just give up acting. I do need a job when I am finished with my program here. I can always find some other career here in Boston, with her.

Charlotte is staring at me waiting for a response. Not sure of what I want to say, so I put my head down and sigh.

" I know, I need some time to think about it", is all I can come up with.

Chapter 47

More than Myself

Charlotte's POV

I have never been one to willingly accept help
from others, which is ironic in a way because I always
tell my patients that is exactly what they need to do to
make them better.

Growing up, everyone always thought of me as
the weird kid. Never asking for birthday presents or
making a Christmas wish list. I always had what I

needed and didn't want anything else. What made me happy was giving something to someone else and watching their face light up with excitement. I did not think that was weird at all.

I want to be the one to take care of others, taking care of everyone else is all I know, now it may end up being the other way around. I will do whatever it takes though to avoid that situation. There is not enough time in the day for me to be sick and run two different facilities, plus spend time with Levi.

"Hold still Miss Thomas, you must not move at all until we are finished here", The nurse instructs me.

I let my eye lids close and my mind drift to the part of my thoughts that are consumed with Levi.

"We are ready to begin Miss Thomas", the nurse's voice sounds like a soft whisper as my head floats high into the clouds where I can dream.

As I lay here, I can picture the way Levi's dreamy eyes make my heart flutter just by looking at them. I think about the amusing ways he makes me laugh, the way his lips caress mine and how his fingers know just where to touch me. I have never felt this kind of love and acceptance, he makes me feel free to be me.

The instant I feel my body getting restless on the exam table, I start to visualize the moments when Levi can stand on his own a little longer, or walk a little farther, and it is so gratifying that I forget about everything else around me.

Three mornings a week I sneak out of my rehab building and make the agonizing trek to the hospital for external-beam radiation therapy. Usually, I inform Levi that I have meetings at the hospital, and so far, he has believed me.

I am going to need to tell Nate soon. He is already questioning my more frequent absences, and he is my second hand when I am gone for long periods at a time. Side effects of the radiation treatments will be difficult to hide from him too.

My first week of treatments were easy. Just lie still on the table for 15 minutes while the beam of radiation does its work. The second week was when the nausea and vomiting kicked in. I told everyone it was the flu, which they didn't question seeing as though I looked like and felt like I had the flu. It was hard to keep with the facade the third week when I continued to rush to the bathroom to vomit at random times during the day, so I blamed it on food poisoning. I know Nate no longer believes my stories at this point; it is only fair that I tell him today.

Luckily for me I have not had any other side effects such as losing my hair and the nausea and vomiting have now ceased.

I realize how unfair it is to keep this from Levi, the one person I absolutely love. It is because I love him so much that I must hold myself together with gracefulness, long enough for him to walk again on his own, so I can let him go back to England. I am not going to be the one to hold him back. After all he has been through and overcome, he deserves every opportunity to return to his home, his friends, and his acting career. That was his goal before he fell in love with me and I am not going to take that away from him.

If Levi knows that I am sick, he will drop everything for me. He will push his goals aside and focus on me instead of himself. He has been quickly progressing and is so close to the end of his program, I just cannot tell him.

He will probably be disappointed and angry with me when he finally does find out, but with any luck, he will find himself content at home when the news hits him.

Chapter 48

The Big Day

Charlotte's POV

Enthusiastic, thrilled, high as a kite; I cannot decide what better describes how I am feeling today. I have that anxious, butterflies in your stomach feeling of excitement preparing for what is going to happen today. Levi has been working towards this day for a little over eleven months and I could not be happier for him than I am right now.

Levi has been on the longest rollercoaster ride of his life, which is probably the best way I can describe his journey here, He has been strapped inside the car, guided by the track through steep inclines and descents, carrying him around sharp curves and changes of speed. At times he found himself stuck in a gravitational force, going around a continuous loop until the track finally changed direction and led him onto the next climb. Just as the car reaches the top of the next hill, there is a moment when everything pauses, when everything felt suspended for him and he enjoyed that moment because the anticipation of the drop was too much to bear. The drop represented everything Levi feared and lost, and he was convinced that this feeling of falling was never going to end and there was nothing he could do to stop it. Eventually he realized that the falls were a normal part of the climb and sometimes he felt the thrill. He found that if he kept on the track, the drops wouldn't feel so bad.

We didn't know exactly how long it would take for Levi to go from walking with one crutch to walking with no crutches at all, so it was decided that we would stream the big event today. His parents, Mark, Landon, Josh, and Andy will all be in London waiting to watch online. They are all coming to Boston in a few weeks for Levi's big graduation party anyway, so they will be able to witness all of Levi's accomplishments then,

There is just one thing that I need to do before Levi's big moment…come clean with Nate, tell him everything that's been going on with me and my new inconvenience.

Nate meets me privately in my office. "Hey Charlie, you said you needed to talk to me about something?", Nate's voice upbeat, I feel bad that my voice will not be when he hears what I'm going to confess.

I ask him to sit down for this and naturally it makes him a little nervous. "Is everything alright?", he shyly asks me.

"No everything is not alright, but I hope it will be", I say, and I see that I am starting to frighten him.

I can't beat around the bush, so I just blurt it out. I tell him about my headaches, the dizziness and blurry vision episodes. I tell him about my eye exam and how it brought me to the neurologist, and I am on my fifth week of radiation treatment now.

After I finish spilling all my secrets, I turn my head to face him. He is completely stunned silent, his eyes wide as he stares at me.

"Nate! are you okay?", I ask him, trying to break him from his frozen state.

"You have been going through all of that, and you are asking me if I am okay?", he says in disbelief.

"That is why you were sick for a few weeks?", he confirms to himself more than asks.

I nod my head up and down.

"Does Levi know?", he questions, his voice beyond concerned at this point.

I move closer to Nate and look straight into his eyes so that maybe he understands the reason why.

"No, Levi doesn't know, and I am not going to tell him".

I can sense Nate's frustration with me now as his voice gets louder. "Charlie, you need to tell him, this is not something you can keep from him, he loves you and you love him. Can you at least tell me why?"

"I have two good reasons and hopefully Levi will understand these reasons when he does find out. The first reason is that if he were to know or if he found out when I did, he would have stopped focusing on his own progress to turn his focus on me, and there is no way I would let that happen. Second reason is that he came here to us knowing that we would give him the best chance of returning to his normal life, as normal as it can be, the life he had before his accident. He needs to go back to his home and his work and figure out for himself if that is what makes him happy. I can't take that chance away from him."

Nate stays quiet for a few minutes before responding. "I won't say anything, you have my word. I only hope that he forgives you for not telling him. You two need each other. You may both be from different places, but your hearts are both the same", he softly tells me. Nate then offers his help to me and reminds me to ask when I need it.

"Okay, enough of this gloomy aura, let's get everything set up for Levi", I bark.

I head to the gym where Levi is waiting for me, sitting in a chair on one end of the room. He looks so happy and the way he is fidgeting with his ankle brace tells me he is nervous as well. I walk up to him and run my fingers through his hair so that he looks up at me.

"Hey", I say and then plant a soft kiss onto his lips.

"Are you ready for this?", I ask him while cupping his face with my hand and brushing my thumb across his cheek.

"With you by my side, I am always ready", he breathes while kissing me again. I press my lips harder onto his trying to suppress the guilty feeling creeping its way into my soul.

Nate has the live streaming all set up and ready to go. We wait until Levi's parents and friends are on the big screen watching.

"Can everyone hear and see alright?", Nate asks everyone back in London.

Levi's parents both greet all of us while Levi's friends shout wisecracks through the mic. "We are ready! Show us what you've got Levi", Landon boasts with excitement.

I turn to Levi and give him my most encouraging smile, "Have I told you how proud I am of you today?" I say softly into his ear.

"Not yet", he gives me a smirk.

Levi reaches his hand out for me to hold while he stands himself up from his chair. We stand hand in hand, perfectly still for a moment. I can feel him tense up a bit, so I give his hand a squeeze before letting it go and whisper to him, "Just breathe Levi, you've got this".

Levi's pace is slow and steady as he takes his first step, then his second on his own, without any crutches, without anyone holding on to him. Levi's mom is screeching and crying at the same time and his friends are rallying him with each step he takes. Levi is grinning ear to ear with every cheer. He almost makes it across the room when he pauses to adjust his gait. His ankle brace causes him to walk with a slight limp, but he has learned how to convert his weight to his right when he lifts his left leg. He quickly regains his composure and carries on, until he reaches the other side of the room.

His mom is hysterically crying happy tears and his friends are yelling and giving each other high fives. I can't seem to move from my current spot, tears are streaming down my face, I am in awe of him and I am stationed in this spot, my mind trying to wrap around what he just showed us. I cannot explain it, the way I feel from watching him walk again on his own, is as euphoric as when I fell in love with him.

He turns around and notices me crying. "Why are you crying?", he holds both his arms out towards me.

"Don't make me walk all the way back over there", he teases me.

I practically jog into his arms and embrace him.

"I love you", he says and kisses my head while I cry into his chest.

"I love you Levi, I am so happy for you", I sniff.

The tears are uncontrollable now, I can only anticipate what is to come next.

Levi lifts my face and wipes my watery eyes, then turns to the screen and thanks his parents and his friends for watching. They all congratulate him and promise to come visit in a few weeks.

"This was perfect! Thank you!", Levi says to Nate and me.

"You were perfect", I say in return, hugging him again. I don't know how I can ever let go.

Chapter 49

Hold My Hand

Levi's POV

I have done it! I can walk again! Knowing that I was paralyzed, at one time trapped in an immobile body having to rely on everyone for everything and wondering if I would ever walk again felt like a surreal mix of reality and illusion. My subconscious wish of being independent again became my ultimate fantasy and it has been Charlotte's unconditional love for me that has helped me shape my dream into actuality.

I telephoned my mum after we finished streaming. She was so emotional that she could not stop crying, even on the phone. Charlotte could not stop crying either and Sarah was noticeably sniffing and wiping her eyes. Apparently, my display of walking stirred up a lot of emotions for all the women. Thankfully, my dad, my friends and Nate stayed grounded because I couldn't handle all the guys crying too. I am sure the lads will be celebrating for me at the pub tonight.

Walking without any support is new and my body tires easily after short distances, so I made sure to sit in a chair to rest my legs while I chat with mum on the phone. After I have managed to calm my mum down a bit, I hold my arms out to Charlotte, convincing her to come over to me so I can pull her down onto my lap.

"So, what do you think of all this?", I search her thoughts.

"I think you are amazing", her expression sweet and her voice muffled from crying.

"Then why all the bawling?", I ask, wiping her tear-stained cheeks.

Charlotte leans her head on my shoulder and softly replies, "I don't know, maybe it is because I love you and how proud I am of you".

I grab her hand and mingle my fingers with hers. "There it is, I was waiting for my daily dose of proud from you", I try and make her laugh.

"Now if you don't mind, I would like you to stop being such a mess so we can go back to your place and I can make you dinner", I chuckle, giving her a kiss on her head.

Charlotte starts laughing along with me, "You, make dinner?"

"I will do my best", I respond and we both cackle in amusement.

She slowly climbs off my lap to stand and I reach out my hand for her to take. I do not necessarily need to hold her hand when I walk, I want to hold her hand. The way her small hand fits perfectly in mine, the feeling of her warm touch, and when our fingers intertwine brings me comfort. I have been longing to walk hand in hand with the woman I love. No crutches, no arm around her shoulder or her grip around my waist to keep me from falling; just her and I, striding side by side holding hands.

"Do you want to drive?", she surprisingly asks me.

Drive! I haven't even thought about driving. It won't be difficult I'm sure, I have complete control of my right leg and both arms, and besides my lack of directions, my driving skills should be on point.

"Sure!", I eagerly shout.

Piece of cake, just like I imagined. I drove Charlotte's jeep back to her apartment without any hiccup. Being behind the wheel, and the feeling of being in control was exhilarating and another triumph for me.

"Can I drive us every day?", I squeal like a giddy teenager driving a car for the first time.

She chuckles at my excitement, "If that is what you want to do".

I am not a creative cook, so I decide to make us spaghetti and meatballs. My legs are tired, but that is not going to stop me from walking around the kitchen like a normal human being and making dinner for my girl. Plus, I have the kitchen counters to hold onto for support if I need it. Cooking should not be this fulfilling to me, but after a year of not being able to carry out this simple task, I am finally capable, and it gives me another sense of achievement and purpose.

I do not need to look at Charlotte for me to feel her eyes following my every move. "Are you making sure I don't burn anything", I jokingly ask her.

"No, I enjoy watching you", she smiles at me.

We both talk and laugh as we eat up the food and later, I am intimately rewarded with Charlotte joining me for a hot bath.

Charlotte's gaze remained immersed in everything I did, from getting myself out of the tub, walking to the closet then back to the bathroom before moving to the bed. It was an awe-struck kind of look she gave me, and I found myself relished in her flattery essence.

The next morning, I drove us back to the rehab center. Boston is a tricky city to maneuver around in a vehicle, but I enjoyed every minute of this new independence. I cannot yet run or even tackle stairs on my own, however, the acts of walking around and driving have made me feel more like myself, more like a man with purpose and hope again.

Charlotte snuck off to the hospital again as soon as we arrived at rehab. I hope her consistent meetings at the hospital are bringing in more clients for her. Only one new patient has come here since Jake left, and that is only because this place is fairly small compared to her California facility.

Nate and Sarah keep my morning occupied with more therapy of course. This time I am working on the stairs. There is a small structure in the gym that represents a form of steps. It looks sort of like a small bridge with a set of three steps on both sides and railings to hold on to. If looks could be deceiving, this stair structure would be it. Sarah stands behind me with her hands on both sides of me while I use all the energy I have to lift my weight up onto the next step. Both of my hands are gripping the rails and I am using most of my arm strength to keep my left leg from giving out. My legs and arms feel like jelly after only those three steps up to the platform. I am frozen in time, anticipating the descent when Sarah catches on to my fear and pushes me to move on.

"Down is much easier, step down with your weaker leg first, then bring your other leg down to the same step and repeat with the remaining steps", she instructs.

I do exactly as she says. With my left ankle locked in place with my brace, this is the only way I can go down the stairs.

"Phew! You were right, that was easier than going up!" I thank her.

Charlotte looks worn out as usual when we meet for lunch. That does not persuade her from continuing my afternoon therapy though. She grabs one of my forearm crutches and then grabs my hand, leading me to the hallway staircase.

"Why do you have my crutch?", I am curious.

"There are 20 steps here and you can only hold onto one railing for support, so you will need to use the crutch with your other arm", she informs me.

"You've got to be kidding me!" I snarl at her.

"Not in the least", she smirks.

My nerves are kicking in, I inhale deeply then exhale my concerns to Charlotte. "You know I only climbed three steps with Sarah this morning, twenty is pushing it."

"Don't worry, you are not going to climb all of them today, but we are going to work at them every day until you make it all the way to the top and then back down", she points out.

That does not calm my nerves any and I sarcastically spit out, "This is going to take hours."

"And I will be right here with you every second", she encourages me.

Charlotte has me start on the left side of the staircase, since my right arm does better with the crutch and my left hand can hold the railing. She instructs me to step up with my stronger right leg first while using my crutch at the same time then bring up my left leg to meet on the same step. Charlotte is behind me holding on to my hips and grasps tighter when she feels me wobble. I make it up six steps before my right leg feels shaky. Looking down, I feel defeated and let out a loud sigh. She takes my crutch and puts my arm around her shoulder and guides me to sit down on the step.

"Six steps! That was great! please do not feel discouraged, just like all the obstacles you have overcome, this will be the same", she takes my hand in hers and reassures me.

"Thanks! my love", I say and bring our locked hands up to kiss her fingers.

"You will conquer this staircase in no time", she blurts out.

She helps me stand back up and hands me my crutch, this time my crutch is in my left hand when I go down the steps. Going down is still easier. I bring my crutch and left foot down onto the step at the same time, allowing my right leg to follow while I cling to the railing with my right hand. Charlotte stands in front of me and walks down the stairs backwards, protecting me from falling. We made it to the bottom in minutes and she congratulated me in typical Charlotte fashion by wrapping her arms around my back and embracing me.

We worked on the stairway every day, adding only one extra step a day. My progress was slow and tedious, though Charlotte inspired me every day to keep at it.

Fighting back my latest mood swings was getting exhausting. Now that I have felt the sweet rush of being able to walk again, I did not want to face the next climb. Not to mention, Charlotte is as exhausted as I am all the time, though she fights harder not to show it and continuously showers me with encouragement.

Today I am going to make it all the way to the top of those damn stairs, and then I am going to celebrate with charlotte by taking her out on a proper date.

Chapter 50

Where it all Began

Levi's POV

Today marks another exciting accomplishment for me at the Charlotte Thomas Rehabilitation Center. I made it all the way up the twenty steps of the dreaded staircase and back down again.

To reminisce about my very first achievement, when Charlotte magically entered my room on my first day here and helped me to move my right hand seems so minuscule compared to what I am doing now. Although Charlotte would disagree, she says that my first accomplishment no matter how small, is what lead the way for all my other ones. She has celebrated each and every one, reminding me that they all took great courage and ability on my part to succeed.

Lately she keeps commenting on how inspiring I am to her and how watching me fight every day to be better helps her fight too. I am not sure exactly what she means by that, she is the one person who has inspired me and has kept me going through all of this. Without her, I would no doubt be confined to a wheelchair alone in my flat taking pity on myself. Her comments recently are subtle but enough to make me worry. I have this nagging pit in my gut warning me that there is something wrong, I just don't know what it is exactly.

It is not like Charlotte is obvious when something is bothering her. She goes about her day as she normally does, she is overloaded with work, but she gets it finished, she meets me for lunch every day, does my afternoon therapy sessions, and we spend every night together at her place. The only thing out of the ordinary with Charlotte are her abstruse philosophical one-liners she has been trying to motivate me with. She has always said the most heartening things to me, and I appreciate how uplifting she is all the time, but the way she has been speaking this week sounds like she is trying to influence herself as well as me. This is overly concerning to me.

This afternoon we are skipping therapy and I am taking her to the place where it all began for me. I have been waiting for this day all week. Charlotte has no idea where I am taking her, I have kept it a surprise. She is always the one surprising me, now it is my turn.

"Levi, where are we going", she asks me all bright-eyed and bushy tailed.

She hops into the passenger seat of the jeep and I tease her by placing a blindfold over her eyes. I know that seems a little dramatic, but I do not want her to know where we are going until we get there. I have already told her how special this place is to me, if I say anything more, she will figure it out.

I pull out of the parking lot and head south on Interstate 93. She keeps us entertained by trying to find and change the radio station without her sight. She managed to press every button and turn every knob before finding the correct one, and when she found it, she turned the volume up and sang the tune. It was comical, we laughed the entire way to the secret spot.

I parked the jeep and walked over to her side to open the door for her. She held my hand as I lead her out and turned her to face the welcome sign. The sign I will always remember, declaring the most ironic name. Charlotte took her blindfold off her eyes and instantly she was all smiles.

"You took me to World's End", she repeats the exact words that came out of my mouth when she took me here almost nine months ago.

I reach out my hand for her to hold and say, "Remember when we were at the park in California and I told you I couldn't wait until I could hold your hand and walk beside you?"

"Yes, I remember", her words are slow as she gives me a curious look.

"I thought this would be the perfect place to hold your hand", I smile at her.

She places her hand in mine and we walk together side by side, down the same carriage path we have been down once before.

We enjoy the comfortable silence between us. I am soaking in this moment, the moment I have wished for a long time. No conversation is needed, only her and I engrossed in the natural beauty of this place. I feel Charlotte's thumb rubbing light circles over mine while her hand is enfolded in mine. I can't take my eyes off her, the way she closes her eyes and breathes in the cool air captivates me. I cannot think of a time I have ever been happier, she makes me feel like my feet are barely touching the ground, like I am floating in air.

This magnificent place looks different in the spring. The vegetation is only starting to bloom, and the grass still resembles a hint of brown from the winter's snow. We gladly explore other areas of the park now that I can walk. We can hike along the cliffs and walk along the rocky shore. The views of the bay are always spectacular no matter what season it is.

We arrive at the same grassy spot where we first had lunch. I spread the blanket I packed across a flat area.

"This is a lot easier than when I was in my chair", I gloat.

Charlotte only nods and smiles. I take a seat down onto the blanket and pull her to sit in between my legs so she can lean her back on my chest. I brush her vanilla scented hair behind her ear and brought my face closer to her so I could gently kiss her neck. She grasped both of my hands and wrapped my arms around the front of her. We sat looking out at the bay while I enveloped her body into mine.

"This is the place where I knew I was falling in love with you", I whisper into her ear.

She brushes her face up against my chest to look at me. "How do you know it was love?", she whispers back.

"I was so deep into the darkness when you brought me here, I didn't understand how I could be worth saving. You held my hand and let me stroll down the path next to you, you lifted me up and sat me on the blanket with you when you could have left me in my chair, and you kept your hold around me so that I could sit up while we ate lunch together. You made me feel human again and not someone who was just crippled", I pour out my soul to her.

She unwraps my arms from her and turns her body to face me. Water is building up in her eyes and she is holding back the tears.

"How do you know it wasn't gratitude you were feeling that day?", her question surprises me.

"Of course, I felt gratitude, but it was love that made my body shiver when you touched my hand, love that caused electricity to flicker under my skin when you wrapped your arm around me, and love that sparked laughter back into my soul. Ever since that day you have been the air that surrounds me, the light in all my darkness and the keeper of my heart", I profess to her.

There it is! the waterfall gushing from her beautiful eyes. I pull her into me again and hold her tight, soaking up her tears with my thumbs.

"Please don't cry, I don't know if you are happy or sad?", I tell her.

"You make me feel all of those things too, Levi. I have never felt this kind of love before", she cries out.

"Then why are you sobbing?", I ask.

Charlotte desperately tries to contain her tears and I waited for what felt like eternity for her to collect her thoughts. she turned her gaze to the water and cleansed her cheeks with her shirt. Her sniffles slowed to a near halt.

I cannot endure the suspense any longer, I need to know. "What is really bothering you Charlotte?", hoping she will engage.

She slowly turns to face me again, this time taking both my hands in hers, softly tracing my palms with the tip of her thumbs.

"It is because of how much I love you that I need you to go back home, to England and give yourself the chance to pursue that new acting role, and the chance to enjoy life the way you did before you met me".

"I do not understand! You want me to leave?", I blurt out.

"No, I don't want you to leave...I love you; I love everything about you, you make me so happy...I just don't want you to give up on any opportunities. You came here to me so that I could help you walk again, so you could return to your life in England", she tries to convince me.

I retract my hands from her hold and cross my arms in front of my chest. "Well things change", I huff.

"Yes, they do, but nothing changes the way I feel about you...please promise me you will give things back home a try", she forcefully unlocks my arms to hold my hands again.

"Fine", I mumble.

I know she is right. Mark is counting on me and deserves my presence since he has convinced the director to give me a shot at a new role. I owe it to my parents and my mates to return home as well, but Charlotte is my everything, just thinking about being away from her is making me panic.

She moves her body to sit next to me and holds her arm around my back, then rests her head on my shoulder. We stay together in this position, silently peering out at the sea, and alone in our thoughts.

Chapter 51

This is Love

Levi's POV

My emotions are boiling up under my skin. I know she loves me; she says she loves me, but everything else she says is confusing as hell. Sitting here quiet on the blanket is not helping either, it is making my anxiety worse.

"We should get back", she says, lifting her head from my shoulder and standing herself up.

Leave it to my panicked mind to cause an excruciating spasm in my left leg when I try to stand. Charlotte sees me shift uncomfortably on the blanket, clenching my fists and wincing and brings herself back down beside me.

"I can't get up", I angrily groan.

She reaches for my leg, attempting to massage the pain away.

"Don't!", I say and move her hand away from me.

She does not say anything, she just remains by my side, watching me trying to fight through the pain.

"I am sorry", she softly says.

After I think that the spasms are over, I get myself to stand while Charlotte folds up the blanket. I reach to take her hand for our walk back, but another spasm sends shooting pains down my leg again. This time Charlotte grabs my arm and brings it around her shoulder and her other arm holds the back of my waist for support. I let her help me even though I do not want her to have to hold me up while we walk.

Our walk back is slow and painful. We had to stop when my next spasm got so bad that I pulled her to face me and put my forehead down on to her head while her arms clutched tightly around my back.

"Levi, breathe", she says while rubbing my back. "I am right here with you", she softly adds.

I cling to her warmth, her touch and maybe that is all I needed for her to do and say to make everything better.

My spasms disappeared by the time we reached the jeep. She instructed me to the passenger side so she could drive. There was no argument about it, only a feeling of shame.

Our drive back was strange. I felt comfort in the fact that Charlotte held my hand the entire ride, but my mind thought I was on a racetrack.

I broke the silence first.

"I am happy staying here with you. I realized my life wasn't always what it was cracked up to be until I met you. Nothing was real, not my fiancé, not my job. I will not be happy there".

"You don't know that you won't be happy until you go and try", she says, squeezing my hand.

She is acting so unusual. All I want is for her to tell me to stay. I feel my eyes well up. I cannot be mad at her, I love her.

She parks the jeep at her apartment and makes her way to my side of the car to try and help me.

"No, I am fine now, thanks", I lie.

I have been having very mild but continuous spasms for the last half of the drive here, but I'm not going to let her notice, so I get myself out of the jeep and slowly walk behind her to the apartment.

"I am going to take a shower", I grunt once we get inside.

Standing in the hot shower, allowing the water to massage my neck, and back is relaxing. I lean my head back on the shower wall while the water flows down my face and try to clear all uneasiness from my mind. I focus on the good from today. Walking with my beautiful girl by myside, treading along the rocks, holding her hand. Visions of her angelic face flood my mind. Just when I feel some peacefulness, my left leg gives out from under me and I slip down to the shower floor.

"Shit!", I yell out.

I reach for the shower chair and pull myself onto it seconds before Charlotte frantically bursts through the bathroom door.

"Are you alright?", she searches all around.

I remain sitting on the shower chair, my head in my hands sulking.

"I'm fine", I mutter back.

My head must have rested in my hands for longer than I thought, because I only lifted my head up when I felt Charlotte's hands pull mine away from my face. Were my eyes deceiving me? Is this my love, my rock, my protector standing naked in front of me, showing me once again that I am not alone.

When my eyes met hers, I didn't see stars, I saw galaxies. When she held my face in her hands, it felt like she was untying all my knots, and when she grazed my bottom lip with her fingers before capturing my lips with hers, it made the whole world stop. She climbed onto my lap, her smooth thighs around mine while placing her familiar arms around my back, her fingers tickling down my spine. She has captivated my mind, and my body presses closer into hers until there is no space left between us. We kiss slowly at first and then passionately, letting the hot water pour over our bodies. When she reaches down and guides me into her, an intoxicating feeling causes my body to shiver in absolute pleasure and ecstasy. It is love that we make, a love that makes me so complete, I cannot bare to lose it.

I close my eyes, my body shaking from giving ourselves to each other. I feel her run her fingers through my hair and tenderly kiss my lips again.

"I love you", she purrs into my ear and brushes her lips near the crook of my neck.

I fold her back into my arms and we are locked in an embrace till the water ran cold.

"Can you stand and walk", she asks concerned.

I kiss her one last time and affirm with a smile, "Yes, I can, our shower sessions always make everything better".

Realizing after hearing our stomach's growl that we have not eaten dinner yet, we change into some lounge clothes and head to the kitchen to make something to eat.

I help her in the kitchen, which is something I have come to enjoy now with my newfound walking skills, plus I like being the one to help Charlotte too. We gulped down our food in no time then planted ourselves onto the couch.

She snuggled her body next to mine while we lay together with my back leaning up against the cushions.

Holding her in my arms is what keeps me sane. She has my heart, a part of me that I will never again give to anyone else. I comb my fingers through her damp hair and glide my thumb down the warm skin of her cheek.

I will give it a try. I will go back to England and give this new acting job a go if that will make everyone happy. I know things will be different for a little while, which makes me hesitant and scared.

Charlotte believes I might find happiness, but she is the reason I have already found it. I may be all the way across the Atlantic, but my heart will always remain here with her.

Chapter 52

Elephant in The Room

Charlotte's POV

"Charlie! Are you feeling alright? You look like you have not slept in days! I am concerned.", Nate caringly points out.

"I have not been sleeping well", I admit.

"My follow-up scans are today, and I am worried about the results."

"Do you want me to come with you for support? I know you would rather have Levi there, but since you have not told him or anyone else about what has been going on with you, I think maybe you need me!", Nate professes his concern to me.

"I will have Sarah keep Levi occupied with some extra stair climbing while we sneak away for your appointment", he tries to convince me.

I find myself nervously pacing around my office. "I don't know", I say to him.

"Charlie, you have gone through this alone long enough, I am coming!", Nate says sternly. "And I am driving you, now let's go", he adds before taking my arm and leading me out the door, unnoticed by anyone else.

I am happy I have Nate here with me, he has become my best friend and I do not know what I would do without him around. My guilt is tearing up my heart though, it is Levi who should really be here supporting me. My lack of energy doesn't only come from the treatments I have been hiding, it is more the bitter fatigue of self-reproach and the anticipation of the regret I will have when Levi finds out what I have been keeping from him.

Two weeks have passed since our day together at World's End park. My emotions have been out of control all week, knowing that Levi's graduation party is tomorrow and after the weekend, he will be flying back to London. Neither Levi or I want him to go, but we have talked about it in length over the last week, and we both have come to realize that he needs to go.

What concerns me the most is the amount of uncontrolled leg spasms Levi has been having during the last two weeks. They are not too intense or painful lately, but they are there. They happen mostly in his left lower leg, where his calf and ankle muscles have yet to return to normal. He has regained enough strength and muscle tone so that he can walk and climb stairs on his own, but when he is tired or anxious about something, that is when the spasms return. I had a new brace made for him a few days ago. The brace reaches higher up his calf, but it seems to be helping with his gait and gives him more support when using the stairs without a crutch. Levi has done exceptionally well during this program, considering this brace is the only assist he needs after such a traumatic injury.

"We are ready for you Charlotte", the nurse breaks my train of thought.

Nate and I have been silently sitting in the hospital waiting room.

"I will be right here waiting for you", Nate says.

After my scans, I grabbed Nate and allowed him to accompany me into the doctor's office to hear the results. Having a friend with me was comforting I must admit. The doctor explained that my treatments were working, but there has not been enough improvement for me to stop. Starting next week, my treatment increases to five days a week for the next four weeks, and then surgery. Nate squeezes my hand assuring me that he will help in whatever way he can. I thank him with a nod, and we head outside to his car. The drive back is so quiet, one can hear a pin drop. Nate is worried for me I can see it on his face. Neither of us want to speak about the obvious.

"Thank you for coming with me today", I smile at him.

"I am here whenever you need me", his smile wary.

"Thank goodness we have a busy night and day tomorrow planning the graduation party, I need a good distraction", I say.

When we return to the rehab center, I found Levi working in the gym with Sarah. She was having Levi stretch on the mat. Levi turns towards me and instantly beams when he catches me staring at him. I cannot help staring, even now. He is more handsome to me every day. His dotting bright eyes, beautiful face, and perfect body, I will never get enough of him. He doesn't mind my gawking either, I think it boosts his manly ego. There is so little time left for me to be able to lay my eyes on him before he leaves.

Levi catches my frown from just thinking of him leaving and raises his hand out to me.

"Come here Love", he says.

I walk over to the mat where Levi and Sarah are sitting. Levi grabs my hand and pulls me down to kiss me.

"Thank you for working with Levi", I say to Sarah.

"No problem! I will catch up with you guys later", Sarah replies.

Levi is still holding my hand as I move in front of him and sit on the mat with my legs crossed. I can see that he has been working hard this morning from the amount of sweat showing through his shirt. He has been around me long enough for me to know when he is trying to hide his pain behind his smile. I know he is tired and sore from his workout and the stairs take a toll on his muscles.

He has not had any spasms in the last two days and I suddenly have an overwhelming feeling of needing to protect him from having any at all. I reach for his lower left leg and grasp just under his knee and his heel, resting his leg on my lap. Levi quietly looks at me with appreciation for what I am doing. I remove his leg brace then start gently massaging his calf muscle. I notice his lips begin to curve upwards and his gaze on me sincere as a feeling of relief takes over him.

I massage his calf muscle a few minutes longer, pressing into and making circular strokes around his tight muscles before moving onto his ankle and then his foot.

"Does this help?", I ask him.

"Yes Love, thank you!", he softly confirms.

"Good! I have been really worried about you, I do not like when you have those painful spasms, and I am worried about you having any more when you are back home", my voice cracking with anxiety.

He reaches for both of my hands and holds them in his, tracing hearts with his thumb on my palms.

"The new brace is working, and you have helped me too, I will be fine, no need to worry about me", his voice is soft and full of gratitude.

I know there is more he wants to say. There is more we both want to say, yet we are either afraid to say it or we are just trying to avoid talking about the inevitable. It consumes our every moment together, the elephant in the room that neither of us want to acknowledge. He is leaving to pursue his dreams and I do not want him to feel bad about it at all.

I look up and peer into his troubled blue-green eyes and can almost feel his trembling heart.

"I love you! You know I love you, right? I do not want you to feel like I am forcing you to leave because you think I do not love you", I slowly and genuinely say to him.

"I know my love, I just do not like knowing we will be apart, even if it is for a short time", he quietly responds.

"How about we spend this weekend enjoying your party, hanging out with your friends and family, and spending our time together having fun!", I smile.

"Brilliant!", he smiles back at me.

I gently pull my hands away from his and attach his brace back onto his leg. He puts his sneakers back on and I stand up beside him, reaching my hand down to him so that he can grab it.

"Come on, we have a lot of work to do to make this party of yours a spectacular one", I smirk.

"Plus, everyone is flying in tonight, so we have plenty to prepare for", he adds.

Levi grips my hand as he stands himself up. He squints his eyes as soon as he shifts his weight onto his left foot, but whatever pain he felt quickly resolved.

"Levi, are you okay?"

He pulls me into his side and kisses my temple but doesn't answer me, he only smiles and squeezes my hand while we walk together out of the gym. Levi looks relaxed now so I will not pressure him any further, he is not going to admit anything even if I ask. We have just agreed to have fun this weekend. The conspicuous elephant will have to remain camouflaged for now.

Chapter 53

Graduation Weekend

Levi's POV

Charlotte and I pick up my parents at the airport first. Their flight arrived early afternoon, so we had time to pick them up and get them settled at their hotel before the lads arrived.

My parents have seen me walk on skype, but they have yet to see me walking in person. I am sure my mum has been driving my dad crazy with the anticipation.

We parked the car so we could surprise my parents inside the airport when they get off the plane. I am just as excited to show them as they are, I think.

"You are shaking! Are you alright?", Charlotte asks me as we are standing hand in hand in the baggage claim area.

I realize that my hand has been fidgeting in Charlottes, but I hadn't noticed my body shaking.

"I am sorry, I am a bit nervous, although I do not know why, and I am excited", I confess.

"You know your parents will be so happy when they see you! Your mum will probably start crying and throw her arms around you from being so happy!", Charlotte smirks.

"Probably", I shrug my shoulders.

"I mean, it is what I do when I see you walking and climbing the stairs, pretty much every other accomplishment as well", she smiles at me.

"For a mother to see her son, a walking miracle! She is going to fall apart!", she playfully nudges her shoulder into me.

I squeeze her hand and give her a peck on the cheek. She removes her hand from mine and brings it to my back and slowly brushes her palm up and down the back of my shirt. Her gesture is comforting, and my body is now relaxed while we stand in the crowded baggage claim waiting for my parents.

Moments later we hear an older woman shrieking my name in a British accent and look over to see my mum barreling towards me, my dad trying to keep up behind her. Charlotte was right! Here comes my mum, arms already open towards me.

"Oh son! I cannot believe it!", my mum wraps her arms around my neck.

She lets go of me for a second but keeps a hold of my arms while she looks over me. "Look at you! I am so happy son!", she is crying now and hugging me again.

Charlotte winks and smiles at me and I can't help but chuckle.

"Hey son! You look great!", my dad finally catches up to us and offers me his hand to shake.

My dad grabs the bags from the luggage belt, and we all walk to where we parked the car. My mum locks her elbow with mine as I escort her to the parking lot. She keeps looking over at me while we walk, studying my every move like she still can't believe that I can walk now.

"You're limping?", she looks at me worried.

"I am alright mum, it is not from pain", I say while lifting my left leg pant enough to show her my brace.

"This is just how I walk with my brace; Charlotte has been helping me correct my gait as much as I can, but I might always have a slight limp", I try and reassure my mum.

"Oh", Is all she replies. Her face turns sad for me, it is probably how a mother feels when she thinks there is something wrong with her son.

Charlotte is the only person who doesn't look at me with pity, she doesn't see me as disabled like everyone else does. I mean, I do have a disability, I can't walk on my own without this brace, I can no longer run or jump either, but that doesn't stop Charlotte from making me try. That is one thing I love about Charlotte, she doesn't treat me like a cripple, she treats me like a person who needs a little help to overcome a few obstacles. She sees my leg brace as something that helps me, not something that labels me as having a disability. I know the way Charlotte views me will not be the way others view me back home and that scares me

We decide to have dinner at a nice little Italian restaurant on the North End called Dolce Vita. The owner is a plump and very loud Italian guy who cheerfully greets us all at the door and personally shows us to our table. The staff is friendly, and the food is amazing. The owner even took time to check on his customers and thanked them by singing a song along with his accordion., my mum really enjoyed that.

I was dreading having to walk up the stairs to get to the loo, but after the wine I drank, I couldn't avoid it any longer. Charlotte had to go to, so she held my hand as we slowly made our way up the steps. I could see my mum and dad focus their attention on us, studying the way I only step up with one leg and one step at a time. This bothers me, the way everyone watches me tackle the stairs, I already feel self-conscience as it is, now my parents are probably looking at me with the same feeling. Charlotte squeezes my hand and smiles at me, reminding me that she is by my side, and reassuring me, like she can read my thoughts. The way back down was just as uncomfortable, the way I would catch my mum pretending not to stare at me.

We had left the car at rehab and walked here, so my mum linked her arm with mine again as we walked back. Whenever we walked over uneven ground, my mum would hang onto my arm a little tighter, as if she were trying to hold me up.

"I am not going to fall mum, I know I may not look perfect when I am walking or going up the stairs, but you do not have to worry about me", I give her an appreciative kiss on her head.

"A mother always worries, son!", she tells me.

Charlotte and I walk my parents to their hotel which is a block away from the rehab center. The lads should be arriving to this same hotel in another hour, so we all sit on the couches in the lobby area having a chat while we wait for them.

It is not long before we hear the loud banter of Josh and Landon as they push their way through the lobby door, Mark and Andy following behind.

"Levi!", Landon shouts loud enough for the entire hotel to hear.

My parents were knackered, so they retired to their room early while the rest of us had a few drinks in the hotel bar. Charlotte did not drink at all though and looked to be as tired as my parents were.

"Why don't you stay here tonight with the guys?", Charlotte's request catches me off guard.

"No! I am spending my last two nights here with you", I tell her.

"We can leave now, get some sleep before the big party tomorrow", I lean down and give her a kiss, convincing her that it is alright.

We get back to Charlotte's place and she is fast asleep by the time I am finished brushing my teeth. I slide myself under the covers and curl myself around her warm body. I softly kiss her smooth cheek and whisper, "Good night my Love", before I swiftly drift to sleep too.

The lads are already causing a ruckus when we arrive back at rehab the next morning. My parents are drinking coffee and chatting with Sarah.

"Let's get this party started!", Josh shouts and makes everyone around him laugh.

Apparently, my two-hour planned party has turned into an all-day affair. All the other patients seem to enjoy that idea as well. We had food and desserts delivered at every hour, it was ridiculous how much everyone ate.

"Time for the best part!", Sarah boasts.

Everyone gathers in the lounge for Sarah's special presentation. Sarah has worked ridiculously

hard trying to create the perfect video of my time here.
I don't know when she had the time to capture all the
pictures and small video clips of me over the past year.
To be honest, I am apprehensive about watching it. I
have been through so much in the last twelve months,
most things I would like to forget, and most things I
will cherish.

Sarah instructs me to sit front and center, in the
middle of the big couch with my parents and friends on
either side. I have no idea where Charlotte and Landon
ran off to an hour ago, but I want them here with me to
watch this.

Sarah starts the video, and everyone watches
intently during the first part. This first part brings up
bad memories of when I could barely move, when I
first moved my arms, when I first drank from a cup on
my own, the first time I attempted to sit up and needed
Charlotte to calm me down from my panic attack. My

mum is crying and clenching on to my arm, my dad

now has his hand on my shoulder, and for once, the

lads are silent. They didn't get to see this part; this is

the time when I tried to shut them out and kept them

from seeing me in this state. I looked around at them,

their eyes wide and mouths hung open in

disbelief. Josh and Andy had real tears forming in

their eyes, and I too felt the tears in mine.

Soon, the music changed, and the video

lightened up. It went on showing my first time

standing, first steps in the pool and first steps using the

parallel bars. Everyone was smiling now and clapping

at times. All of the sudden I feel Charlotte standing

behind me, she leans down and wraps her arms around

the front of me, bringing her face close to my ear and

whispers, "Do you know how inspiring you are to

everyone here? I am so proud of you", then she kisses

my cheek.

I do not know where she just came from, but I am not letting her go. She can keep her arms wrapped around my neck with her face so close to mine. I need her close, she is the reason I am able to walk again.

Sarah threw in a few funny pictures of the lads fooling around in the wheelchairs and bantering with me in the gym. Everyone had a good laugh. When the final clips showing me walking on my own and my mates yelling for me on the streaming video came to view, everyone stood up and started cheering along with the TV screen.

The very last scene was of me and Charlotte walking up the staircase together, hand in hand. Charlotte catches the lone tear that has escaped my eye and I turn to her and kiss her lips.

"I know I do not need your help all the time now, but I will miss your help, I will miss you always holding my hand, I will miss you Charlotte!", I softly

say into her ear and kiss her again.

Chapter 54

Missing Him

Charlotte's POV

It has been strange not having Levi here. Two weeks have gone by already and even though I am busy throughout the day and my treatments at the hospital have increased, I still feel empty inside.

Before meeting Levi, I thought I was happy, that my life was fulfilled. I didn't mind not being in a relationship at the time because I had so many other things to do.

But Levi showed me there is more to life than just my work. He helped me realize I was missing one of the most important things in life...love.

I have never had this type of intimate connection before, someone to love me and accept all that I am, someone to share my free time with, laugh with, cry with. I miss him.

There is a piece of my heart missing now and I find myself just going through the motions of living and it is lonely.

Nate notices it too. Not only am I sick again from having radiation every day now, but I am also exhausted and cannot keep up with the demands of my work.

I ended up having to hire another fulltime therapist so that she can take over for me and I can focus on only the paperwork and running the facility. Nate has demanded that I do no more patient therapy until I am feeling better.

Nate also has convinced me to tell my parents about my situation. Of course, they flew here right away and were not only terribly angry at me for not telling them in the first place, but they also became immensely helpful to me.

My mom has been keeping my apartment tidy and cooking all the meals and my dad has kept occupied with fixing whatever he finds broken around here. They also sit with me during my treatments, which is comforting for me. Them being here by my side makes me feel guilty as well. I am wishing it were Levi here helping me through this, but I am the one who pushed him to go back to England. He is going to be upset with me when I finally break the news to him, maybe he will not talk to me or even want me anymore. I am hurting him by not telling him, but I am helping him at the same time, I hope. I feel stuck between a rock and a hard place. Either I keep this secret for as long as possible so he can enjoy life back home and finish this new acting role he has or spill the beans. Either way, it may be too late at this point, and I will probably end up by myself the rest of my life.

Levi and I have spoken on the phone almost every day. The six-hour time difference has made it difficult for us. Between his acting job and my job here, as well as my grueling treatments, finding the right hour during the day to chat has been a challenge. I have found a few moments here and there to speak with Landon though.

Landon found out that I was sick when he was here for Levi's graduation party. I did not tell him the extent of my struggles; all he knows is that I have been ill, and I didn't want to worry Levi with my problems or make him lose focus on his goals. Landon seems to understand where I am coming from, but he also feels guilty about hiding something from his friend. Andy moved out of Levi's flat to live with his new girlfriend, so Landon decided to move in with Levi so he can keep an eye on him and help him out. It makes me happy knowing Levi has a friend living with him, he will not feel lonely that way. Plus, Landon fills me in on how Levi is really doing back home.

I feel bad calling Levi at this hour of the night in London, but I need to talk with him before my two-week stay at the hospital that is happening day after tomorrow. I am scheduled for surgery in two weeks and my doctor has scheduled extensive treatments for me prior and says it is a good idea for me to stay there during this treatment phase. I will be sick and exhausted, I will not be able to work, and I even might lose some of my hair from this, which I am not looking forward to at all.

"Hey Love!", Levi answers his phone, his voice groggy. I probably woke him up seeing as it is two in the morning over in London.

"Hi! I am sorry I am calling so late!", I apologize.

"Don't worry Love, how was your day? you sound tired", he says.

"I have just been busy and have a lot on my mind. Enough about me, how was therapy today? How was your second week on the new set?", I divert the conversation to him.

"Therapy is fine, we have worked out a six in the morning time slot for me, it works better than after a long day on the set.", his voice more pronounced now.

"Oh good, and how about the movie, how is it coming along?", I ask again.

He pauses for a moment before answering which makes me think there is something he is trying not to tell me. Lately, he hasn't wanted to talk about his new movie.

"Levi, what is it?", I press.

"It is only a supporting actor role they gave me, nothing special, it is going fine", he sighs.

"That sigh doesn't tell me it is going fine", I point out.

"I knew it would be like this, I knew everyone would treat me different. My co-star Emily spotted my leg brace the other day and ever since, she looks at me like she needs to be careful around me. This morning she witnessed me go up the stairs and she grabbed my arm like she needed to help me", Levi says to me with defeat clear in his tone.

"Levi, it sounds like she is trying to be nice. Maybe she was just caught off guard. I mean you are unavoidably attractive and a great actor, maybe she was surprised at how well you are able to move about on your own", I try and lighten his mood.

"I do not know about that, only you and Landon treat me like a normal person. Mark even treats me like I need special treatment, that is probably why he keeps trying to find me small roles to play", he says.

"Sounds like they just care about you Levi".

"God, I miss you Charlotte!"

"I miss you too Levi".

"Please keep calling no matter what time it is over here, I need to hear your voice", he pleads into the phone.

"I love you Levi, I am proud of you for making a go at this and for sticking to your daily physical therapy!", I encourage him the best I can from all the way across the Atlantic.

"I love you Charlotte", he says before I hang up on him.

It bothers me that Levi is struggling back home, trying to get adjusted. He hates the fact that he still needs to wear a brace and he thinks that people will only see his limp and not see him. I know this is hard for him, he is known all over the world because of his job and has camera people following his every move, waiting to judge him. I wish I could be there to help him through this. Good thing he has Landon, I think to myself.

The following week had been hell for me. I have received a triple dose of medication to prepare me for the best possible outcome during surgery. If I was not sleeping from sheer exhaustion, I was in the bathroom emptying my insides into the toilet. I had only managed to phone Levi once that week. I am sure I sounded awful when I spoke, he is sure to believe there is something wrong with me now. I do send him text messages every day to make up for the lack of him hearing my actual voice and I hope that is good enough for now.

This current week has not been any better for me. I have been just as sick and tired; I can barely move my limbs. I feel like I have the never-ending flu. My parents have visited every day and Nate has come by every other day to fill me in on everything going on at the rehab center. I tried calling Levi this morning, but he didn't answer. I got a hold of Landon though. Our conversation was not what I expected.

"Charlotte, I am worried about Levi, he is not in a good way this week!", Landon says.

"What do you mean?", I ask him.

"Last week he looked depressed and this week he looks in pain! He is constantly rubbing his left leg and has been using his crutch this week, so I know his leg is bothering him, he also skipped his physical therapy sessions the last few days! He misses you

Charlotte! Why haven't you called him?", Landon hysterically informs me.

Shit! the spasms are back. This is my fault, he is worried, I have only been texting him. I need to at least tell Landon what is really going on, maybe he can help Levi without actually telling him about me.

"Landon, I am having surgery on Thursday morning to remove a brain tumor, I have been in the hospital the last two weeks preparing for the surgery".

"What?", Landon blurts out.

Landon continues to yell at me through the phone, "Charlotte, you need to tell Levi, he should know! you could die!", Landon exaggerates that last part.

Before I could respond back, I hear Levi shout something in the background and the line goes dead. I lay back down against my pillow on the hospital bed, my hand shaking as I try to place my cell phone on the nightstand next to me. What did I do? Landon is right, I should have told Levi. He is back at home and in pain because of me, he is going to hate me now. I have never felt so afraid and so alone.

Chapter 55

Missing Her

Levi's POV

"Levi, try that part again, this time get up from the stool, walk slowly over to Emily and reach for her hand as you say your lines", the director instructs me.

I move to stand up from the stool and quickly adjust my pant leg to cover my brace. Emily catches me and she gapes wide-eyed at my left leg brace, then gives me the uncomfortable pity look. I glare at her

628

with slanted eyes and she clears her throat before fixing her posture and looks away from me.

Great! this is all I need I think to myself. Emily is the leading actress in this particular movie, and I am only in a few scenes. Mark thought it best that I slowly get back into bigger roles, to prove to the producers that I am capable, I guess.

I follow the director's previous instructions and get the scene done to his satisfaction. Emily gives me that questioning look, like why am I wearing a leg brace kind of look. I do my best to ignore her, but she decided to follow me up the stairs to the dressing rooms.

"Do you need some help?" Emily asks and grabs my free arm while I make my way up the stairs, one step at a time.

I shake her hand away, trying not to be mean, but I am annoyed at the way she is acting towards me after catching sight of my disabilities. She didn't treat me this way the first two weeks, so why all the sudden?

"I do not need any help, this is how I walk up the stairs", I blankly tell her.

"Oh", is all she responds in a shy tone.

I sigh loudly. If this can't get any worse! Where is Charlotte when I need her? Oh right, thousands of miles away because I decided to let her talk me into coming back here so I can pretend everything is back to normal, when in reality, everyone here is treating me like a cripple. Everyone except Landon that is. Great! Here comes Mark walking towards me, probably going to ask if I need any help.

"Hey mate! everything go alright today? Do you need anything? You look like you are limping more!", Mark says to me.

I am beyond irritated at this moment. No, everything is not alright, I have been having leg spasms all day, Emily is treating me different, and Charlotte hasn't spoken to me over the phone in a while...Is how I really want to answer Mark.

Instead, I only reply with, "Yes, everything is fine, no need to worry about me".

"Good! I will see you tomorrow then! Not much left here, you are just about done with your scenes", Mark states before leaving.

I am happy to be done with this small role, this is a better time than any to go home and lock myself in my room for a while. I need to call Charlotte! I miss her voice I miss everything about her.

The following days were not what I expected. Landon tried to keep me occupied, but the only person I wanted to see and hear from was Charlotte. She hasn't answered my calls in days, only a few brief text messages have been exchanged and I was worried. Worried she didn't want me anymore; worried she no longer loves me.

I can barely walk on my left leg; the spasms are frequent and cause me so much pain. I had to resort to using a crutch to help me get around. Skipping PT was probably a bad idea, but I did not care at the time. Landon is concerned for me and keeps pushing me to see the therapist here, but I ignore him as well.

Today seems to be the worst day for me so far, pain wise. I cannot stand to be in my room any longer, so hiding out on the balcony feels like a better idea. Landon hasn't figured out I am out here yet, he probably thinks I finally left the flat, which is fine for him to think. Sitting out here in the fresh air helps, it is peaceful out here listening to the birds and the small amount of traffic in the distance.

"What!" I hear Landon shout at someone from inside.

I open the balcony door and slowly head inside to see what the commotion is all about. Landon continues to yell at someone over the phone.

"Charlotte! you need to tell him! you could die!", I hear him shout.

Both Landon and I freeze in place and stare at each other, eyes wide, mouths almost dropping to the floor. Was he really just talking to Charlotte? And why did he say she could die?

It takes me a moment to secure my thoughts before I walk right up to Landon and grab his cell phone from his hand. He doesn't put up a fight, he lets me take his phone. There is no one on the line, but Charlotte's name appears on the screen. He was just shouting at Charlotte.

My jaw clenches and my hands ball up into fists at my side. "Why were you yelling at Charlotte? Why were you even talking to her? and what about going to die?", I angrily question him.

Landon puts his head down; he is visibly shaking. Good, he should be scared I think in my head.

"She is sick Levi, she has been sick for a few months", he nervously tells me.

"What do you mean Landon?", I ask him with an angrier tone.

"She has a brain tumor, she is having surgery to try and remove it on Thursday", he blurts out.

I am not sure what came over me at that moment. Rage, fear, hurt were only a few of the things I was feeling when I lunged at Landon, grabbing him by his shirt collar and throwing him against the wall.

"And you didn't think to tell me that the love of my life could be dying of a brain tumor!", I scream at him.

" I am sorry, I did not know how bad it was until now on the phone, I only knew she was sick, and she didn't want you to know... she did not want for you to worry about her, she wanted you to succeed, to walk, to climb stairs, to be able to go back to acting again!", Landon yells back at me.

I let go of him and fall back onto the couch. We both stay silent for a while, neither of us knowing what to say. Landon not sure of himself, takes a seat onto the couch next to me.

My face is hiding behind my hands. I feel so stupid. How did I not realize that she was sick for the past few months! No wonder why she was always tired, and her so called flu was not really the flu or food poisoning for that matter. Her headaches too, that was a sign to worry but she convinced me she only needed glasses.

"Why did she tell you and not me?", I finally ask Landon the real question that bothers me the most.

"Did she not trust me? Does she not love me enough to want me to be there for her? Did she convince me to come back home because I was a burden on her?" I ask him, mostly just rambling every thought that crosses my mind.

"Don't be daft! It is because she loves you so much that she only cares about making sure you are better. She only told me because she figured through me, she could keep tabs on you, she is always making sure you are ok Levi".

"What kind of a person am I? I let her spend all of her time helping me to walk and everything else while she has been sick and tired, and probably in pain!", I ask Landon who notices the tears forming in my eyes.

"I am angry!", I add.

Knowing full well that I am angrier with myself for being so naive than I am with Charlotte. I am upset that she didn't want me to help her through this. She is the most selfless person I know, sacrificing her sickness and pain so she could help me.

"You cannot be too angry with yourself you had no way of knowing; she was exceptionally good at hiding it. And you can't be too mad at Charlotte, this is the way she wanted it", Landon tells me.

"That is exactly why I am upset!", I retort.

"Levi don't you see! this girl has unconditional love for you! I have never seen that kind of love before and you have been lucky enough to experience that love firsthand!".

" You need to get your arse on a plane right now and go see that girl before her surgery", Landon states after I didn't respond to his last statement.

"She does not want me there, she has made that clear", I groan.

"Now you are really being a wanker! She needs you as much as you need her, whether or not either of you admit to it, now go!", Landon points to the door.

As much as I feel like a twit for having no clue as to what was going on with Charlotte, Landon is right, I need to see her. I need to be there for her like she has always been for me, even if she doesn't want me there. I cannot let anything happen to her. This surgery she is having scares the hell out of me, I might lose her!

Chapter 56

Road Home

Levi's POV

"Levi, sweetheart! Are you sure about this", my mum asks me.

"Yes, mum, I have never been so sure of anything in my entire life", I answer her.

I booked the first flight I could find to Boston. There was just one stop I needed to make first, I needed to see my mum, she had something with her that I needed before I left England.

The flight from Heathrow to Boston felt like it took centuries. My nerves made my leg spasms return and there wasn't enough leg room between these seats for me to stretch or massage my leg.

I asked the flight attendant for a drink because it was the only thing that might calm me down. I am anxious to see her, anxious to know how she feels, scared that she will be upset with me for coming. Maybe she really doesn't want to see me? I cannot stop thinking about her surgery and all the risks involved. I should not have left; I should have known about this and been with her this whole time. I am so stupid! I am never leaving her again!

She is going to be so disappointed when she sees me using my crutch, why did I skip PT? What is wrong with me? This plane needs to fly faster.

I sucked down two drinks before closing my eyes so I can try to take a nap before I freak out on this airplane.

Finally, my plane lands in Boston and I catch an Uber to the hospital Nate told me she is staying at.

I hate the smell and feel of hospitals. I do not have any good memories about being in a hospital. The front lobby directs me to Charlotte's room. She is on the fifth floor, room 514.

My head is spinning, and I feel as though I might faint. Worry is overwhelming me. I feel sick to my stomach knowing how sick Charlotte has been. I lean against the corner of the elevator in case I have the urge to collapse. I need her to be okay, I need her to be safe, and I need her to make it through the surgery.

The fifth floor looks like any other hospital wing. Plain walls, cold air, nurses, and machines everywhere. I am shaking uncontrollably on the inside; I am so nervous to find out what will happen when I enter room 514. It is a good thing I brought my crutch because I cannot control what my body is doing at the moment.

Her door is slightly open, so I slowly push it open a little more until I see her tiny body wrapped in covers, lying on the bed. She is facing the opposite way from me, thank goodness. She is wearing a pink beanie on her head covering her hair.

I walk into her room, my body still shaking, and she turns her head around to face me when she hears my crutch touch the floor.

"Levi! What are you doing here?", her voice squeaks.

"I... I am here for you, my Love", I stutter.

I am stuck standing near her door looking at her, waiting for her to get mad at me or something. I did not expect her to sit up and reach her arms out for me. I am awestruck and my body doesn't know how to move from this spot.

"It's ok Levi! Come here!", she says to me.

I lean my crutch against the wall and limp over to her. Her eyes look sad as she examines me. I reach her arms and she grabs ahold of my hands with hers, pulling me to stand right in front of her.

" I am sorry", I look down and tell her.

She is not yelling at me or scolding me for the way I am limping or upset that I came here unannounced. She feels me shaking of course and squeezes my hands in hers to calm me like she always has.

"I am sorry too Levi, I should have told you, I just was so excited for you and all of your accomplishments, I didn't want you to worry about me", she confesses.

Her skin is pale in color and cool to the touch, she doesn't have her usual warm feeling. She has lost weight too, not like she ever had to, she was always so fit, now she looks tired and sick.

"I would have been here for you Charlotte, I would not have left, I will always be here for you", I cup her face with my hands and rub my thumbs across her cheeks.

"I know, that's why I talked you into going back, so you could be happy, so you could be home", she says.

" I may have thought I had everything and that I was happy before my accident, but I was wrong. Only after meeting you did I realize I was not truly happy there. England may be where I am from, but with you Charlotte is where I belong", I pour my soul out to her and kiss her softly on her cool lips.

She slides over on the bed and motions for me to sit down next to her.

"You have been having terrible leg spasms, again haven't you?", she asks me, but I just look towards the floor not answering her.

I am here for her, not so she can ignore her own problems to try and comfort me, so I will ignore my pain the best I can for now.

" I am fine Charlotte, I am not here so you can worry about me", I mutter.

"Please lay down with me?", she asks softly, and moves her fragile looking body towards the side of the bed to make room for me. I kick off my shoes and brace and climb in next to her. She takes my arms and wraps them around her body and intertwines her legs with mine. God, how I have missed snuggling with her.

I hold onto her tight, too scared to ever let her go again.

"Please tell me about your surgery you are having in the morning?", I nervously ask her.

"Well, the extensive treatments I have had over the last two weeks has shrunk my tumor enough that the surgeon feels he can remove it all", she explains.

"So, you will be fine after? What are the risks?", I didn't want to ask but I need to know.

" I hope I will be fine after", she chuckles a bit.

"And every surgery has risks, but seeing as though this is my brain, there are lots of risks like stroke, or bleeding, or ..."

"You might not make it", I choke out, finishing her sentence for her.

"Or I might not make it through", she sadly confirms.

I can feel my tears escaping and wrap my arms tighter around her.

"I am such an idiot, I should have realized what was going on, I should have been here for you", I whisper while I bury my tear-stained face into her neck.

Charlotte releases my arms from her body so she can turn around to face me. We are both lying on our sides face to face. She brings her hand up and runs her fingers through my hair then wipes my tears away with her thumb.

" I have missed your handsome face and those mesmerizing eyes of yours", she says, trying to cheer me up, but instead more tears start to flow.

" I do not want to lose you Charlotte, ever!", I tell her.

" You won't lose me Levi, I promise! I love you!", she says to me and presses her lips to mine.

That is all I needed to hear for me to do what I needed to do next.

"This is not what I had envisioned, but here we are", I smile.

I climb off her bed and stand up mostly onto my right leg while pulling her up so she can sit on the bed in front of me. She gives me a puzzled look and I probably will not be able to get up again once I kneel, but I give it a go. I get down on one knee in front of her and pull out a small white box from my pocket and place it in her hand.

I am shaking again and begin to speak, "The day I met you, the day you walked into my room when I thought I had lost everything, there was something there between us. I didn't know it was love then, but you never left my side, you pulled me out of the darkness and gave me hope. Falling in love was not part of the plan, but when you held my hand, I knew I belonged and that I was loved. It only took one look into your beautiful eyes to know that I was home, one gentle kiss from your soft lips to wash all my sorrows away. You have my whole heart Charlotte. I would give up anything in the world for you and would do anything to keep you safe. I love you".

Phew! I am glad I did not mess up that mouthful. I am still shaking though, hoping she feels the same way I do. She looks at the small box then looks up at me and slowly opens it. Tears now flowing from her eyes.

"Will you be my wife and let me love you for the rest of my life, Charlotte Thomas?", I ask her.

She takes the diamond ring out of the box and feels it with her fingers. Silence takes over the room as she beams at the ring.

" The ring is beautiful, elegant and different! Where did you get it?", she asks.

"This is my grandmother's ring, she wanted me to give it to the person who I was sure to spend the rest of my life with", I tell her.

She gives me a puzzled look again, and I think I know what she is thinking but she refrains from asking me. I guess deep down I was unsure Emma was really the one when I proposed to her, so I didn't give her this ring. Plus, Emma wanted a bigger, fancier, newer diamond on her finger. I knew Charlotte would love this ring, it represents an everlasting love, like her.

"What if I don't make it through the surgery, or what if something goes wrong and I end up blind or worse?", she asks, still focusing on the ring she is holding.

I take the ring and hold her left hand while I slide it onto her ring finger.

" I will love you and want you as my wife no matter what... and you will make it through the surgery", I say and then pull her close so I can kiss her.

She cups my face and feverishly kisses me back.

"Is that a yes?", I ask her before locking lips again.

"Yes", she breathes.

I use my arms to lift myself back up onto my right leg and pivot myself back onto her bed, trying to avoid any pressure that would cause pain in my left leg.

"Under one condition", she surprisingly says to me.

"What is that?" I ask.

" That you continue your daily PT so we can get you back to walking pain and spasm free", she states.

I kiss her cheek, " Just being here with you, my leg already feels better", I smile.

We lay back down and snuggle ourselves tightly around each other. This time I brush my fingers along her cheek and then her arm and hug her again and kiss her neck.

" I am scared for tomorrow", I shyly confess to her.

" I am too", she says back.

The night does not last long. I held her all night in my arms, hoping she was able to get some sleep in between nurses coming in to take her vitals. I stayed awake feeling worried for what is to come. I know she worried too so I kept my body close to hers to comfort her.

Morning arrived and I made sure I was up before the doctor came in. I attach my brace and put on my shoes. For the first time in over a year, I do not feel self-conscious about wearing this damn brace. If it is something I need to wear the rest of my life, if my left leg is never fully functional ever again, so be it! As long as Charlotte is safe and healthy again, I will be happy, and I will make sure she is happy too.

"We are ready for you Miss Thomas", the tall slender guy in scrubs says when he walks into the room with a wheelchair, waiting to take her away from me.

Charlotte's parents arrived moments earlier to wish her luck and to wait with me.

I help her into the wheelchair and kiss her lips again. "I love you and I will be right here waiting for you when you wake up", I assure her.

" I love you too, and don't worry, I will be fine", she smiles.

"Please take good care of my fiancé!" I direct towards the man in scrubs as he wheels her away.

Charlotte's parents and I look at each other, we all have the same worrisome expressions on our faces.

She better be alright!

This is going to be the longest day of my life.

Epilogue

Levi's POV

Six months later...

"Levi sweetheart!", my mum walks over and hugs me.

"What's wrong mum? Is she alright?", my mum is making me nervous with all her hugging and crying.

" Everything is fine son! You look very handsome in your tux", she smiles while straightening my bow tie.

" Everyone is waiting son, you better get in there ", my mum adds.

My left pant leg keeps getting caught on my new brace and I don't know why. I think it is the material causing some static with the brace. I have kept up with my PT like I promised Charlotte I would. My muscles in my lower leg and ankle have strengthened but not enough to walk around all day without my brace. This new material is ultra-thin and so light, I can barely feel it attached to my leg. There is a hinge in the ankle area so that I can bend my ankle just enough to allow me to navigate stairs like a normal person and walk with a barely noticeable limp, but still gives me support so I don't trip and fall over my non-compliant foot.

I do not wear my brace when I am at home. Thankfully, I have learned how to walk without it during therapy. I do need to be extra careful though when I step so that I plant my foot properly and do not twist my ankle. In the house is the only place I do not mind looking like a fool. Charlotte doesn't look at me or treat me like a cripple when she watches me limp around ever so slowly without my brace, she only smiles at me with those encouraging and proud of me eyes of hers. If I cannot run or jump again, it is fine with me as long as Charlotte is by my side reminding me that I am not as disabled as I think myself to be. That girl is always pushing me to never give up or feel down about myself.

I thought when Charlotte said yes to my marriage proposal that it would be the happiest moment of my life, but after anxiously waiting nine hours for Charlotte to make it out of surgery... it was the surgeon telling me that she was alright, and he removed the whole tumor which ended up being the happiest moment.

I am now here on my wedding day ready to marry the love of my life. We have had so many happy moments together and this one will be sure to top the list.

After Charlotte recovered from her surgery and was told she was completely tumor free, we decided to find our own home together.

We actually found two homes, one in Boston near her rehab center and one in Los Angeles near her facility there. Charlotte promised that she would not take on any patients herself like she did with me, and only oversee the two facilities, splitting her time between the two cities. I would always travel with her of course.

Mark agreed to find me small acting jobs for whenever we were in L.A. and when we are in Boston, I help Nate at the rehab center. The patients have taken a liking to me knowing that I went through a similar ordeal to what they are going through. Charlotte suggested I take some counseling classes and use my knowledge and experience to help her patients. Her suggestions worked out perfectly for me and I find joy and meaning in helping others. I finally have a sense of why Charlotte enjoys it so much.

We visit my parents and mates often and they come here to visit us. I do not miss what I had in England before my accident. Well, I do miss having fully functioning legs, but I do not miss my flat or the nights out at the pubs, or the life I had there.

Charlotte's selflessness and unconditional love showed me that life will always be better with her. And even though she spends her time taking care of everyone else, including me, she knows that no matter what struggles either of us face, life is better when we are together.

Landon punches my shoulder, snapping me out of my trance, " Here she comes!", he says to me.

Landon, Andy, Josh, Mark, Nate, and Jake are all standing up with me by my side at the altar. I asked Jake to stand up here with me too because he was the one who helped me face my fears and accept Charlotte's love.

The music plays and everyone rises to get a glimpse of my beautiful soon-to-be wife.

She is absolutely stunning in her long white dress, walking down the aisle with her dad. I have the biggest grin on my face knowing that this amazing girl is mine.

Her dad gives me her hand before walking to his seat to sit with the rest of her extended family. Her sisters are standing up here with her. We both turn towards the priest, hand in hand, my gaze locked onto her. I cannot peel my eyes away from her beautiful face, small tears running down her cheeks as we recite our vows.

"Do you Charlotte take Levi as your wedded husband, to love and cherish him, in sickness and in health, until death do you part?", The priest reads from his book.

"I do!", she whispers behind her happy tears.

For a moment, the entire church is silent until the priests says to me, "You may kiss your bride", and the entire place erupts in cheers when I lean down and place my lips onto hers.

"Thank you for everything my Love", I whisper into her ear.

Made in the USA
Monee, IL
13 December 2020